8x 9/14 LT 9/14

PRAISE FOR *SELF-INFLICTED WOUNDS*

"If you're the type of sicko who enjoys a hilariously talented person debasing herself for your amusement, then *Self-Inflicted Wounds* is the book for you."

—Andy Richter, comedian, actor, writer, announcer, man Friday on *Conan*

"Aisha Tyler's book *Self-Inflicted Wounds* is an uplifting, hilarious trek through her life of insults, agonies, and failures. Each story is not only painfully funny, but it's also thoughtful and stunningly candid. I really do love this book."

—Jay Chandrasekhar, director of *Super Troopers*, *Beerfest*, and *The Babymakers*

"We all do stupid stuff, sometimes on purpose. But rarely do we ever talk about it, let alone publish an in-depth retelling—leave it to Aisha Tyler to help us all feel a little less dumb and a little more connected."   —Seth Green, comedian, actor, creator/writer/director of *Robot Chicken*

"Aisha Tyler is queen of the blerd nation and living proof that for nerdy little outsiders things really do get better. But in her case, before they got better they got a whole lot worse. It's impossible not to laugh while reading *Self-Inflicted Wounds*, stories of one epic fail after another. It's also impossible not to worry about Aisha's mental health."

—Touré, author, critic, host of MSNBC's *The Cycle*

"What Aisha says about embracing your fear and using mistakes to forge character is beautiful. What she says about Oprah is unforgivable."

—Baratunde Thurston, *New York Times* bestselling author
of *How to Be Black*, CEO/cofounder of Cultivated Wit

"Aisha Tyler's incredibly vivid stories of going for big air only to land flat on her face (or possibly a rusty spike) are a unique combination of cringe-worthy and inspiring. That she shares these stories makes me love her all the more."

—Bill Burr, comedian, actor,
host of *Monday Morning Podcast*

"Self-inflicted wounds. We all have them, but no one exploits their own pain for the funny like Aisha Tyler."

—Wayne Brady, comedian, actor,
star of *Whose Line Is It Anyway?*,
host of *Let's Make a Deal*

"Aisha Tyler's brain moves faster than a shock spell from the hands of a lightning mage. She is hilarious and hyper-articulate, and will kick your ass in Call of Duty. She is the life of the LAN party."   —Chris Hardwick, comedian,
host of *Talking Dead* and *Nerdist*

SELF-INFLICTED WOUNDS

Also by Aisha Tyler

Swerve

SELF-INFLICTED WOUNDS

Heartwarming Tales of Epic Humiliation

aisha tyler

itbooks

AN IMPRINT OF HARPERCOLLINS PUBLISHERS

*it***books**

HarperCollins books may be purchased for educational, business, or sales promotional use. For information please e-mail the Special Markets Department at SPsales@harpercollins.com.

FIRST EDITION

Designed by Renato Stanisic

Library of Congress Cataloging-in-Publication Data
Tyler, Aisha.
   Self-inflicted wounds : heartwarming tales of epic humiliation / Aisha Tyler.—First edition.
      pages   cm
   Summary: "On the wildly popular podcast 'Girl on Guy,' comedian and actress Aisha Tyler asks her guests to recount moments from their lives when they've done something boneheaded, ill-conceived, dangerous, or just plain stupid . . . to themselves. In *Self-Inflicted Wounds*, Aisha turns the lens on herself—recounting her most egregious mistakes—to hilarious result. Laugh-out-loud funny and totally relatable, *Self-Inflicted Wounds* highlights a new comedic voice on the rise"—Provided by publisher.
   ISBN 978-0-06-222377-7 (hardback)—ISBN 978-0-06-222378-4 (paperback) 1. Tyler, Aisha—Anecdotes.   2. Women comedians—United States—Anecdotes.   3. Podcasters—United States—Anecdotes.   I. Title.
   PN2287.T89A3   2013
   792.7'6—dc23   2013013538

13   14   15   16   17   DIX/RRD   10   9   8   7   6   5   4   3   2   1

Dedicated to my parents, Robin and James,
who raised me to be brave.

Maybe *too* brave.

Contents

Preface

Despite the fact that much of what I write about in this book has been cribbed from my life experiences, this is not an autobiography.

I am self-involved, but not so self-involved to think that my life merits comprehensive documentation. I will wait until I am an old and tragic drunk for that. (Or until I make the terrible mistake of cheating on my husband with an appallingly young backup dancer. I absolutely do not intend to do this, but it would surely merit some pompous and tearful introspection.)

I talk about real people in this book, and real occurrences. That being said, everything here has been retrieved from the annals of my spotty and highly unreliable memory, and for all I know, may be complete fabrication—due either to severe retrograde amnesia (the early throes of which the Internet assures me I am in), or, more likely, my intense desire to have lived a life more thrilling than the one I've shambled rather aimlessly through thus far.

For that reason, please do not take this book as any kind of documentarian portrait of my life, or try to use excerpts from this book to judge me, my family, my childhood, my friends, or as example of the broad and inexorable decay of Western civilization. All names have been changed or omitted, both to protect the innocent, and because I can't remember who the fuck most of these people are anyway.

Furthermore, it would be spectacularly futile to try and use this as an evidentiary document with which to convict or exonerate criminals, figure out what happened to the Lindbergh baby, uncover the truth about the Kennedy assassination, or divine where Jimmy Hoffa may be buried.[1] If you take this as gospel, you will be sorely disappointed. This book is not a salacious tell-all full of celebrity secrets and tearful confessions. This book is just a book; one I hope is serviceably funny and relatively free of grammatical errors.

My hopes and dreams for this book: I hope it will be amusing. I hope it will be entertaining. I hope it will make you laugh, and maybe make you think. I hope that it will be the only book you ever read by an African-American comedian/actress/television host/podcaster/gamer/intense lover of pancakes with such a lush and heady surfeit of fine curse words.

I hope this book will inspire you to be yourself. I hope this book will encourage you to follow your dreams. I hope this book will impress your friends when you display it prominently in your home, preferably on a coffee table or in the bathroom next to that dog-eared (and unread) copy of *Mensa Magazine* that you put there to intimidate your guests as they pee.

I hope, all else failing, that this book will provide a stable surface upon which to place a refreshing beverage when you are watching television.

Above all, I hope that you, like me, will embrace your fears, learn from your failures, celebrate your victories, and run headlong into (metaphorical) danger. Get up, go out into the world, and do awesome shit.

I'll be here on the couch if you need me.

---

1 This book *may* help you figure out where my yellow banana-seat cruiser is. If you find it, please let me know. I *really* miss that bike.

Introduction: What, Exactly, Is a Self-Inflicted Wound?

"It is through being wounded that power grows and can, in the end, become tremendous."—FRIEDRICH NIETZSCHE

"Holy crap that fucking hurt."—AISHA TYLER

I am not a psychologist, but I do know some shit about people.

This is not a boast. This is just the truth.

If you were to question why the hell I think I can write a book about human failure and its power to transform people with the strength of its sheer awesomeness, I would have to plead no contest. I am uniquely unqualified to pontificate on the behavior of others and its significance. My undergraduate degree is not in psychology, or human behavior, or sociology, or even anthropology. My undergraduate degree is in government, with a double minor in environmental studies and drinking shit.

I have no letters after my name.[1]

I possess no qualifications to indicate I have any special or unique insight into the human condition. I have spent no amount of time

---

1 Other than H.N.I.C., which is a *very* easy degree to get.

studying socio-cultural norms or human behavior. I've never even gone through therapy.[2]

What I have done is been a person—for quite a while now, in fact. I think of myself as an expert on being human, especially as I have never been anything else. So while I cannot speak to the experiences of others, I can talk a whole hell of a lot of shit about myself. And since I am human (last I checked, anyway; it's entirely possible I've been body snatched or am a blissfully unaware assimilate of The Borg),[3] I am more than willing to extrapolate wild and totally unscientific conclusions from my personal experiences and apply them to the human race as a whole.[4] Whee! Science!

So, upon this ill-considered and alarmingly flimsy foundation, let me present the concept of the self-inflicted wound—its origins, nature, structure, and subsets.

To commence, there is an axiom that applies pretty universally to the human psyche when it comes to spectacular failure. For expedience, and because it sounds awesome, let's call it *The Tyler Fuckup Principle*.[5] It goes like this: when something goes terribly wrong, the human mind instinctively casts about for something *other* to blame. The mentally unpalatable concept that we might have massively screwed up is so difficult for the mind to grasp, so utterly cognitively dissonant, that we immediately decide—no, *recognize*—that there is no way this could have occurred without negative outside influence.

As a result, our own failures are always, by their very nature of being "failure," someone else's fault. When one is undone—sprawled across the cold tile of a public bathroom in a pool of one's own vomit, or shivering in the back of a taxi in a pair of urine-soaked skinny jeans with no money for cab fare and a dead cell phone battery—much like a wobbly toddler or an unhinged politician, one immediately looks for

---

2 It's not that I don't like talking to strangers, I just prefer to do it on a stage where they have assembled into a group and are visibly intoxicated. One-on-one interaction? *Ick.*

3 Resistance is futile.

4 A wholly unscientific method first successfully pioneered by Oprah.

5 *Tyler's Razor* felt a bit derivative.

someone else to blame. God. Your parents. Ex-girlfriends. Undocu-
mented immigrants. Marvin in Human Resources. China.

This is natural. This is the way the mind works. "I know I am
standing in a pool of milk and broken glass, but that is because someone pelted me with milk bottles. I could *never* have spilled this milk
myself! I am *living perfection*!"[6] We do not take responsibility for our
actions, not because we are weak willed or devoid of character, but
because we are just not wired that way. Even tiny children know it is
much wiser to point at that *other* kid rather than step forward bravely
when asked, "Who ate the cookie?" Children are not taught this, and
contrary to the claims of the Parents' Television Council, they do not
learn it by watching cartoons or interacting with atheists. It is just
something they *know*. Deflection is in our genes, much like a predis-
position to retain abdominal fat and a love of crunchy orange foods. It
is just how we are.

We are born this way.

With a self-inflicted wound, one is clearly both perpetrator *and*
victim. The damage is so severe and spectacular as to be unavoid-
ably apparent to others, and when one casts about for someone to
blame, one finds, to one's great chagrin, that there is no one to blame
but oneself. The self-inflicted wound, whether physical or (much more
common) psychological, is a demon entirely of one's own making—a
self-conjured gorgon pulled from the netherworld, if not voluntarily,
then at the very least unbidden. Eventually one has to wake up and
smell the metaphorical blood; *you did this to yourself*.

Sometimes the self-inflicted wound is entirely of your own making,
and sometimes others empower or hasten it along, as if adding accelerant to your fast growing pyre of self-immolation. Everyone enjoys a
spectacular meltdown, which is why we are so addicted to shows about
people who extreme coupon, dress their children up like hookers, or
live in a hoarder's paradise of vintage magazines and Ziploc bags of
cat poop. It is supremely fun to point and laugh at the foibles of others,

---

6 Or more relevant, "I know I was caught tickling another man's foot with my pants down in
a bathroom notorious for being the locale of homosexual trysts, but I just have a wide stance
and a twitchy extremity. *I was in no way soliciting gay sex!*"

and if we can stick out a foot to trip someone into a murky puddle of their own damp mistakes, all the better.

But in the aftermath of a self-inflicted wound, when you sift through the embers for the arsonist's tool, the propane canister or half-burned lighter, much like the nameless narrator in *Fight Club*, you discover that Tyler Durden is just a figment of your fractured imagination, that you blew up your own apartment and burned your life to the ground, and you've been punching yourself in the face like an idiot the entire time.

Don't fight it. Accept it for what it is. You screwed the pooch. All you can do now is try to turn it into a learning experience.

Or, at the very least, into a killer story you can tell your friends.

Prologue: Why Am I Doing This? Why?

"I'm a little wounded, but I'm not slain; I will lay me down for to bleed awhile, Then I'll rise and fight again."—JOHN DRYDEN

"Just give me a second to get my wind back. Who the hell put that pole there?"—AISHA TYLER

Comedians love a good story. Unnaturally so. So much so, in fact, that we will subject ourselves to any amount of self-torture and humiliation to get it.

I have often heard a comedian tell a story of such abjection, such pure and unadulterated shame, that any normal person with even a modicum of self-respect would do everything in his or her power to first forget, then make others forget, it had ever happened.

Burn every photo. Kill off witnesses. Bribe law enforcement. Change names, addresses, phone numbers, entire lives, to make sure no one will ever, *ever* repeat that story to others.

A comedian, however, cannot *wait* to belt that story out in front of strangers, replete with sound effects and wild gesticulations. The most crushing and humiliating of these stories will send a comedian barreling into a party with sweaty palms and a jelly jar full of bourbon, screaming, *"Holy shit, you are not gonna believe what happened to me Saturday night! I am such an asshole!"*

It is a sickness.

Why are comedians like this? Being a comedian requires an extremely high threshold of psychic pain. You must be able to tolerate humiliation, learn to resist it, defy it, crave it even. You must make love to embarrassment, tongue kiss abjection, clasp emotional injury close to your heaving breast. You cannot fear the mocking of others; you must face it as a brave, if utterly doomed, Roman soldier. Because the truth is that sometimes the audience may actually be laughing *at* you and not with you. And that needs to be okay. For the comedian, laughs are *much* more important than one's own psychic comfort—the goal is to entertain, not cultivate a prayer circle. You must be immune to bloodshed, even—no *especially*—when the bloodshed is your own.

You must give the people what they want.

Pursuant to this, you will find, almost universally, that we comedians have no shame. This critical internal trigger, one that makes others behave in discreet and proper ways in the company of others, just does not work in us. We do not have it. We do not need it. Much like people born without a spleen or tibia, this is just the way we are built.

Do not pity us, however. Much like Daredevil, who turned his blindness into a crime-fighting tool, we have turned a shortcoming into our greatest weapon. Lack of shame is our superpower. Comedians feel nothing when dumped, snubbed, fired, or told off. Or if we do, we shove those feelings deep inside, down by where we keep the memories of that time we peed ourselves at show and tell, right alongside our big burlap sack of lifelong rejection. Every terrible experience is fodder for discussion, subject to dissection and examination, foundation for a joke, a rant, or other exploitation, whether it is on stage or in the corner at your brother-in-law's barbecue, when you would *really* rather us shut the hell up.

I suppose a more accurate description would be that we *do* feel, but not in the way a normal person does. When shamed, we actually feel two things: the feelings we should be feeling at the moment—sadness, rage, disgust, dull ambivalence—and a second, stranger and more singular feeling, which is: *man, this is going to make a killer story.*[1]

Humiliation is fuel for art, and there is nothing more strangely satisfying than exploiting our own cringe-worthy experiences for others' enjoyment and our own itchy brand of self-satisfaction. Much like picking at a scab or pulling a hangnail to the quick, there is a prickly pleasure in telling others that you urinated on yourself just steps from your front door due to an overindulgence in German wheat beer, or that you screwed up the courage to feebly punch a guy you believed to be sleeping with your ex-girlfriend, only to find out that not only did you punch the wrong guy, but the "Taylor" your girlfriend left you for was a girl.

It hurts at the moment. *Man*, does it hurt. It burns like a mouthful of napalm on an empty stomach. But then, doesn't hurt also taste just a tiny bit like winning?

This book is about those moments. Those massive failures that are yours, and yours alone, to claim. No one made you do it. No one cheated you, tricked you, forced you to be a dunce, a chump, a klutz, a butthead, an asshole. You did that shit *all* to yourself.

And by *you*, of course, I mean me. And by *yourself*, I also, of course, mean me. This is not a collection of my triumphs, my best moments, my gilded seconds atop the winner's podium, my halcyon days in the metaphorical sun. No.

This is a collection of stories about all the times I shit the bed.

I can't wait to tell you all about them.

---

1 This is more like a thought and a feeling smashed together. A *theeling*. A *fought*? No, a *theeling*. Definitely a *theeling*.

(1)

The Time I Cut Myself in Half

"The wound is the place where the Light enters you."—Rumi

"This is gonna need ointment."—Aisha Tyler

When I was about five years old, I stabbed myself in the chest.

Well, not exactly *stabbed*. More like sliced. Yes. I sliced myself nose to navel, as if conducting a frog dissection in science class. Only without the relatively sanitary tools, face protection, or pursuit of scientific truth.

And, also, on *myself*.

I could say it wasn't my fault. I could protest that it was an accident— unforeseen, unpredictable, unkind, unfair. None of that would be true. I did this on purpose. I knew exactly what I was getting into. The entire debacle was calculated, focused, and gleefully headlong.

Before you gasp in horror and thinly disguised pity, this was no suicide attempt.[1] I was not *trying* to gut myself. At the same time, I can blame no one else for the bloody vertical striping that occurred.

I courted that stabbing, poked at it with a metaphorical stick,

---

1 People have called me a lot of things, but one word they have never used is depressed. I am, fortunately or not, depending on your perspective, nauseatingly upbeat, disgustingly cheery. Please, withhold your disdain. This is a genetic condition. Much like synesthetes or people who love musical theater, this is just how I was born.

taunted it like a rangy pit bull behind a wobbly storm fence, mocking and laughing as it slavered in captivity—right up to the moment the dog leapt, snarling against the wire, knocking the fence to the ground like a structure of drinking straws and me face-first into the dirt. Or, more accurately, face-first into the hot, abrasive summer pavement.

Some might call such behavior stupid. They would be one hundred percent right.

Here's the thing. I am uniquely, and occasionally quite stupidly, fearless. I have never been afraid. Well, not *truly* afraid. I have had moments of trepidation, acted tentatively on occasion. Tiptoed toward my fate timorously, doubts creeping, internal alarms blaring. Occasionally, I exercise a bit of caution. But more often, and to my sustained chagrin, I run sprinting toward my own demise, without consideration or forethought. I like to shoot first and ask questions about why there is a bullet lodged deeply in my own foot much, much later.

So on this golden August day in my fifth year, I had been playing outside in my Oakland neighborhood with a dusty scrum of local kids in a completely unsupervised group, the way we used to in the good old days, before the Internet told parents that this was a terrible idea[2] and likely to result in your child being abducted by aliens or devoured by wolves. We were all in various states of typically dirty late-summer disarray: faces sticky with rivulets of many-hours-dried melted Popsicle and festooned liberally with dirt, most shoeless and many shirtless, including (inappropriately I suppose in hindsight) me.

Yes, I was running around a city neighborhood unchaperoned, on hot pavement with bare feet, and worse still, a bare chest.[3] Now, before you jump into your time machine and call Child Protective Services, get over your prissy self. It was the seventies. Kids ran around unsupervised. This is before people felt the need to meticulously curate every

---

2 Along with kids riding the bus, doing their homework without parental "assistance" (read: "doing it for them"), using a kitchen knife or an open flame before the age of seventeen, or anything else that builds character, instills mental toughness or makes kids into actual people.

3 I was a five-year-old girl. I still had a "chest." If you think it was inappropriate, you need therapy. Also, you may need to look out your front window and see if Chris Hansen from *To Catch a Predator* is lurking in your bushes waiting to strike.

minute of their child's day. In the morning during the summer, parents opened the front door and forcibly ejected their children into the street with five dollars and a firm admonition to come home when the streetlights came on and not to run into oncoming traffic. This is just how things were done. I suppose if we were rich, the nanny could have followed behind us in the family's second minivan, but we weren't, and she didn't, and that, my dear friends, is that.

So we were running around barefoot, narrowly avoiding puncture wounds from the abundance of rusted nails and broken bottles strewn liberally about the streets, fleeing rabid dogs and hissing cats and the occasional loitering ne'er-do-well, and having the time of our fucking lives. We climbed some trees, chased an ice cream truck, terrorized a squirrel, picked up dried dog poop, threw rocks at things that break when they are hit with rocks, and were generally on raging kindergarten fire, when we found an alley. *Sweet.*

Naturally, it being an absolutely terrifying place, and me being feckless and wild,[4] I decided to go into that alley. And why the hell not? After you've touched dried dog feces with your bare hands, nothing much else troubles you. And in that alley, among empty fruit crates and mosquito-infested puddles, we found . . . an abandoned hobbyhorse.

Abandoned! Who the hell leaves a perfectly good hobbyhorse just lying around? I announced to the group. *Heathens! Profligates! Godless people, that's who!*

I was a dramatic child.

We dragged this hobbyhorse from its dank hiding place and into the street, the better to surround it with hard surfaces that might embrace a small person's tumble. We surveyed it briefly from all sides to confirm that it was, indeed, in functioning order. And then, in turn, we each hopped on board and rode that thing like a Hapsburg prince on a Lipizzaner stallion. Springs have never clung to life so dearly, nor groaned in protest so loudly. We played quite orderly, waiting politely in line for our turn, which may seem surprising considering all the tree

---

4 And needing desperately to show a certain neighborhood boy who was fond of picking up dried poo and throwing it at me that I wasn't afraid of anything, not dogs or alleys or least of all, poos. Yes, that is the plural of poo. *Poos.*

climbing and poo flinging we had engaged in prior, but this was the seventies, and pre-Internet, and the unique self-involvement of the You-Tube era had not been invented yet. We were relatively well-behaved, and when appropriate we shared, and I'm sure most of us brushed twice a day because that Yuck Mouth guy on TV had admonished us to, and who were we to disobey?

And because I had found the horse and was feeling particularly magnanimous, I went last.

Oh. I forgot to mention. This magical hobbyhorse had one flaw. Just a *tiny* one. The horse was old, and its fragile plastic body had begun to decay, revealing its metallic skeleton. Bits of metal poked through the horse's sides and hind flanks, and a massive rusted metal bar protruded violently from its head, like some jagged, ferrous horn.[5] This toy was a little plastic unicorn just built for destruction. I couldn't wait to climb aboard.

Please, try to reserve your judgment for the end of the story, where it will be truly well placed.

So we are riding, and we are whooping, and we are feeling the kind of warm self-satisfaction that comes only from courting danger in a pair of sticky Underoos in the afternoon sunshine, and life is good. And I hop on this thing, and I am full of joy.

Now, as I was easily a foot taller and fifteen pounds heavier than all of the previous riders, this horse was taxed beyond capacity. If it had been a real horse, its tongue would have been lolling pendulously from its froth-framed mouth as its eyes rolled wildly in socket, whites exposed to the blue summer sky. But I am happily oblivious to the strain I am placing on this decaying plastic toy, and I rock away, springs groaning, frame creaking ominously, and I ride, ride, back and forth, farther and faster now, until the tail and nose scrape the sidewalk, leaving chips of brown and white in their wake, little plastic button horse nose skittering now across the pavement. And I ride on, dipping farther back now, laughing, eyes closed, face toward the

---

5 This did absolutely nothing to diminish the appeal of this toy to us, but made it feel like we were riding some kind of death metal narwhal. The fact that it made the thing potentially deadly was just an added level of awesome.

heavens, the sun on my sticky little-kid face, and forward now, so far forward, like I am on a *real* horse, a real true life horse . . . and I am *flying*.

And then I actually am flying. Forward, over the horse's head, and that metal spike, and a bunch of negative space, and I tumble to the ground, smacking into the cement headfirst. This is followed by an awkward somersault, and I am flat on my back, my Popsicle-and-dirt-bearded chin quivering with impending tears.

When you are a kid, there is that moment after you've fallen, when you can't decide *how* you feel. Things hurt, but not that much. Not yet. You can't breathe, and you're a little confused, because just a few minutes ago you were having SO much fun, but now you're lying on the ground in a heap and all that joy has turned to sawdust and Bactine in your mouth. You have to take a minute to gather your thoughts, because an injury means the end of fun for the day, and maybe a lot longer than that. So you ask yourself: Am I really hurt? Sometimes it's up to you to decide, and sometimes the injury decides for you. In this case, I wanted to keep playing. But the injury decided for me.

I staggered to my feet, ready to finish my ride.[6] But as I stood there, thinking I could "walk this one off" as my father often admonished, the faces of my friends said it all. I was getting a crowd-sourced diagnosis on this one, long before the term had been invented. Their expressions provided ample nonverbal evidence that I was in deep, deep *poos*.

I looked down. A spreading stain, a bright and crimson line, ran downward from my chin to dangerously near where my junk might be, if I had been old enough to have developed junk, or even know what junk was. It was a long and continuous streak, and growing increasingly bloody by the minute. Even my five-year-old brain knew that a rusty spike slicing you open longways couldn't be a *good* thing. My mom had squawked enough about the threat of tetanus and lockjaw coming from dirty metallic items for me to know that I couldn't just lick the back of my hand and wipe this one away like I did a skinned

---

6 No fair cutting! I wasn't done!

knee or a rivulet of boogers. This was a job for someone with gauze and ointment and a bottomless supply of kisses for my boo-boo.

The dreaded truth settled in my head with a thud; the thing no kid ever wants to accept. It was time to go home.

And as I realized that, the five-year-old part of my five-year-old brain finally kicked in, and I did what a normal little kid would do. I burst into tears and ran all the way back to my house.

When I arrived there, looking like a mad scientist had tried to flay me open like a tiny Frankenstein, my mother freaked out in appropriate fashion. When I told her what had happened, as she was dabbing my torso with bubbling peroxide and wiping my salty tears, she asked, in that annoyingly reasonable way adults do, "Why would you play with that toy when you knew it was broken? Why would you do something you knew was clearly dangerous?" To which I gave an answer I was sure was apparent to all but the most dim-witted of people. "Mommy. It looked fun."

In retrospect, it *was* fun, once it was confirmed that I wasn't going to get lockjaw or tetanus or leprosy or cooties. Courting danger, facing fear, and engaging in life fully without caution or conservatism was a fantastic time. And, yes, the possibility existed that I would get hurt, but the possibility also existed that I would have a shitload of fun. And that was just too strong an enticement to ignore.[7]

"And whose fault *is* this?" my mother demanded. "Did one of the other kids push you to ride? Was it that hoodlum Malik? I always knew he was bad news. I am calling his mother."

"No." I shook my head. "It was my fault."

Even then, I knew I had no one to blame but myself.

Did I learn my lesson, my mother wanted to know? Did I realize that the world was dangerous? That I needed to be careful? That I

---

[7] Fun, back then, as now, is a powerful enticement. It is why we jump out of planes, drink too much, drive too fast, fake illness to skip work, wake up in bed woozy and pants-less next to people we have just met. And no matter how mature or responsible we become, fun is always there, just out of sight, trying to lure us from our responsibilities—a nude and voluptuous siren holding a bottleful of bourbon and two tickets to Vegas, reeking of jasmine blossoms and cookie dough and doom. She is a foxy evil bitch queen, that Fun. She is not to be toyed with.

should approach foreign objects with caution, and wear shoes, and put on a sweater, and avoid rusty nails and never ride broken hobbyhorses again? Did I? *Did I?!?*

Yes. I nodded. I had learned my lesson. I would be more careful.

But the truth is that all I had learned was that it might be a good idea to wear a shirt occasionally. And that the next time I found a free hobbyhorse lying around, I was damn well going to jump on that thing and teach it who was boss.

This was a harbinger of things to come. The first time I ran headlong into danger, not just fearlessly, but gleefully embracing what would surely and inevitably be my demise, without caution or restraint. That horse was corroded, barbed, and threatening, its tiny horn tipped with rust and the bloody remnants of a thousand tiny broken dreams.

And it would be mine. Oh, yes. It would be mine.

For that experience, for the ride, the injury, and the scar I still bear to this day, I can only blame myself. It was no one's fault but my own. I did it to me.

This is the essence of a self-inflicted wound, metaphorical or other. You'd like to project blame, point the finger, claim accident, bad luck, confluence, coincidence. But the truth is the blame lies squarely with you. And the only way to salvage the experience is to try to find a way to learn from it, to grow as a person, take responsibility, and move on.

That kind of personal examination and growth is what self-inflicted wounds are all about. A long, slow movement toward adulthood, and the learning and growth that can only come with a few scrapes and scars.

As for me, I blame the horse.

(2)

The Time I Almost Set Myself on Fire

"As the eagle was killed by the arrow winged with his own feather, so the hand of the world is wounded by its own skill."—Helen Keller

"I just fucked up my hand slicing a bagel. Stupid bagel."—Aisha Tyler

When I was seven years old, I set my house on fire.

I realize that this sounds vaguely *Carrie*-like, only without all the religious zealotry or repressed sexuality. Also, *way* less blood.

In my defense, it wasn't *totally* on fire, and it wasn't my entire house. Technically, it wasn't even a house but an apartment. An apartment with shag rugs, marbled mirrors, and sparkly cottage cheese ceilings. An apartment just begging to be dirtied up a bit. It's possible I may have been harboring a bit of misplaced anger at the apartment that had less to do with interior décor and more to do with the fact that my parents had just separated. But in my mind, at the time, that apartment was just asking for it.

My parents were in the middle of their first trial separation, and my mom, sister, and I had moved into a two-bedroom apartment in a decent neighborhood in the hills of Oakland, California. Safe, quiet, walking distance to the bus stop. A nearby 7-Eleven provided easy access to neon-blue frozen drinks when needed. A secure underground parking spot offered protection for my mom's badass 1974 Mustang.[1] Not too shabby, considering the solemn circumstances under which we made the move.

I can't say I was happy about my parents' separation and impending divorce, but I honestly can't say I was sad, either. I was a kid, for chrissakes. I didn't know how the fuck to feel. People often lament about divorces and what they do to children. There is a lot of hand-wringing about nuclear families and dual parenting and kids needing continuity—and about the damage divorce does to their sense of stability, their belief in the permanence of things, their tender, nascent optimism, and a bunch of other misty-eyed laments.

But I'll tell you what else fucks with a kid's optimism and sense of stability: when your parents fight all the time. That shit can really suck. Listening to your parents yell, or cry, or stomp off in anger, or worse, that deafening silence that falls over a home when the two biggest residents aren't speaking to each other, and only reply in jagged monotone when the kids ask for seconds or beg to be excused from the dinner table[2]—*that* is damaging. That shit is no fucking fun at all.

This may be heresy, but as a child of divorce, I can say it wasn't *that* big a deal. I'm sure at the time I found it a bit more traumatic, but looking back, it all seems much ado about nothing. My parents didn't get

---

1 The loss of this Mustang is one of the great stinging regrets of my life. This car was powder blue. It had pleather bench seats. It had an 8-track inside, in which a cassette of Bootsy's Rubber Band's *Ahh . . . The Name Is Bootsy, Baby!* was permanently lodged. This was not a problem. This made the car perpetually funky. Riding in this vehicle to and from Montessori made me feel like a tiny, brown, female Bullitt.

I do not know where this Mustang finally came to rest—my mom eventually traded it in on a much more practical and family-friendly powder blue Volkswagen Rabbit. Thinking of it being slowly crushed into scrap makes me die a little inside. In my fantasies, it is living on a farm, gamboling in green pastures alongside the cars from *Streets of San Francisco* and *Christine*.

2 Hostage negotiators would be driven screaming from the dinner table of a family in the throes of divorce. There is nothing as frostily off-putting as two adults trying to act as if things are fine for the sake of their kids, who in all probability can totally sense the complete bullshit being slung across the dinner table. Kids aren't stupid, and their bullshit meters are much more highly calibrated than adults'. Grownups aren't fooling anybody.

along. They wanted different things. They broke up. They both seemed moderately happier afterwards. That was good enough for me.[3]

So. Was I sad about the divorce? At the time, I couldn't say. What I did know was that all of a sudden I had a lot more unsupervised time on my hands, and that time was ripe for getting into trouble. Epic, thunderous trouble.

Starting with setting some shit on motherfucking fire.

I didn't actually *mean* to set anything on fire. This was not some destructive act of rebellion. I just liked to cook. Or, more accurately, I liked to eat. Cooking was a means to an end, and that end was eating awesome shit. I have always loved to eat. I am a large person and I have been this large, essentially, since birth. A big baby. A robust toddler. A giant, stumbling kindergartner who could destroy a roast chicken in seconds, crack the bones for their marrow, and come back for more. I looked old enough to buy beer when I was thirteen. I am the go-to in any group when some shit needs getting off a high shelf. A girl this big needs sustenance.

And when I was a kid, my favorite thing to do was the thing I was absolutely forbidden to do: put a big pot of oil on a flaming stove, and fry shit up. Let's face it, kids love crispy foods.[4] They are always in search of a chip, or a fry, or a crunchy extruded shape of some kind. Once I figured out that crispy food did not come exclusively from the store or drive-through, that one could *make* these morsels of delight in the comfort of one's own home, in almost unlimited quantities, I was hooked. No matter the time, I was always down to get high on my own supply.

Maybe I was drawn to the danger of it, too; the irresistible lure of the forbidden. Because while I was older now, and entrusted with more responsibility, I was still a child of only eight years, prone to accidents both unforeseen and entirely predictable. And each day I was given

---

3 When you are a kid, you don't really have a sense of what adult happiness looks like. As a result, you kind of don't care. As long as they aren't yelling and you get stuff like money and toys, shit is good.

4 This is the first of the primary and immutable truths about kids, followed by 2) they never want to go to sleep, and 3) some part of a child will always be sticky.

very specific instructions by my mother, repeated slowly and with meticulous diction every time she left the house.

No oil. No stove. No fire.

So of course, the second my mother would leave the house, I would find a pot, fill it to meniscus-challenging capacity with oil, and turn that bitch on high.

I never had a problem, either. I was careful, I told myself. And more than that, my mom was just being controlling, overprotective, and a poo-poo face besides. She had no idea what she was talking about. I could fry just fine. I didn't need supervision. And I wanted French fries. No one would stand in the way of me engaging in the heat-catalyzed sorcery that turned two small brown tubers into the most extraordinary and life-changing pile of crispy heaven sticks ever to be dipped into a tomato-based condiment. My mother and her admonitions were dream-killers, to be dismissed without regard. And I had done so, hundreds of times, to no ill effect. I made French fries, my mom remained blissfully ignorant, and the balance of power in the universe was maintained. Who was hurt in this transaction? No one.[5]

So on this particular day, I was flouting my mother's wishes once again. But this day was different. This day I was in a hurry, because I was flouting not one rule, but two: 1) do not cook, and 2) do not wear your mother's favorite white chiffon top. *Ever.*[6]

I was feeling fancy,[7] so I had gone into my mother's closet with an eye to turning this morning into a solitary fashion statement. I first took care to check any pockets for forgotten change,[8] and then searched out

---

5 Maybe the potatoes.

6 But *especially* while engaging in fire- and/or grease-related activities.

7 I don't know why. Sometimes a girl gotsta get her floss on. And yes, I do immediately regret writing that.

8 "Forgotten. Who forgets money in the pockets of their clothes?" scoffed the six-year-old me. "Obviously this woman is extremely wealthy and profligate enough to cast good money after bad without regard. It is also abundantly clear that her admonitions about 'money not growing on trees' are a pile of lies she peddles to get out of sharing her immense fortune with me. This woman is not to be obeyed or trusted. On the bright side, this is just enough for a Popsicle shaped like Ms. Pac-Man and four packs of Now and Laters, so the lady can't be *all* bad."

her favorite top. Not coincidentally, as this was my favorite top, too. I was at the age where everything my mother liked, I liked. I was constantly trying to emulate her in every way. From adoring the Ohio Players (whose adult-themed music I did not even *begin* to understand) to cinching my belts so tightly they gave the impression, however painful, that I had hips, to copying the way my mom laughed—an adorable little scream-shriek of surprise followed by openmouthed peals of delight—I wanted to be like her, and I would stop at nothing. Nothing at all, including sneaking into her closet and wearing her clothes like some tiny, creepy serial killer.[9]

And on this morning, I went for the gold: her prettiest, most expensive top, one she saved for special occasions. It was white, layered chiffon, with flowing satin ribbons and a watercolor painting of cranes and irises on the front. It was the closest thing my mother had to a princess dress in her closet, and since I was a little kid, it pretty much was a dress on me, albeit short and a little slutty, as if I was going to a late night kegger for woodland faeries.

Since I was circumspect and modest, even at that age, I decided to rock it tunic style. I pulled her mommy-sized white chiffon frock down over my seventies-era gauchos with the flowers on the butt pockets (don't hate) and sauntered into the kitchen to prepare, then enjoy, a greasy platter of Idaho's finest.

Realizing that I was compounding my trespasses, I thought it would be smart to get all this criminal activity done and over with alacrity. My mother was running errands and had taken my little sister with her, but who knew how long they'd be gone? The worst possible arrangement of events would be for my mom to walk in while I was eating clandestinely produced French fries dressed in her date-night finest. So to move things along, I turned the oil up on high, the better to get it ready to fry quickly.

In my head, this makes sense—medium heat, fun soon; maximum heat, fun *now*. So there I stood, hair in tiny afro-puffs, barefoot in gauchos and chiffon, perched daintily atop a perilously wobbly chair,

---

9 It puts the lotion in the basket.

waiting for a large pot dangerously full of grease to reach the proper temperature, which in my murky child mind was "volcanic."

When smoke started to rise from the pan,[10] I figured it was time to add the potatoes. Nice, wet, freshly sliced potatoes, cut in jagged hunks with a dull blade, and dropped into the oil in big, grubby, first-grader handfuls. Wet potatoes hit the hot grease, and did the thing that physics and chemistry demand. Sizzling droplets of grease sprayed angrily outward—onto stove, chiffon, and open flame.

Hooray! And also Yikes!

The fire flared up immediately. In seconds, it went from a tiny fire on the stove to a huge fire in the pot, and young as I was, I still knew this was a big fucking deal. Even then, I had the composure to think to myself, "You little asshole, you knew this could happen." But I clung to confidence as I yanked the pot off the burner to the cold side of the stove, certain the fire would go out. Instead, it flared up higher. "Hm," I thought. "That kills that theory."

Then I jumped back in fear, and freaked the fuck out.

Now, I *did* know something like this could happen. I shouldn't have been cooking when my mom was out. I definitely shouldn't have been cooking food in scalding-hot oil. Indeed, as I suspected, I *was* a little asshole. But I had done it like a hundred times before, and nothing had ever gone wrong. I had a flawless track record up to that point.

As a result, all I had learned about little kids, shoestring-cut potatoes, and scalding-hot oil was that if you put them all together, you got a French-fry filled, happy little kid. As far as I was concerned, the voice in my head—along with my mom's admonishments and that idiotic bear on Saturday morning TV blathering about lit matches and forest fires—was totally full of shit. I was careful, and even more than that, I was smart, and I was special. I could break the rules, because I was better than everyone else.

This would be the first time I learned that this was not true. It would not be the last.

---

10 Smoke! Dude. *Smoking grease.* If I saw a seven-year-old doing this now, I would put them in a straitjacket and call the authorities. Looking back, I was clearly out of control from the first grade onward.

The fact that the stove was on fire was a shock. Stuff like this was supposed to happen to other people. Dumber people. People not dressed up so fancy, or so hellbent on their own satisfaction. But it *was* happening to me, and it forced me (after climbing down off the chair to frantically get some water, throw it on the fire, learn irrefutably that water does nothing to grease fires but aggravate them and terrify you, get out the fire extinguisher from under the stove, put out the grease fire, and cover half of the kitchen in a fine white layer of regret) to confront my heretofore deeply held faith in my own superiority.

Reality is a bitter, bitter pill.

One thing was certain. I was not going to get away with doing the dishes and hiding the evidence this time. Unless I could sift through the Yellow Pages[11] and find a house painter who could cover the damage before my mom came home for the low, low fee of my weekly allowance, I was screwed. There were burn marks on the stove hood. There was a discharged fire extinguisher lying limp on the grease-spattered kitchen linoleum. Worst of all, there were oil splatters on my mom's favorite chiffon shirt. I was more than screwed. I was dead.

And in it crept. The sneaking suspicion that maybe I didn't have it *all* figured out. Maybe others had something to teach me. Maybe . . . just maybe . . . I still had a few things to learn. It seemed farfetched, but possible.

I got in a hellstorm of trouble that night. An early (and painfully brief) moment of tearful relief on my mother's part was followed by a reckoning not seen since in that household. Grounding. Restriction of television. General elimination of fun. There may have been cold gruel. It was a long time ago, and hazy, but I distinctly remember some kind of manual labor. And I took it all without complaint, because I had brought this on myself, and for once, I had learned my lesson. Never, ever, prepare fried foods in chiffon.[12]

My kitchen fire era came to a close that day. I never made that

---

11 Remember those? Yeah, neither do I.

12 This rule probably has larger metaphorical implications, but even taken literally, it is still pretty good advice.

unique set of mistakes in that precise order again. And from that experience grew the first silvered glimmer of an overarching axiom that I have come to embrace lustily, after having proved it to myself (and others) hundreds—no thousands—of times in my life. Stark and egregious errors, the truly epic failures, forge character. They burnish your edges and make you the person you are.

Not burning your hand 100 times in a row teaches you nothing but self-satisfaction, smugness, and wild-eyed arrogance.

But burn your fingers terribly just one time, and you will stay the fuck away from that stove.

Winning is awesome. Winning is the goal. Winning is what you should pursue unfailingly, unflinchingly, without pause or compromise. But to truly win, to become the kind of person who both knows how to pursue excellence and can recognize it once achieved, you *must* fail. You mustn't just be able to *deal* with failure, you must *embrace* it, wrap your arms around its shoulders like a frigid bedmate who rejects your every sexual advance, yet lashes out in rage and knuckle-punches you in the nuts the minute you turn away.

Failure doesn't want you. It wants you to want it. And only when you can look it in the eye and stare it down like a gladiator in the blood-soaked arena with a mix of both contempt and bemusement, can you truly win.

Winning doesn't teach. Winning *rewards*. You can only really *learn* from failure. And in the end, after you have taken a prolonged physical and psychological beating that would destroy a lesser man or woman, you will understand that success is not the absence of failure, but rather the presence of not quitting when you do fail. To win, you need to fail, and fail hard.

Pursue failure, and you will trip over success along the way.[13] That, or you'll trip over the dangling train of your stained chiffon tunic.

Either way, you're going down.

---

13 And also probably chip a tooth. What're you gonna do? That's what veneers are for.

(3)

The Time I Was a Human Maypole

"Do not show your wounded finger, for everything will knock up against it."—Baltasar Gracian

"I probably shouldn't have said that out loud."—Aisha Tyler

I was a weird kid.

Not entirely by my own choosing, either. Movies always like to portray weird kids as "quirky" or "offbeat," marching to the beat of a different drummer, listening to emo-dubstep through duct-taped headphones and screaming into a ravine in the rain with their oddly attractive yet adorably quirky friends.[1]

Unfortunately, my life was not a Wes Anderson movie, so I was just weird. *Weird* weird. A fucking weirdo. Unnaturally tall, tragically bookish, gawky, horsey, slouchy, loud. I interrupted conversations. I snorted when I laughed. I bit my cuticles obsessively.[2] I loved reading so much that daylight hours could not contain my love of literature, and

---

1 Because somehow movie weirdos are still socially adept enough to have an actual group of friends, one of whom is hot enough to have sex with. If they are female, she wears colored tights and dances on the lawn at night without shoes. If they are male, he is emotionally tortured and rides his bike through the city in the pouring rain. These people are not real.

2 Not my nails. Nail biting is for amateurs. Cuticle biting is where you draw real blood. That's what separates the simply odd from the truly and desperately compulsive.

I would take a flashlight under the covers and read far into the night, usually some very dense and impenetrable science fiction that invariably involved time travel. I played the *violin*, for chrissakes.

I was also a loner. And I didn't just play alone by default. I *liked* it. One of my favorite things to do was to go to the library on a Saturday and spend the entire afternoon looking at pathology books. If you don't know what a pathology book is, it is a reference book for doctors who need to see pictures of what diseases look like. Some of these books are so large that you cannot hold them in one hand, or even two, but instead must ask assistance from a librarian to lift them onto one of those large and dusty podia in the corner of the reading room,[3] so you can stand atop a footstool and turn pages gingerly as you gawk at the incredible, and often nausea-inducing, misfortune of others. I would look at everything. Infectious compendia. Venereal disease anthologies. My favorites were the ones that showed startling growths, tumors, and goiters in vivid detail. *Goiters.* No idea why I was into this; I just was.

I was the oddest child.

Compounding my oddity was the fact that my parents were kind of weird, too. Not in the tragically complex way that I was, but they had their moments. My parents were of that generation that migrated west in the seventies, in search of personal freedom, patchwork corduroy, free love, and joints the size of babies' forearms.

They had grown up very differently. My father lost his own dad during World War II and was raised by a single mother, engulfed by four sisters in the hardscrabble streets of Pittsburgh. He eventually fled all that estrogen for the relative calm of Washington, D.C., where he met my mother, a Howard University homecoming queen and civil rights activist. They were young, beautiful, and politically aware, which meant, of course, they needed to pack all their crap into a puke-green Chevy and move to California.

---

3 I don't know *why* I am using words like "podia" and "librarian." And "books." Like anyone's ever heard of that stuff nowadays. If you are struggling with these concepts, just imagine the Internet was really heavy and you had to carry the whole thing around in your hands and there wasn't any porn or videos of cats in toilets inside it, just words and a few scant illustrations. That's what going to the library was like.

And they did just that, driving west from D.C., meticulously avoiding the South, which at the time was not the most hospitable place for two young brown people with devastatingly fierce afros, and landing eventually in the San Francisco Bay area. It was progressive, it was culturally vibrant, and, most of all, it didn't snow there, which was a major attraction for my parents, as they both hated cold weather and vowed never to shiver through another East Coast winter again.

They also decided, once fully committed to California as a choice, to just push this hippie thing all the way to the wall—why not?—and burn incense, study meditation, put pictures of dead Hindu guys around the house, and stop eating meat. I have to applaud their commitment—there's a reason you never saw many black Hari Krishnas[4]—but this was not a recipe for popularity. Coming to school each day smelling like carob and Nag Champa incense is not a mark of normalcy. I didn't have much to work with from the start.

The icing on the honey-sweetened carrot cake was that when I started first grade, my parents sent me to a private school. This was commendable on their part. They wanted a better life for their daughter, to provide a safe learning environment where their kid could play a string instrument, enjoy opera, and speak with white people in their native accent. There is nothing wrong with these dreams. They are utterly valid. But to be not just the one black kid, but also the one tall kid, the one vegetarian, the one kid railroaded into Transcendental Meditation, the one kid most likely to show up at school with a bag of date rolls and a copy of the *Baghavad Gita* under her arm, well, this was just straining the capacity of human comprehension. When you're a kid, you may be able to get away with being one kind of weird. But being seven kinds of weird is putting gravy on your ice cream sundae. It's just. Not. Allowed.

Don't feel sorry for me. I got very good at playing alone. I loved to read, and to build sand castles, and erect little villages made out of sticks and mud, where the cowboys and the Indians would live to-

---

4 It's hard enough being a minority in the regular world, without actively choosing to be a minority within an even tinier minority of people who danced around airports asking for money. Way to self-isolate!

gether peacefully, and the Indians would give the cowboys tobacco and maize, and the cowboys would give the Indians blankets infected with a virus that would make their descendants many generations hence impervious to alcoholism and fluent in their ancient tongue. I was a happy kid. I needed no one.

There is a funny thing that happens when you reject the social hierarchy and go off on your own. People start to resent you. They don't know why, they just do. When you are a weird kid, people think you should want to be like them. Why wouldn't you? They are popular and awesome, and you are offbeat and struggle with eye contact. When it becomes apparent that you don't *want* to be like them, they start to wonder. "What the hell does she know that we don't know?" "Why doesn't she like us when we are so very enamored of ourselves?" And, "What's so interesting about that pile of sticks and sand shaped like a teepee?" And rather than ask you about your rigorously authentic, well-constructed sand structure, they smash it, because that is just what kids do.

Kids are assholes.

Once I got on the radar of the other kids at school, who didn't know *why* they didn't like what I was up to, they just *didn't*, my reverie was shattered. Long periods of nattering harassment were punctuated by intense bursts of physical taunting that bordered on operatic. It culminated (for the first time, anyway) one day when one enterprising young child, who had no doubt seen this done on an ABC after-school special the week prior, decided it would be satisfying to mount a more concentrated effort at my ridicule—something more organized, collaborative, and with more, I dunno . . . *oomph*.

He gathered the others, who up until this point had been coming at me erratic and scattershot, and together they concocted a coordinated attack. These kids got me alone, during a rare moment of reflection,[5] joined hands, and started (I kid you not) to taunt me while dancing

---

5 Oh, who am I kidding? I was standing by the fence biting my cuticles and reading *The Left Hand of Darkness*.

around me in a circle. Very quickly, as they gathered speed and intensity, it began to resemble a May Day dance, with my classmates in the roles of the towheaded Nordic cherubs celebrating the abundance of burgeoning spring, and me the confused and sullen maypole, who wished this discomfiting jubilation would end so she could get back to reading about life in an alien society in the year 4870.

When I say they were dancing in a circle around me, I am being altogether literal. They joined hands, formed a circle, and skipped around me clockwise in a circle while chanting my name. Not my family-given name, but my *meditation* name. When my parents got into meditation, we all got spiritual names. The one I received was *Sujata*, which in Sanskrit means "from a good family origin." [6] I have a feeling none of this irony was lost on my parents. They are nothing if not funny.

Anyway, somehow, in a moment of severe weakness about which I will always feel a deep regret, I told one of my classmates about my meditation name. This was like placing an unpinned grenade in the hands of a poo-flinging monkey, one incapable of sympathy or mercy, but very good at dancing clockwise in a circle while singing.

So there was me, the wretched human maypole, and them, the remorseless children blind with glee, and the singing of my meditation name, and the dancing. This went on far longer than any amount of taunting should without devolving into violence and tears; me observing dispassionately, them doing their best to mimic the Von Trapp kids, only without all that wholesome earnestness. I would not show weakness, and they had rotational inertia on their side, so this thing went on for what seemed like an eternity.

In retrospect, I have to give it up to these kids. They were organized, they were all moving in the same direction, their chant was

6 In real life, Sujata was a pretty awesome chick. She brought the Buddha a bowl of milk rice when he was starving to death after six years of extreme austerity. In doing so, she helped him distill the concept of "The Middle Way," which is a pretty important principle among Buddhists to this day. So I suppose there's that.

both haunting and melancholy with a slight mordant twinge,[7] and it was well concepted and perfectly executed across the board. And it sure did make me feel like crap. Which I'm sure was their intended result.[8]

Now, you may be asking, "How exactly is this wound self-inflicted? Seems to me like these kids were the crass bullies and you the dainty innocent." But you see, my friend, you have missed a crucial element to the story: I *gave* them the ammunition with which to bombard me. I couldn't control the fact that I was tall, or odd, or a nerd, or a creepy loner, but I could control the level to which I allowed my tall, odd, nerdy aloneness to be weaponized.

I pretty much just handed over the detonator on that one.

The fact is that there will always be predators in the world, heartless dead-eyed thugs just waiting to exploit even the slightest show of weakness on your part. And you may not always be able to avoid predation. Some of these assholes are *good*. But what you can do is avoid feeding their fire. They will dig for days or weeks to find the chink in your armor; don't lift up your chain mail the first day and show them where your soft parts are. If they're going to drive a blade through your delicate heart, for god's sake, make them *work* for it.

Don't get me wrong: hold fast to who you are without apology or compromise, because the things that make you odd as a kid make you *unique* as an adult. Don't ever let anyone make you feel ashamed of who you are, no matter how outside the main. But if you can, try to avoid throwing metaphorical gas onto their flame of incomprehension. In my case, I was already a tall, bespectacled, vegetarian girl who was the only person of my ethnicity in the student body, didn't have a television, and was obsessed with reading. I didn't need to throw one more straw of oddity onto my camel's already strained back. People have a hard enough time understanding each other as it is. The last

---

7 Which is hard to do for a second-grader. Mordancy is a pretty difficult concept to grasp at seven, or any age for that matter. I doff my hat to them.

8 And clearly is some shit I haven't been able to let go.

thing you should do is actively make yourself seem stranger than you already are.

Because there is another axiom that holds true for human beings, and it is simple and universal. Much like the Incredible Hulk, what we don't understand, we don't like.

And what we don't like, we smash.

(4)

The Time I Got Boobs Way Before Everyone Else

"An insincere and evil friend is more to be feared than a wild beast; a wild beast may wound your body, but an evil friend will wound your mind."—Buddha

"Mean girls suck."—Aisha Tyler

If you were tuned into popular culture at all in the year 2010, you may remember the "It Gets Better Project," a campaign launched to help young people gripped in the throes of bullying. Adults who had been bullied as children, many of them gay, spoke to a generation of young people, telling them that no matter how desperate, how isolated or ostracized they felt now, things would get better. That they would grow up, find themselves and like-minded people who would love them for who they were, develop confidence and a sense of self, and the taunts and jeers of youth would fade into the background like so many vuvuzelas at the World Cup. That campaign was awesome.

This chapter is not like that.

I do wish, however, that the adult me could talk to the third grade me, and use those three words (without infuriating people for whom the phrase "it gets better" has real meaning and substance). Because the fact is, it *did* get better, but at the time, when I was *eight years old*, and getting boobs, I thought the world was coming to an end.[1]

This seems counter-intuitive, I know. Girls are meant to get boobs. Hell, they are *dying* to get boobs. An entire literary career has been built upon the concept of preteen girls praying to some busty unseen deity for cleavage.[2] Middle-schoolers get training bras far before they need them, when the only things filling out the cups are house keys on one side and a very sweaty Android phone on the other. Adult women purchase more boobs than they can ever hope to carry or their husbands hope to handle, and then assault the rest of us daily with the human equivalent of a steel plow soldered to a Smart Car. Boobs are all we ever think about. Honestly, if we as a culture put a quarter of the mental effort into world peace and sustainable energy that we put into thinking about, talking about, touching, fantasizing about, visualizing, augmenting, and trying not to stare at boobs, we'd be Klingon—a planet with no hunger, no violence, and no war.[3]

So it seems silly that I would be sad about getting boobs. Much like Lorraine Baines to Marty McFly, boobs were my destiny. But when you are already a giantess, have cornrows and glasses and wear clothes from the free box at the Goodwill while everyone else is rocking inky Jordache® jeans with the contrast trim, one more thing that makes you stand out is not what you pray for under the covers while feverishly trying to finish *The Silmarillion* by flashlight. No, you are praying for a cloak of invisibility, even though the *Harry Potter* series hasn't been written yet. And breasts on a third grader are like a cloak of "Hey everyone, check out the mad rack on that gigantic eight-year-old!"

When my boobs came in, they came in fast and furious. There was no budding growth, no hint of décolleté. One day I was a slightly masculine preteen, and the next I was a slightly masculine preteen with

---

1 My problems are not real problems.

2 See Judy Blume's infamous "We must . . . we must . . ." borderline limerick-couplet.

3 Also not much sex, but hey, something's gotta give.

huge boobs.[4] This was alarming, as I *felt* no different. I was still obsessed with the Scholastic newsletter. I still liked to feed mud to my Baby Alive doll. I still hid in the cubby room so I could eat my lunch uninterrupted while poring over Martian fiction, and possibly eat portions of others' lunches as well (more on that later). I was still very much a kid but, suddenly, I had the body of a teenager. This is like waking up one day and finding out that your golden retriever puppy shoots lasers from its adorable puppy eyes. Someone is bound to get hurt.

Most likely, it will be you.

I did not know what to do with my newfound anatomy. They were unexpected and unwieldy and wholly unmanageable, and they made all my favorite tee shirts too tight. Despite all my best efforts to control them, which included crossing my arms supportively and wearing multiple shirts at once, they wiggled and waggled and were entirely disobedient. I was at a total loss as to what to do.[5]

I *definitely* did not want to close the door on my rapidly receding childhood by purchasing a bra. A *bra* was for old people and white ladies like Jayne Mansfield and strangely white black ladies like Grace Jones. A bra was not for little kids who dreamed of being astronauts. What are you gonna do with boobs in space? Unless they are currency for some far-flung civilization, all they're going to do is interfere with proper oxygen flow inside your space suit. I was not interested in having boobs, and I was *definitely* not interested in giving them support, moral or otherwise.

The awesome thing about getting boobs when you are a little kid is that people tend to ignore them. There is something weird about a little

---

4 It's all about proportion. I was a big kid, so even my starter rack dwarfed the efforts of others. My breasts were the Manute Bol of boobs: maybe not the best compared to others, but most definitely the biggest.

5 I know this is well-trodden ground, but when you are a kid, your particular crisis is the worst thing that has ever happened to anyone in the world ever. The fact that plenty of women everywhere seemed to be managing their boobs without much difficulty was completely lost on me. I was in torment. Torment!

kid with breasts, the way there is something weird about a little kid in a suit and top hat, or a little kid who is too precocious and articulate. You can't help but feel that the time-space continuum has been gruesomely ruptured in order to make this little human strangely adult, and it is better not to look directly into his eyes for fear of being mesmerized and sent stumbling into a cornfield to your death. Preternaturally mature kids are either instruments of the devil or speeding toward a ripping drug habit. They are best avoided.

So thankfully, no one really noticed the boobs, or if they did, they didn't say anything. My parents, angels that they are, kept telling me, as they always had, that I was perfect in every way.[6] And as I became more comfortable with these new members of my inner circle, I decided that I did not have boobs at all, but rather interstellar communication devices that would, at any moment, turn on and connect me directly with an alien race in a neighboring galaxy.

I was *very* into Ray Bradbury novels at the time.

So there I was, clinging as desperately to my childhood as my ever-tightening clothing clung to me. I staunchly refused to accept what was happening. I was cultivating the kind of denial construct normally reserved for alcoholics and politicians' wives.

Until one day I was slapped, painfully and directly, back to reality.

When someone wants to humiliate you, they will say something cruel. When they want to decimate you and throw you into a psychological tailspin, they will say that cruel thing loud enough for everyone in the vicinity to hear it, and with such dismissive derision that you have no choice but to curl up into a tiny ball and blow away.

And so it was that a little girl in my third grade class, whom I'll call Ashley,[7] walked up to me, and with a tone better reserved for speaking over a pile of steaming shit or freshly puked vomit, said, "Ew! You're getting *boobs*! They're huge! Yuck!" And then she walked away, gig-

---

6 Well, my mom would drop little sugar nuggets like that. My dad had more of a "fuck 'em if they can't take a joke" approach. Which was pretty inappropriate language at the time, but still, surprisingly effective.

7 Seriously not her real name, but somehow it just oozes mean girl, doesn't it?

gling in the way that only third grade girls can, emitting a sound that is at once delightful and depressing, a combination of soap bubbles popping, flower petals opening, bells tinkling, and golden retriever puppies plopping tiny plops of ploppy puppy poop.

That sound was the soundtrack to the end of my innocence. It was time to face the facts. I had boobs. I was not a woman, but I was certainly not an ordinary third grader anymore. And it was highly unlikely I was ever going to get to travel into space. Not with *those* bazongas in the way. I was who I was, and who I was was an insanely stacked third grader who wore tight tee shirts and loved science fiction.

I can't say that my boobs were self-inflicted, at least not in the *active* sense. I mean, I did actually grow them myself, but that would have happened with or without my consent. The body does what the body does unbidden, growing wide hips or stork legs or ears that could double as badminton rackets while you howl in protest, dismayed and powerless. You have nothing to do with it, and you can do nothing about it. But my frantic discomfort with my changing body, and my refusal to accept what was happening, empowered others—namely a super-mean third grade harpie with a tinkly laugh and a heart made of carbon—to turn what was a natural human development into a prickly psychological weapon. That, and I needed to suck it up and get a training bra.

What is the moral of this story? Nature will deal you a mixed hand, and in all likelihood, you'll get something you didn't ask for—large boobs or small ones, big feet or freakishly long fingers, buckteeth, a giant head, a laugh that can strip paint. Be proud. No one in the world can open a jar, use their giant shoe to drive home a nail, shade others from the sun with their cranium, or laugh wildly at a joke quite like you. These may not end up being your favorite traits, but they are yours and yours alone. So don't be ashamed. Rock what you got.

And know that—with the boobs, as with everything else—it will definitely get a whole hell of a lot better.

5

The Time I Foolishly Tried to Trade Vegetables for Meat

"How poor are they that have not patience! What wound did ever heal but by degrees?"—William Shakespeare

"I would literally do anything for a slice of bologna."—Aisha Tyler

Throughout one's life, one often attempts a feat that one knows, in advance, will be an exercise in futility. Tying a sheet around one's neck as a cape and leaping from the garage roof. Asking the hottest girl in school to the prom when the sum of your previous contact was bumping into her in the line for pierogies on Ethnic Food Day. Exposing one's breast on national television in the hopes of kick-starting one's career. It is a critical and fundamental component of the human psyche that we believe unwaveringly in the fantastic, the mysterious, the transcendent—and the wildly improbable.

And so it is that when I was a child I believed blindly, hopelessly, that someday I would be able to convince one of my classmates to trade their lunch for mine.

This would prove to be utterly naïve.

As previously lamented, for as long as I could remember, my family had been vegetarian. My earliest memories are of vegetables. And fruit. And carob. And tears.

We were vegetarian at a time when vegetarianism was neither cute, nor fun, nor hip, nor even particularly nutritious. There were no gourmet veggie restaurants, no hipster gluten-free bakeries, no meat-less patties that tasted eerily like industrial hamburgers, not even a single celebrity vegan with a come-hither smugness and a fancy cook-book. Soy was something you used to feed cattle or thicken industrial adhesives. Almond milk was just a glimmer in some infant hippie's lactose-intolerant eye. We were early adopters, trailblazers; we were completely on our own.

My parents weren't even particularly meticulous vegetarians. We still ate eggs, milk, and cheese, but refused dairy butter.[1] We ate a lot of vegetable casseroles and buttered toast, but would then voraciously devour the occasional twenty-pound ling cod my father would bring home from his deep-sea fishing trips (including the eyeballs, a favor-ite move of my father's that never failed to gross out my mother and completely delight my sister and me). Their approach managed to be inconsistent yet draconian at the same time; I was denied meat, but also fruit juice and processed foods. I could order a Filet-O-Fish at McDonalds, but the rest of the menu was completely off-limits, as if the fish sandwiches took some circuitous and altogether more virtuous path toward their paper-wrapped end. And I was not allowed to have sugar, which as far as I could tell, was just plain mean.

To top it all off, at this time, my father worked as a meatcutter at a massive beef plant in Oakland. This irony wasn't lost on even *my* young, developing brain. I may not have understood cognitive disso-nance yet, but I did understand *unfair*.[2] My dad had access to an un-

---

1 This led to a dramatic riddle for me as a child. I loved to eat butter. My mother would open the butter compartment to find two child-sized finger marks dug ferally through the stick, as if a tiny werewolf had mounted a dairy attack. I would often steal sticks out of the fridge for furtive ingestion later; I was hooked. But this was not even real butter, but soy margarine, a terrible trick played on me by my parents and the world at large. The first time I had real dairy butter, I was like a methadone addict getting a first taste of black tar heroin. They found me in a glistening heap, reeking like a dirty theater lobby popcorn machine, weeping quietly for redemption.

2 This was like telling a panhandling hobo you don't have any money, and then climbing into your Maybach filled with gold bars and freshwater pearls. I mean, you don't owe the guy anything, but there's no need to rub his nose in it.

limited supply of delicious steaks, and yet was making me eat bricks of tofu and fermented wheat gluten. This was injustice on a high order. This outrage would not stand.[3]

There was no reason for me to lust after meat so badly, other than the fact that it was forbidden. Kids always want what they can't have, and in my case, meat represented something more than just a food-stuff. It symbolized my intense desire to fit in. All the other kids at school were eating bologna and American slices on white bread, softly slicked with neon smears of yellow mustard, a sandwich that embod-ied everything that was mainstream and wholesome and normal in the world, while I was picking alfalfa sprouts from between my teeth. Meat meant normalcy. Meat meant *belonging*.

I was vaguely aware of the fact that meat was bad for you, but the whole "meat is murder" meme had yet to be coined, and no one had thrown blood on a creepy old fur-festooned rich lady yet. There was not much known in the mainstream about vegetarianism, and it cer-tainly was not *cool* in any way. Whenever I would have furtive access to a television,[4] they would flash that nutrition pyramid during *School-house Rock*, taunting me with that tantalizing block of meats and pro-teins. The entire world was aligned against me.

Making things worse, I couldn't think of one good reason for us to be vegetarians, other than to make my life a living hell. As far as I could tell, we didn't eat meat because meat tasted delicious and gave me hap-piness, and my parents' goal in life was to deny me all human joy. This was the motivation for our abstemious lifestyle: to ruin Aisha's life and destroy whatever modicum of normalcy remained to me.

And so I was a vegetarian along with my parents, but with a deep and abiding reluctance. And since I did not make money, purchase groceries, or prepare meals, I really had no choice.

There were meals my mother made that I really did love: big piles

---

3 My father once took me to work with him to show me how disgusting the meat production industry is, how bloody and dirty and shot through with the stench of death. This only made me want meat more. I don't know what that says about me, other than that I am impervious to lesson learning and have a highly developed ability to sublimate.

4 Oh yeah, my parents also didn't believe in TV. Our house was a barrelful of awesome.

of spaghetti (what we called it back then, before the heady days of *pasta*), blanketed in that chemist's excuse for cheese shaken from a big green canister; omelets filled with sautéed peaches and strawberries at the height of summer and doused in maple syrup (I was a fan of the savory-sweet trend long before it became hip); grilled cheese sandwiches broiled to bubbling and stuffed with thick slices of juicy tomato; carrot cakes packed with raisins and walnuts and piled high with real, homemade cream cheese frosting. It wasn't that my mother couldn't cook—she was a fantastic cook. It was just that I felt I was being put through a childhood-long test of some kind, training to prepare me for a long adult life of discipline and deprivation, perhaps as a missile silo operator, an international spy, an Antarctic research scientist, or (I still clung to hope) the first black astronaut to make Mars landfall.[5]

This training extended to my time away from home, when I was forced to enter groups of normal, carnivorous kids, and act as if I was one of them. I approached this like an ongoing sociology project, a series of experiments in early espionage and infiltration. Could I act like them? Could I persuade them I was one of them, blend in and fade away, like the last living soul in a world of flesh-eating zombies? I assigned myself this task each morning, like a tiny agent of a vegetarian sleeper cell, or an alien occupying a freshly body-snatched human. *Act normal.*

This worked for most of the morning. But as soon as the lunch bell rang, the tofu salad hit the fan.

You remember what a big part of socialization trading lunches is when you're a kid—exchanging the food you don't want in your lunch for the stuff in your buddy's lunch, of which he or she is equally disdainful, but which to you looks like ambrosia sent from Mount Olympus in a tiny golden chariot. This is a big part of making friends, keeping friends, and, if you refuse to trade, sending friends into a shame spiral of self-hate and dejection. You can imagine how desperately I wanted to be included in this sacred ritual. You can probably also imagine how frustrated I felt that the only thing I had to trade were foods

---

5 "One small step for me, one giant leap for mankind, you jive-ass sucka."

that, while edible, could easily be used for industrial doorstops and NHL-strength hockey pucks. It is hard to convince someone to give you their container of Jell-O squares or extra Ring Ding when you cannot even muster up adjectives to properly describe what you offer in return. I struggled to make my case, but had very few descriptives in my arsenal: chief among them "soft," "bitter," "slightly acrid," and "doesn't taste as much like dirt as you might expect." I was woefully outgunned.

This did not deter me from trying. I was one against an army, a wrench in the machine, and I would fight until my very last breath, or until I was forced, once again, to eat my avocado sandwich and date-coconut rolls alone on the tetherball court. Each day was an opportunity to try anew, to get back behind that rock and roll it incrementally up that hill, to prove that I, all respect to *Glengarry Glen Ross*, could *always be closing*.

I tried everything. Seduction. Subterfuge. Threats. Bribery. None of this was even remotely successful. In a world of carnivorous A-Rods, I was a vegetarian Adam Dunn.[6] No, I was worse than Adam Dunn. I was batting a perfect zero.

I don't know when it was that I resorted to supplication. It was truly dismaying to realize that in a world ruled by extortion, bargain, and leverage, I was weaponless, without enticements of any kind. I had nothing anyone wanted. When you have nothing to bargain with, you resort to what honorable yet impoverished people have done for centuries—alms-seekers, ne'er-do-wells, freeloaders, and bums—you beg.

This was as pathetic in practice as it sounds in retrospect. To be a little kid, roaming at recess, begging for scraps of bread like a Benedictine friar at the tail of the Plague is tragic on a very high order. But desire and hunger soon overcame any shreds of pride I had left, and wolfish bites of a crème-filled golden cake can sweeten even the bitterest dregs of shame. Fortunately, kids have as much capacity for

---

6 No. I did not know, before Googling it, that in 2011 Adam Dunn (.159) was on his way to beating Billy Sullivan's record for lowest batting average ever (.170). But now I do, and I am marginally richer for it. Just marginally, though.

extreme generosity as they have for dead-eyed cruelty. And when you fling yourself upon their mercy, and maybe promise to organize their cubby or do their homework, they will give you their castoffs freely and with open hands. As easily as they can be cruel, kids can also be kind; a direct appeal to that buried bit of nice can tease it quickly to the fore. All I needed to do was drop the wheedling and manipulation and *ask* for what I wanted—a practice that has served me countless times since. Sometimes the most effective path to a destination—be it boardroom, bedroom, or lunchroom—is a straight, direct, unabashed line. The only thing someone can do to you when you ask for something is tell you no. But ask enough times and *someone'll* finally say yes, if only to get you the hell out of their face.

I lived through most of fifth grade on half-eaten bologna sandwiches, orange Skittles, Dorito dust, Twinkie heels, and those weird-shaped Boston Baked Beans from the bottom of the box.[7] And I learned that every once in a while, if you ask for what you want, you'll get it. Or at least, a third of it. Maybe with a few bite marks.

I have not always depended on the kindness of strangers. But for one long and delirious year, I cast my fate, and my awful hippie lunches, to the wind. And the wind blew castoff pizza crusts back into my face.

It was a fair exchange.

---

7 Boston Baked Beans is the worst name for a candy since Nut Milk. Yes, there is a candy bar called Nut Milk. Let it wash over you. Well, not literally. Ew.

6

The Time I Almost Seared My Flesh to My Dad's Motorcycle

"A wounded deer leaps highest."—EMILY DICKINSON

"Holy crap I'm on fire. Again."—AISHA TYLER

For many, childhood is about puppies and cupcakes, running through meadows chasing kittens, candy, dreams, rainbows, and puppies again.

I say childhood is about tragedy. Crushing, tear-stained tragedy.

For me, childhood isn't something you savor so much as something you survive, a litany of tragic episodes and cosmic insults, birthday letdowns and social rejection, skinned knees and heartbreak compounded exponentially and punctuated only briefly by wee slivers of cake-induced joy, until one day you wake up and you're twenty years old and you got so drunk the night before that you passed out on your best friend's futon in your underwear, slept through midterms, and will probably flunk out of college and be forced to manage an all-night diner or park cars for a living.

Oh, and while you were sleeping, someone wrote on your face. In Magic Marker.

Childhood—it is not for the meek.

Since childhood is so punishing, such a hazing gauntlet writ large, it only makes sense that one should make as many grand gestures as possible—to "go huge," if I may coin a lame and not particularly compelling phrase.

So that is what kids do. They throw tantrums, explode into screams, hurl and squeal, cry and giggle, until they near asphyxiation. Everything is the "best thing *evarrr*" or "the end of the world" or "if I don't get this I will *die*." There are no half measures in childhood. Everything is cataclysmic.

For me, this extreme expression took many forms, but none so painful as the year I decided to dress like a ballerina. *All the freaking time*.

Not at a cute age, either. This was long after the age of three, when I would have looked totally adorbs in a tiny pink leotard, ballet shoes, and a tutu dusted with chocolaty fingerprints that could either be a dancer's skirt or a princess dress depending on what struck me over my Wheatena that morning.

No, I was the hoary age of ten when I decided I wanted to dress like a prima ballerina (or perhaps a weird old SoHo hippie who made her own granola and never wore pants because "they interrupted the flow of my *chi*, man"). I wanted people to know that I was serious, not about ballet necessarily, but about art. Somehow I had decided that the best way to showcase my seriousness was to wear a ballerina outfit at all times, and to all places.

Why did I fixate acutely on such a specific fashion choice? I have no idea. Kids seize upon things. Favorite shoes. Special dolls. Compulsive hand washing. Eating paste. Who knows why? The juvenile mind is a mystery. I may have watched a PBS special on dancers one afternoon. It might have come to me in a fever dream. But one thing was sure— despite the total impracticality of this concept, I could not be swayed. I was hell-bent on my own slow and very soft destruction.

I wonder, looking back, if perhaps I needed to order my life, to control it in some way, because so much of it had changed so dramatically. My parents' divorce had finalized, and I was living full-time with my father. Before you nod your head in wistful understanding, it wasn't that traumatic. There was no mayhem, no blowups or Kramer vs. Kramer dramatics. I went with my dad, my sister went with my mom, and we all still saw each other as much as possible. Life went on. But there may have been a part of me that needed to control what I could control. And wearing the same outfit, or a variation on that outfit, every single day, certainly qualified as *controlling*.

First, I needed the outfit. I went to my mom for this. I wanted a series of coordinated ensembles: leotards and tights, with a matching ankle-length wrap skirt that tied at one side. These all had to match perfectly in color, which meant we had to buy the leotards and tights, find matching fabric, purchase a skirt pattern, and have the wrap skirts built from scratch.[1]

We then had to find a seamstress with the skills, ability, and patience to sew these things up for me. My mother had long ago tapped out of being my bespoke couturier, as I was never satisfied, and she had things to do, like go to work so we could eat and shit. So we found a seamstress in Oakland's Chinatown. I will not say any more on this subject, because no matter what I do, you will find a way to make it racist.

My parents were kind enough not to stand in the way of my weirdo dreams, and ponied up the money for this exercise in sartorial suicide. And so I had five of these outfits constructed in a variety of colors, all of them various shades of dun, none of them flattering. Somehow, I believed brown tones made me seem more serious, but in reality, they made me look like a tiny dancing version of Hanky the Poo.

I began to wear these outfits everywhere, regardless of place, time of day, or contextual appropriateness of my attire. I wanted to make a statement. I was going to be like Thomas Wolfe or Christopher Hitchens, universally known for my distinct sartorial style and my utter lack of concern for others' feelings or happiness. I was more than a ballerina, I was a tastemaker, and I was going to make myself *known*.[2]

This crazed approach immediately posed problems. For instance, it

---

1 Even as a child, I was very exacting. Some might call it anal. I might call it go fuck yourself. Yes, even back then I would have called it go fuck yourself.

2 Why are kids so freaking dramatic? Nothing's even happened to them yet!

is very difficult to play dodge ball in a wrap skirt. You may cut a fine figure in the beginning, skirts flapping elegantly as the ball handler picks off the weak and the slow, but the minute you need to engage in any type of evasive action, that fabric will wrap around your tights-clad legs like a lasso around a rodeo calf, and you will fall to the ground, there to be pelted about the face and chest violently and repeatedly by the stinging slap of red rubber.

This is also not a practical outfit for: sleeping, walking, running, swimming, digging in the dirt, climbing trees, picking blackberries, riding a bicycle, swinging on a swing, playing jacks, or anything requiring dexterity or practicality—pretty much anything one might do as a kid.

It *was* pretty awesome when I played violin. I looked like a Russian tsarina in afro puffs. The outfit would also have worked in ballet class, but I had quit that shitshow months before. Pulling my hair into a tight bun every weekend was giving me headaches, as was all the random and poorly pronounced French. So I became an impostor, a poseur in Lycra, waltzing around looking for all the world like a ballerina when the best I could deliver on that front was a crooked second position and a few wild gesticulations. But man, did I look *good*.

This extended piece of performance art came to a spectacular halt when my grand ballerina fantasy ran face-first into my father's dude-on-a-fast-bike fantasy.

One was bound to get creamed.

My father loved motorcycles, and had always wanted to ride them. And nothing, not propriety or social norms or the oppressive yoke of fatherhood would defer his halcyon dream. He had been working toward this fantasy for years, as having kids required a slow and measured approach. When my sister and I were very young, my parents had Italian scooters: Vespas, to be exact. This made them the coolest parents ever; even now they'd be awash in hipster points. They had a custom cart built that attached to the back of their scooters so my sister and I could ride along with (or actually behind) them. We sat backwards, facing traffic, strapped in with seat belts, shielded from the sun by a custom canopy and shielded from auto exhaust and potential impact by shiny optimism. We loved riding in this cart, and would sit happily side by side, laughing, playing games, and giving as many passing cars the finger as we possibly could.[3] Sometimes we went for the double finger for extra impact—this could be compounded by aiming all four fingers at one driver, or spread out among several motorists for maximum efficiency. We were a rolling two-kid wrecking crew.

We loved riding with my parents on their Vespas, and when my dad graduated to first a small, and then bigger and bigger motorcycles,[4] I was no less enthusiastic. It was insanely cool to walk to the curb after school and watch your classmates crawl into their boring old Volvo wagons or VW buses, then pull on your helmet and jump on to the back of a revving crotch rocket. Add to that the fact that my dad was an insanely handsome black man with more than a passing resemblance to Action Jackson, who wore a brown leather jacket and motorcycle boots with no sense of irony and had a mustache so thick he needed to comb it with an afro pick, and you can see how this was really working for me. I might have been a weird kid, culturally off-piste and socially isolated, but at least my dad looked like Dolemite and rocked a badass ride.[5]

Despite my love of riding motorcycles, I was only average at being a motorcycle passenger. I held on with passable surety, my gaze often drifting toward cars alongside or distant passersby. I would use my father's back as a podium, placing *The Lord of the Rings* or *The Phantom Tollbooth* atop his capacious lats. More than once, I fell asleep on the back of my father's motorcycle, listing frighteningly to one side or the other before being elbowed violently in the ribs by my terrified dad. This led him to have a custom harness constructed, one that strapped

---

3 This is one of the unsung joys of childhood: being able to give people the finger and having it be seen as at once both shocking and cute. There is no way an adult can get away with shocking *and* cute at the same time. Russell Brand thinks he has this dialed. He does not.

4 By the time I was in high school, my father had owned, in succession, three different and progressively larger and more intimidating Kawasaki Ninja bikes. This made him very popular among my male friends, and in defiance of all his efforts to the contrary, I am confident got me laid more than once. This was wholly unintentional and supremely disappointing. For *him*.

5 Not that any little kids knew who Blaxploitation film superstar Dolemite *was*. But they could sense the *badness* blowing off my dad.

me to his back so that even in full coma state, I would not tumble from the bike to the pavement at high speeds.[6] I ended up liking this very much, as it allowed me to use both hands to read—one to hold the book and one to turn the pages—whereas before I was reduced to turning pages with my nose. So his solution to my somnolence worked out quite well for both of us.

It wasn't my drowsiness that ended up being the problem.

Despite his almost daily admonitions to watch the exhaust pipe, the temperature of which went from ambient to Earth's molten core in about sixty seconds upon ignition of the engine, I was always dallying perilously close to hot metal. This was not intentional. I was a kid, distractible and preoccupied with important things, like whether peanut butter and olives would make a good sandwich. So I would hop on the bike, arms full of books and peanut butter dreams, and almost always touch my leg to the exhaust pipe, letting out a startled yelp, after which my father would roll his eyes and erupt, "I *told* you to watch out for that pipe! I don't say this shit for my health!"[7] I would nod and agree, and we'd be on our way, Daddy Dolemite and L'il Ballerina, off to fight crimes in the ghetto and stick it to the man, or at least make a whole wheat peanut butter and honey sandwich and watch the Sugar Ray Leonard–Floyd Mayweather fight.

At this time in our lives, I was acutely focused on my artist phase, and rocking my ballerina outfits daily. With all the work it took to swirl my skirts while maintaining a haughty air of culture and refinement, taking time to avoid the exhaust pipe was simply not on my very full agenda. So on this day, I climbed on to the bike in my brick-brown ensemble, thinking about how elegant I looked, and how after I did my homework I was going to rip through some Ray Bradbury, when I smelled smoke. *Interesting*, I thought. *Just thinking about* Fahrenheit 451 *made me smell fire. My imagination is like, magic or something.*

---

6 No. At no point did my father consider not riding bikes anymore. This was no more an option than him becoming a dairy farmer or joining the priesthood—he would sooner have lain down to die. We would be *cool* at any cost. Children be damned!

7 My dad was extremely loving, but very, very straightforward.

At that moment, I looked down to see that the right hem (and, well, most of my skirt) had melded itself with the exhaust pipe of the motor-cycle, and was aflame. Aflame in that kind of way where the burning spreads quickly, turning a small hole into a very big one, and making you question how much longer you will be on this earth. A thoughtful person would have remained calm, stepped from the bike, and as those 1970s preparedness commercials admonished, stopped, dropped, and rolled. A less thoughtful person, say, a dream-addled ten-year-old, would have lost their shit.

This is what I did.

Which made my dad lose his shit.

Which was *not* a good thing.

Dads are big. This is one of their most awesome qualities. No matter what their size in relation to the rest of the world, when you are a kid, dads are huge, imposing, and highly effective. They block out the sun, have unlimited supplies of quarters in their large and bot-tomless pockets, and can eat your entire plate of spaghetti in the time it takes you to reach down and tie your sneaker. Dads are leviathans. They are magnificent. They are not to be fucked with.

Mine, in particular.

In one move, he put the bike kickstand down, leapt from the seat, ripped me from the moorings of gravity, and threw me to the grass, in a fashion that was at once caring, gentle, and insanely terrifying. He patted out the flames with the sleeve of his jacket in what would surely have won the world record for patting out flames on one's burning daughter, should there have ever been such an event. And then he stood me up and gave me the kind of scolding that nowadays would have earned him a viral video on YouTube, and perhaps a public scolding from Nancy Grace.

This all happened in about fifteen seconds flat.

Coincidentally, this was also the last fifteen seconds of my ballerina phase.

Luckily, I was not burned. There was no physical damage. I did have to spend the rest of the day looking like the chimney sweep from *Mary Poppins* (my father would not take me home to change, as he was not my chauffeur, he was fond of telling me), but I was not burned. Psychological damage is harder to measure, but I can say with confidence that the delicate part of my brain related to pretentious artiness died a fiery death that day. I went back to dressing like a normal grade-schooler instead of an affected Manhattan art dealer that trades only in experimental oils. I had learned my lesson.

Watch that fucking pipe.

And I learned the futility of stylistic rigidity. I mean, come on. Even Thomas Wolfe wears sweatpants once in a while.

(7)

The Time I Peed on Myself
and My Surroundings

"Dogs are wise. They crawl away into a quiet corner and lick their wounds and do not rejoin the world until they are whole once more."—Agatha Christie

"When you gotta go, you gotta go."—Aisha Tyler

I have always wanted to be hardcore. Incredibly disciplined, immovably resolute, unrelentingly focused. I have wanted to be one of those people whose mind was always one hundred percent in control of their body, someone who could jump out of a moving train without flinching, scale a skyscraper without rope, walk barefoot across a room strewn with broken glass, should the situation arise.

I have always dreamed of being a badass.

Like most human hopes, this desire is incongruous, unrealistic, and completely inexplicable. That does not make it any less real.

From the time I was little, I have wanted to be tougher, meaner, less vulnerable, more disciplined than others. I don't know why this is. Maybe it is because I am a firstborn kid and thus, true to all stereotypes, an A-type personality haunted by fears of failure and inadequacy. Maybe it is because I have always been an outsider, and so have fantasized about "showing them"[1] with my athletic feats of prowess, dazzling intelligence, and triumphant victories as a billionaire playgirl superhero.

I have also always loved action movies. I think people who love action movies have a very specific personality trait—or flaw, more accurately—which is that whenever we watch an action film, we immediately put ourselves in the place of the hero. With each one-on-seventeen bar brawl, each reckless leap down a burning elevator shaft or hairline escape from a listing helicopter leaking fuel, we remove Bruce or Jet Li or that kung-fu Belgian with the loads of plastic surgery, and put ourselves at the center of the action. The more Hollywood action we consume, the more we fantasize, until every moment is pregnant with the possibility of ninjas dropping from the skylight, or an armored car loaded with bank robbers and stolen bearer bonds smashing through plate glass directly in our line of sight, and we will have to grab loose paper clips and hastily construct a fistful of makeshift caltrops. We are always ready for whatever may come, even though what usually comes is traffic, homework, bills, dirty dishes, and lukewarm macaroni and cheese.

But we are ready, my friends. We are fucking *ready*.

Maintaining this constant state of heightened readiness requires unwavering focus, self-denial, and sacrifice. Things must be learned. Other things must be renounced. Skills must be mastered. And many, many things must be endured. Because one never knows when one may be called up for service by relentless destiny.

When I was a kid, this preparedness took several behavioral forms. I was precise, obsessive and very peculiar. For long periods I would only eat cereal, or grapes, or scrambled eggs with ketchup for breakfast.[2] I would pack my backpack for a quick getaway, secreting away snacks, juice, Band-Aids, a warm sweater, and perhaps Popsicle sticks

---

1 It does not matter who "them" are. Bullied people know who "them" are. And "them" are gonna pay. "Them" are going to let us into their club and be nice to us and give us the respect and the cookies we deserve.

2 This seemed to me a very heroic breakfast.

and glue in case I had to construct a weapon or shelter of some kind. I would hoard food, keeping cans underneath my bed, along with sleeping bags, Mylar blankets, and, of course, copious reading material. Who knew—I might have to bivouac in some remote place without entertainment for several hours or even days—a Bradbury compilation or *Little Men* would keep me occupied while I waited for rescue and planned my next move. Even a heroine needs a little diversion.

What was crystal clear to me, even then, was that being a hero was a 24-hour-a-day job. One never knew what kind of obstacles life, or an evil international league of villains, might throw my way. The eventual test of my mettle could be anything, so I needed to be ready for *everything*.[3]

This knowledge pushed me to put myself in terrifying or difficult situations with the goal of trying to endure them mentally. I don't know why I was so hell-bent on pockmarking my childhood with potentially psychologically and even physically damaging episodes, but I liked the idea of mental toughness as well as physical toughness. It was one thing to be able to take a punch. It was another entirely to be able to withstand crushing disappointment or emotional devastation and still push forward. Did David Lightman in *WarGames* freak out when adorable Joshua turned out to be the sinister yet earnest WOPR, wanting to play Global Thermonuclear War for real?

No. He grew a pair and hightailed it to some island in the Puget Sound looking for Professor Falken, a guy he believed to be dead. And then he went to NORAD. Fucking NORAD. If Lightman could try to get into the most defended military bunker on the globe to save the world, I could put up with being a little chilly, or wet, or hot, or hungry. And I could certainly deal with a bit of physical discomfort, say for example, having to pee.

---

3 This behavior has not diminished in my adult life. My car is a wonderland of food bars and portable water. My purse is so stocked with first aid implements that EMTs could use it as a triage kit. As the Preppers and Millenialists and doomsday obsessives proclaim hysterically, when the shit hits the fan (WTSHTF), I will be ready. And as my friends have pointed out—partially in awe, partially in alarm—no paper cut, stubbed toe, or other pedestrian injury obtained at a dive bar or elsewhere has ever gone untreated in my presence. Got a boo-boo? I got some ointment for your ass.

What did I care for bodily functions? Peeing was for humans and weaklings. I was an action hero. John McClane. Sarah Connor. Storm. Starfire.

And so it went, deep in my young survivalist phase, that I often found myself on the long bus ride from school to my home high in the Oakland hills,[4] a trip that required three bus rides and a punishingly long walk up a very steep hill. Usually on this half-mile crawl, I engaged in elaborate fantasies about summiting Kilimanjaro or bisecting the Mongolian steppe. Every experience was an opportunity for personal growth.

Yes. I am as disgusted as you are.

The walk was long but beautiful, passing blackberry patches and plum trees as it wound into the hills, and I would usually bookmark whatever sci-fi I was reading to forage, filling my backpack or lunch bag with fistfuls of sticky, smashed fruit that I could use later should the Bay Area power grid go offline, or the food delivery systems be disabled by pestilence or wildfire. In reality, I wasn't going to be saving any lives or feeding hungry masses. However, I would be wiping streaks of moldy fruit juice and furious ant populations out of my Trapper Keeper for weeks to come.

On this fateful day in late spring, despite all my training for the apocalypse, I had miscalculated terribly. In my haste to start that day's adventure, I did not pee before I left school. On the three bus rides home, separated by long waits at transfer points, I ignored the pressure building in my lower quadrant, telling myself I was stronger than my body, that I could hold it, I was no little girl, I was a Jedi, a ninja, a bushido warrior. Peeing was for suckers. And peeing in one of the many locations available to me on my trip home wasn't just for suckers, it was for people who liked touching surfaces that in all likelihood were saturated with the pee of strangers, the Bubonic Plague, or, even worse, the Bubonic Pee of Strangers, which was about the worst thing

---

4 This sounds fancier than it was. My father and I moved around a lot, based on how his work was going. This place was high in the hills but trust me, no Hearst castle. It was more like the place where the people who shined the shoes for the people who occupied Hearst Castle lived—*Bootblack Manor* (murky racial overtones completely intended).

my little mind could possibly conjure, and even now sounds pretty fucking awful.[5]

So, true to my life philosophy, I held it in. But on the third bus ride, as we jostled and bounced and jiggled and skittered along Telegraph Avenue on a bus that should have been condemned to the junkyard a decade prior, my resolve began to weaken. Or, more accurately, my ten-year-old pelvic floor began to weaken.[6]

I was no weakling, I told myself. I thought of Luke Skywalker on Dagobah, trying to raise that infernal x-wing out of the swamp. He didn't give up, and neither would I. I turned all of my mental power inward, on whatever muscles would keep the most terrible of tragedies from happening to me on this bus. And I *believed*. As Yoda admonished Luke, not believing is why we fail. So I would *believe* that I could make it, *believe* that I could get to my stop before the trickle became a torrent and I was reduced to a sad little lukewarm puddle of a girl on the bus. I would *believe* that my mind was stronger than this ever more urgent, more pressing matter. And—as liquid is wont to do when affected by the inexorable pull of gravity—man, was it pressing.

I stumbled off the bus at my stop, eyes pressed shut against the building internal storm, and started jogging up the hill. Never had my trek up Kilimanjaro seemed more insurmountable. The once welcoming blackberry patches were now dark and haunted thickets, the plum trees mocking me as I half-ran, half-bobbled past, legs twisted in agony. My destination quavered in the distance like a receding mirage, every mailbox a toilet, every patch of grass offering sweet relief. But still I pushed on, *believing* that I could make it.

At least my mind believed. My body was calling bullshit.

About two-thirds of the way home, I started to realize that perhaps I required additional Jedi training (or *any* Jedi training at all) before I would be ready for such a herculean task as carrying a full bladder

---

5 I had a germ thing when I was a kid. It has matured into a pretty fun, full-blown neurosis as an adult. The greatest moment of my life was when they invented that liquid hand sanitizer. Seriously. It was like my Diamond Jubilee.

6 I was far too young for Kegels.

home with my person unmoistened. This was the real world. I could not raise a spaceship with my mind. I could not lift a pebble with my mind. And I certainly could not hold this pee in for very much longer. I began to sprint. It was too late.

I made it as far as my front porch, and that infernal x-wing went crashing back into the swamp, sending water sloshing everywhere.

Yes. That was a *Star Wars*–urine metaphor. Welcome to the Fortress of Blerditude.[7]

After I cleaned myself up, and the landing, and the stairs, and a little bit of the living room floor, I took thin solace in the fact that I had made it all the way to my front porch. That was almost as good. With practice, I could do better. Like Kyle Reese in *The Terminator*, I didn't make it back home, but there was honor in the effort. And, much like Reese, in defeat was spawned new hope for the future.

Mental toughness is all fine and good. But when you gotta go, you gotta go.

---

7 Black + Nerd = Blerd.

(8)

The Time I Asked a Boy on a Wildly Inappropriate Date

"It takes a lot to wound a man without illusions."—Ellis Peters

"My illusions are all I have."—Aisha Tyler

I have a sneaking suspicion that my father wished I had been born a boy.

I don't have a problem with this. People want lots of things they can't have. Unlimited wealth. The ability to fly. A magical bowl of soup that never empties no matter how much you eat.

Life is rife with disappointment.

Dads want boys; moms want girls. All that dreck about just being happy the kid has all ten fingers and toes is all very well and good, and just the right tone to strike in mixed or judgmental company, but if cornered and alone with no possibility of discovery, most parents would admit to wishing for a little Mini-Me to shape and mold and railroad into doing all of the things they were too busy or lazy or terrified to do themselves when they were young.[1] Of course parents love

---

1 And this is why I don't have kids, because I would be one of those moms who dressed her daughter in adorably inappropriate miniature versions of her own clothes and forced her to attend her alma mater without a droplet of remorse. I would be mad with power, my child

their children, no matter the gender. But they also long secretly for a child whose body and emotions are similar to theirs, and therefore easily molded and understood. Now, you may be a parent, and disagree with me one hundred percent on this. You may be simmering in outrage right now, ready to fling the book across the room. But for the sake of argument, for the time being at least, work with me.

I definitely don't believe my dad was disappointed. I was deeply loved and fiercely protected by a father who believed I could do anything I set my mind to and often encouraged me to try everything, no matter how daunting or outrageously ambitious. But for a parent, there are naturally a different set of fears and expectations with girls. The threats are more numerous, the potential pitfalls more abundant, and perils menace every turn. With a girl, you worry about predators and pregnancies and intolerably maudlin teenage angst, with the requisite terrible poetry and Taylor Swift on repeat that accompanies it. Girls are complicated and wonderful and messy and emotional and nuanced and delightful and devastating.

With a boy, you just hope he doesn't turn out to be an asshole.

Because a girl's life can be fraught with so much more peril, they are naturally terrifying to a father, who has never been a girl, and so can only see the dangers she faces but cannot put himself in the shoes of his daughter to understand how they might be overcome. Some fathers react by trying to control every aspect of their daughter's life, restricting where she goes, what she does, who she sees, and turning her, inevitably, into a slutty alcoholic loudmouthed tramp with rebellion issues and a daddy complex.

The other way to go is to mentally and physically equip your daughter to face anything the world throws at her, to make her thoughtful, tough, self-possessed, and independent. She may still turn out to be a slutty alcoholic tramp, but at least it'll be her *own* money she's spending on flavored booze and Magnum condoms.

---

forced to dress in pencil skirts and power suits while delicately sipping bourbon-based cocktails, which would be especially objectionable if my child was a boy, or a natural scotch lover.

My father has always been about independence. From the time I was big enough to walk to the front door and open it, he encouraged me to explore the wide world on my own, and develop the skills to attack it headlong. He worked hard to raise a girl who was bold and fearless, who never felt sorry for herself and who could overcome setbacks with grace and determination. Upon retrospect, I realize that he was also trying to get me to be independent enough to get the hell out of his face so he could woo a special lady friend or watch the freaking game in peace. His approach served its purpose nonetheless.

One of his favorite things to do with me when I was a kid was to start the day with a kind of motivational call and response. These were akin to a coach's locker room speech before the big game, a general's rallying cry before a major assault, or a drunken heckler's hurled taunt. These were different in that they involved a little girl in a mis-buttoned cardigan running perpetually late for school. And they were shot through with age-inappropriate language, as my dad had a daughter to raise and money to make and no fucking time to screw around. They often went something like this:

Dad: Whose day is it?
Me: My day.
Dad: And what are you gonna do?
Me: I'm gonna grab it by the balls.
Dad: Louder!
Me: I'm gonna grab it by the balls!
Dad: That's right! Grab it by the short hairs and twist!
Me: Twist!
*Dad: Have a good day, baby. And remember, keep your grades and
    your drawers up.*

There were variants on this theme, usually having to do with telling people who doubted you to fuck off, or kicking the corpses of your defeated foes, but they were all equally rousing and similarly outrageous. My dad was arming me for a world full of predators, obstacles, and disappointments.[2] He didn't have time to craft a butterfly-soft approach. He had shit to do.

I respected it then. I respect it now.

My dad's approach to cultivating independence in a child was simple and straightforward: do as little as possible to make your child's life easier. The world is terrible, people are terrible, and no one is ever going to make things easy on you, so why should your parents trick you into thinking that for the rest of your life you'll be enjoying crustless sandwiches and tubes of drinkable yogurt lovingly provided by others? This included stuff that most kids take for granted, like getting rides to places, or having activities planned or meals prepared. It wasn't that he was cruel; he was incredibly kind and supportive. I was a very loved kid. It's just that I never got a fucking ride anywhere besides school. *Anywhere.*

I remember once wanting to go to a party in high school. It wasn't in a particularly bad part of town, but you did need to go through a rather heinous area to get there. I *really* wanted to go to this party. It was all I could think about. I rarely got invited to anything, and certainly not anything I actually wanted to go to. But this was at a popular kid's house, and other popular kids would be there, and I had it on good authority that there would be *beer.* This party needed attending.

I asked my father about this party constantly. Weeks in advance, I primed this guy to be prepared to take me to this thing. I even worked it out so if he would take me, I could get a ride home from someone else. I couldn't have made it easier for him. It was a night he was home; his vehicle fueled up. I had cleaned not just my room, but the entire apartment and several lengths of adjacent sidewalk. There was no reason for him not to take me to this party. Providing this small kindness would require little effort for maximum reward. This is how I saw it.

This is not how he saw it. As he saw it, he was not a chauffeur, he did not work here, he did not have me so he could wait on me hand and foot, and if I wanted to go to a party, I could get there myself. I had

---

2 Looking back, I can see that this might have something to do with the obsession with mental preparedness I mentioned previously. Interesting how that works.

money, I had a brain, I had the bus schedule, and if I wanted things in life, I knew how to get them.[3] And I wouldn't get them blocking his view of the television.

Looking back, I realize he was cultivating initiative. I will admit, at the time though, it just felt super mean.

His goal was to train the fear out of me, to make me someone who went after her goals without hesitation. If I wanted things in life, I would need to go out and get them myself. Better to learn that early before the world punched me in the face with it. The brazen self-motivation he instilled me with was invaluable, and has served me in every aspect of my professional and personal life to this day. It has made me brave and risk-taking in my creative life and fearlessly loving in my private life. It has also made me highly accident prone (the freakishly tall thing doesn't help, either).

Unfortunately, in training the fear out of me, he also trained out any shred of cautiousness, circumspection or reservation, any inner voice that might have said, "Hey, maybe you'd like to think this through before you leap headlong into a room full of armed bear traps?" I don't have that twinge, which for the most part—minus a few dramatic injuries, literal and metaphorical—has been a good thing. For the most part.

My dad was right. Fortune favors the bold, and he was trying to make me bold. He was almost always right.

Except for this one time.

When I was a kid, I liked a boy. And because I never did anything in half measures, I liked this boy a lot. Like, *a lot* a lot. I liked him so much it was all I could talk about, think about, do. I obsessed about this boy constantly, so much so that I was becoming a thorn in my father's side, even more of an annoyance than I typically was. I loved

---

3 The requirements of parenthood have changed profoundly. In the olden days, if your kid was fed, relatively clean, and had all their digits, you had done your job. Nowadays, if your child is not dressed like a silvered butterfly and eating gluten-free cupcakes with an ice-cold glass of organic almond milk for breakfast, you are fodder for CPS. I occasionally long for the days when your mom's arm, flung in front of your chest as she narrowly avoided a collision, was seat belt enough. Those were heady days. You could feel life in the center of your marrow.

this boy (I thought), but because I was a kid, and had no idea what love was, or what to do about it, I would just wail and gnash and babble about it constantly like an alarm clock of unrequited love with no snooze button.

My father wanted desperately to smash me in my snooze button.

Being focused on problem solving and personal empowerment as he was, he came up with an even better solution to the problem, one that he engaged in repeatedly throughout my childhood and still occasionally uses to this day. He threw money at it.[4]

He decided he would give me some money, and I would ask this boy to dinner. I could pick a restaurant and pay for everything. It was a grand idea, a sweeping gesture, modern, forward thinking, feminist even. It was a very big idea.

It was also a terrible idea, as I was ten years old.

My dad gave me sixty bucks to execute this nefarious and dazzling plan. For weeks that sixty bucks burned a hole in my pocket, the way my love for this boy was burning a hole in my soul. But even then, I knew this plan wouldn't work. I sensed that my father was probably the only father at my school, in my neighborhood, or the universe, *encouraging* his daughter to take a boy out on a date at the age of ten.[5] I knew there was a terrible rift in the space-time continuum, and though I couldn't figure out exactly why this scheme would fail, I didn't need Velma to tell me this plan would go terribly awry, meddling kids or no.[6]

Nonetheless, my father had issued a challenge, and I had both a deep need to please him, and an intense desire to buy sixty dollars' worth of Chinese food. So after several weeks of paralysis and delay, I mustered up the tiny girl nuts to ask this guy out. I cornered him against the putty-colored stucco of the fifth-grade classroom during recess, and asked him if he wanted to go get food with me after school sometime.

---

4 This was his answer to almost everything. I never complained.

5 Most men don't encourage their daughters to date at *thirty*. My dad has a unique mind.

6 Ruh-roh, Raggy.

He cocked his head. *Like, outside of school?*

Yeah! I showed him the money. *My dad gave me this.*

His eyes bugged. Sixty bucks was a lot of money to a fourth grader, then and now.[7]

It just seemed weird for me to have that much money. I don't know what the boy was thinking, as this was pre-gangsta rap, but if he had any stereotypical rap/drug/black people tropes available to him mentally, they were bobbing wildly around his head like apples right now.

So, like, just you and me? He squinted.

Yeah, just you and me, and we can order and eat whatever we want. I'm going to get a huge plate of sweet and sour pork and eat out all the pineapple.[8] *And you can have whatever you like. My treat.*

This didn't have the intended seductive effect.[9] He just stared. So I tried to sweeten the deal.

My dad's gonna give us a ride. On his motorcycle. He never gives me rides, so this is a pretty big deal.

Both of us? He was squinting more tightly now.

Both of us, yeah! On his motorcycle! It'll be cool.

The amount of danger involved in this proposition was now too insurmountable to overcome. Going on a date, with a girl, without adult supervision, and our own money, and getting a ride on the back of a motorcycle? With a guy who looked like a leather-clad Apollo Creed?

I could see him shut down.

I'll uh . . . I'll ask my mom. He slowly backed away, eyes focused on some distant and suddenly interesting horizon point.

---

7 Adjusted for inflation, my dad had given me a golden hubcap and two Franklins. I was *rich*, bitches.

8 Left to my devices, with spending money and no supervision, I would purchase and eat as much meat as I could obtain legally. To assuage any feelings of guilt, I would eat all of the plant matter out of a dish first—say, the veggies in a stir-fry or the parsley garnish on a steak—so as to demonstrate at least a nominal commitment to vegetarianism.

9 In retrospect, it may be relevant to mention that this boy was Japanese, and I had asked him out to Chinese food. This may have been my first and most fatal mistake. It wasn't racist, just thoughtless. In my defense, at the time, Americanized Chinese food really was my favorite thing to eat.

I watched him go, that sixty bucks a fistful of lava in my pocket.

He wasn't going to ask his mom. I knew it. I somehow also sensed that we wouldn't ever be speaking, or making eye contact, ever again.[10]

That was the first time I ever asked a boy on a date. It definitely left a bruise.

And while I have engaged in many wild acts of bravery in my life, including scuba diving, ice climbing, spelunking in winter, and telling jokes to rooms of intoxicated strangers, it was a very long time before I ever did anything that truly reckless again.

I did, however, get to treat my dad to an amazing Chinese lunch. $61.37 worth, in fact. He spotted me the extra $1.37. And I ate every single piece of pineapple out of my order of Sweet and Sour Pork.

Nothing ventured, nothing gained.

---

10 I was one hundred percent right about that.

(9)

The Bunny Fiasco

"All honor's wounds are self-inflicted."—Andrew Carnegie

"Trying to do the right thing sucks."—Aisha Tyler

Despite my desire to be tough, I have always had a tender heart.

Or maybe it's the other way around. Maybe because I have always been an emotional cream puff, I have tried to harden myself to the inevitable knocks that life brings. But deep down, I am a giant bowl of marshmallow fluff with feet and glasses and a penchant for maudlin Korean pop.[1] I have always been a softie, and I fight it with every fiber of my being.

Sadly, my being's fibers need to hit the gym.

I have always wanted to save things: animals, plants, bugs, butterflies, people, hobos, rabid dogs, wayward rodents. There is no living thing for which I cannot find sympathy, no animal I cannot anthro-

---

1 If you want to see the best distillation of how other cultures view American popular culture, watch Korean pop videos. K-pop has appropriated our shit and done us one thousand times better. And if imitation is truly the sincerest form of flattery, Americans are all ripped-jeans wearing, neon-tank sporting, trend-obsessed teenyboppers who care deeply about casual sex, drinking in nightclubs, and walking provocatively down high school hallways in short skirts while being shot in the face with high-velocity wind (not far from the truth).

Additionally, Koreans are way blacker than our black people could ever hope to be. They are rapping, krumping, stomping, dapping, and generally out-blacking us as if they came to one of our meetings and bought ten copies of the handbook. They are *killing* it over there.

pomorphize.[2] I cry at children's movies. I cry watching the news. I cry during Nike ads. I cry reading cereal boxes.[3] I am constantly welling over with heartrending compassion. I am a total and complete sucker.

When I was a middle-schooler, my mother moved into a house that shared a fence with another family who owned a lot of animals. Their property was a veritable barnyard wonderland. And because the homes shared a perimeter, their yard was our yard, and we were suddenly surrounded by domestic wildlife. They had absolutely no business doing this shit. They lived in Oakland, not Ohio. The block was surrounded on all sides by industrial buildings, cement, cyclone fencing, and the beginnings of the East Bay rap scene.

This was no place for chickens.

But chickens they had, and ducks, and a goose, and probably some other animals they kept chained up in their basement, because they were weird, and clearly didn't understand contextual appropriateness when it came to animal life. They also had bunnies. Two bunnies, in fact, that lived next to the chicken coop, and seemed pretty pissed about it, as chickens make terrible neighbors. They are rude, insensitive, and never know when to stop talking. Chickens are dicks.

Whenever I went to stay with my mom, I actually kind of liked having all of these animals around. As discussed, I had a lot of survivalist fantasies, and one of them involved homesteading (of course), so I thought it would be good to study these animals and figure out how they worked, in case I had to steal a few in the dead of night and strike out on my own to make a life for myself in the post-apocalyptic wasteland. So I observed the animals closely, to learn what I could about their care and feeding. What I learned is that bunnies don't do much but shit and fuck, chickens will eat absolutely anything you feed them, including cigarette butts and small coins, and geese are total assholes.[4]

---

2 Reading *Charlotte's Web* really didn't help.

3 *If only the entire world could taste how fucking awesome this organic granola is! And only four grams of sugar!!!*

4 This is scientifically provable. Geese are out to get us.

Don't feel sorry for the goose. That goose would chase me around the yard without relent every single time I stepped outside. He was like a fowl model of the T-2000—resembling an ordinary bird but without fear, remorse or mercy, seemingly tireless and hell-bent on the destruction of the human ankle. Eventually we had to keep a broom by the back door so we could make it to the car. You can see how this would be frustrating, especially since *this wasn't our goose*. Trust me, if it had been, my mother would have broken her vow of vegetarianism and we'd have eaten Rusty Pete for dinner with some fava beans and a glass of grape juice. Alas, he was the pet of another, and so to be feared and avoided, and occasionally pelted with shoes.

While we were doing all of this goose evading, the bunnies did what bunnies do, and had bunny babies. And I quickly realized that geese are not the only assholes in the animal kingdom. Geese may be the most aggressive, but chickens have their own brand of lazy evil.

Soon after the baby bunnies were born, the chickens starting eating the baby bunnies alive.

They pecked at them through the wire of their cage, which was pushed perilously close to the walls of the chicken coop. And they were terribly, heinously, ghoulishly effective. In about a day, they had pecked all the baby bunnies to death.

All but one.

Of course, upon discovering this ghoulish tableau, I immediately tried to save that baby bunny. Separated from its mother, who had rejected it due to what I can only imagine was some deep and irreparable psychological trauma involving murderous chickens pecking her family to death, the baby bunny was alone in the world. So I set about saving that bunny, knowing nothing about rabbits, babies, or living things in general.[5]

The neighbors were nowhere in sight, which I took as tacit permission to take possession of their infant rabbit. I lifted the bunny from the bunny cage and placed it gently in a shoe box lined with blankets. I do not know whether this was what the bunny needed,

---

5 And *certainly* nothin' bout birthin' no baby bunnies.

but it did sure make the bunny look cuter. I tried to feed the bunny milk. Why? Because babies drink milk. Don't they? I had no idea. I took that baby bunny everywhere, because from what I could tell, you didn't just leave babies lying around to fend for themselves, no matter what their species or phylum. I didn't know what you did with babies when you had them, but I know you didn't just prop their shoebox in front of the television and let them watch the soaps while you were away.

I took the box to school, and carried it from class to class. I tried to conceal the box from the prying eyes of teachers and other kids by holding it inside the flap of my jacket, pretending it was an art project or a diorama for some imagined homework assignment. But the halls of a middle school between classes are a hectic and treacherous place. I, and my delicate bunny, were pushed, jostled, and occasionally smashed violently against the wall as we navigated the corridors. The box and its precious contents were dropped. More than once. I am not proud of this. I was eleven. I was an idiot. An idiot with good intentions, but an idiot nonetheless. That bunny was on a slow inevitable slide toward darkness that started when chickens attacked, and accelerated when a well-intentioned but entirely bewildered preteen took the reins. That bunny never stood a chance.[6]

It did not take long for that last bunny to die. It wriggled slower and slower, every leg twitch or head turn a silent protest against the world that had forsaken it, little eyes blinking in mute judgment of my failures. When at last the tiny bunny lay still, we buried it in my dad's backyard, under some marigolds, and I cried for at least a day at how unjust the world was, and how cruel, and how chickens fucking sucked.

But somehow, even though my act of compassion had failed mightily, and my heart had been broken by cruel fate and fowl, I never lost my desire to be kind. I had tried to save something. I had tried to do good, and the fact that one light had been snuffed out didn't mean that

---

6 I would argue that idiots with good intentions are more dangerous than any other idiots, as they are so much more aggressive with their dumbness. It's like they can't wait to spray their dumb all over you. They're like dumb-dumb cannons.

others couldn't be kept burning. I might have failed this bunny terribly, but I knew somehow, someday, I would not fail the world.

Because out of the young and hopelessly stupid, much like baby bunnies from the womb of a willing and fertile rabbit, hope springs constantly anew.

(10)

The Time I Desperately Wanted
to Get My Period

"It is usually the imagination that is wounded first, rather than the heart; it being much more sensitive."—HENRY DAVID THOREAU

"If wishing makes it so, I should start wishing for better stuff."—AISHA TYLER

I had a lot of time on my hands as a preteen. My dad worked crazy hours, long and punishing, sometimes at more than one job. He was in constant need of a break. The minute my overworked, overwhelmed, overtired single father got the faintest whiff of the idea that I could take care of myself and stay home without supervision, the cat was out of the bag. Or, more specifically, the dad was out of the apartment. Like a shot.[1]

This was not abandonment. I was sufficiently stocked up. There was food and water, and a tiny door to crawl out of in case I needed to escape. I had homework. Phone numbers. Emergency plans. I had come to understood that fire burned. I knew that strangers were evil. I would be fine.

---

1 There is nothing that strains at its moorings more plaintively than a single parent trapped in an apartment with a middle-schooler.

And I was fine. I didn't mind the solitude. I had always been a solitary kid, first forced to, and then electing to, play with myself (stop it) so this was nothing new, nor particularly daunting. By this point I was on nerd autopilot; the idea of not doing what was expected of me never even crossed my mind. Ever the apple polisher, I would come right home after school each day and immediately do my homework, read recreationally, and, if I was feeling a bit rebellious, nap.

By this time, it would only be four-thirty. I was a little *too* effective at time management. My dad wouldn't be home for hours. I needed to formulate a game plan or descend into a swirling eddy of crushing boredom.

I started to devise all kinds of time-killing activities. I crafted. Did puzzles. One of my favorite pastimes was to save my allowance until I had enough money amassed to afford an impressive assortment of frozen dinners, which I would then purchase, carry home, prepare and eat.[2] This, if augmented by a lengthy selection process at the supermarket freezer wall, could easily kill several hours. My favorite was the deluxe turkey dinner, because digging into that cranberry dessert made it feel like Thanksgiving no matter what day it was. And the associated feeling of danger involved with secretively eating so much meat felt akin to getting wildly drunk.

Or maybe that was the tryptophan.

I was a big kid for my age, so when I did put my latch key around my neck and venture out into the world, I was generally left alone. The supermarket was directly across from our flat—I could practically run there and back without encountering one single adult—and the neighbors and vendors in the neighborhood all knew my father. And from what they knew, he was a large man with an intimidating mustache who rode a motorcycle, wore leather for function rather than style, and for all they knew could kill a person with a set of *nunchakus* or several silently thrown ninja stars.[3] As a result, they gave me a wary yet

---

2 Another reckless favorite was turkey potpie *followed* by a turkey dinner. Turkey twice! What what? Hedonism. Followed by a nap.

3 Who highly resembles a black private dick who's a sex machine to all the chicks? My dad. You're damn right.

protective eye, along with a wide and generous berth. No one wanted to wake up with a mouthful of *shuriken*.[4]

So for the most part I was left to my own devices, which included reading a lot of speculative fiction, eating an ungodly amount of frozen "delicacies," doing my homework far in advance of its deadline, and hanging out at the stereo store next door to our apartment building, where they had huge televisions, an entire wall of killer Pioneer stereo amps, a soundproof speaker room, a languid staff of twenty-year-old salespeople slowly dying inside from acute boredom and low wages, and a big leather chair that reclined when you pulled a lever on the side. Because I was a kid, no one dared ask me to leave; either they feared my dad irrationally or they were sure I was a street-faring waif who could use a few hours in a warm place. I lived in that chair, and every time I pulled that lever, I pretended my own personal Enterprise was hitting warp speed.[5]

I spent most of the seventh grade, and the following summer, like this: reading, hanging out at the stereo store, eating unsafe amounts of processed turkey, and imagining I was the captivating yet resolute captain of an intergalactic space vessel. And then somewhere in there, with all that free time to ruminate, I decided I was officially a teenager, and it was time to get my period.

As I also believed in mental power, having just finished a book on telekinesis,[6] I thought the best way to get my period was to start acting as if I already had it. But as I was living with my father, who would as soon discuss menstruation as gouge his own eye out with his *shuriken*, I had no freaking idea how to do that. I didn't know what a period felt like, what it did, how long it lasted, its point of origin, none of it. All I knew was that it heralded the onset of womanhood, and doggone it, I

---

4 Japanese throwing stars. You know you wanted some when you were a kid. You want some now.

5 I once watched an entire movie in that chair while eating a mixture of sunflower seeds and sour apple Now and Laters out of a plastic grocery bag. No one had the heart to throw the little black girl who had nowhere to go out of the store. I *really* took advantage of these people.

6 *Firestarter*. Read it twice. I feel no shame in admitting that.

was done with being a kid. I had eaten all the potpies I could stomach. It was time to kick this shit up a notch.

I stopped buying frozen dinners and started buying Jean Naté, mainly because there were one thousand ads for it on television all day long, and that was all I saw at the stereo store. I would splash it on like the lady in the ad, liberally, as if I was trying to exterminate skin mites or drown a small rodent, and then jump immediately back under running water to rinse away the extraordinary feeling of burning skin.[7] I would then mist myself liberally with Love's Baby Soft, because I was weak-willed and any kind of targeted advertising had an immediate and propulsive effect on my impressionable preteen mind. I would finally grab my bag of sunflower seeds and neon sour candies, toss in my dog-eared copy of John Christopher's *The City of Gold and Lead*, and head over to the stereo store to loiter like a street urchin.

I spent most of my seventh grade summer dehydrated, green-tongued, and smelling like a Malaysian whorehouse.

But I was hell-bent on becoming a woman, and if not a woman, at least less of a girl than I had been thus far. I was propelled forward by recklessness and the insuppressible impatience cultivated by a summer without the distracting influence of camp. I decided that the best way to kick this whole thing off was to just go and get some sanitary pads and start wearing them around. I was already wearing grownup cologne. Why not rock the undergarments as well?

I went to the drugstore across the street and purchased the most imposing menstrual pads I could find, because I was going to be a real woman, and real women needed maxi pads. Not mini-pads, or slim liners, but *maxi* pads. For the *maximum* woman. Which I was. And I took them home, along with six turkey potpies and a bag of Sno Balls, and opened up the box.

Holy shit.

I inspected the pads as if I was an alien life-form who stumbled upon a pepperoni Hot Pocket and was trying to use it to make a phone

---

7 I had no frame of reference for this. I just thought this is what all adult women did. Splash cologne all over their naked bodies, and then run screaming back into the shower stall.

call. I had no idea what these things were. They looked like a tiny hammock for a bird, or an upholstered slingshot, or insulation material for a nuclear submarine. There was no adhesive, no instructions, and definitely no signage indicating "this way up." And because my father was at work and my mother was at work and I shouldn't have been spending my money on sanitary products I didn't need anyway, I had no one to ask. I was on my own. I delicately placed one of these salami-sized zeppelins into my undergarment, zipped up my pants, and prayed for my period.

After a while, when nothing happened, I decided it might be a good idea to take this thing out for a spin. People walked around while they were getting their periods, right? You always saw people doing things and being surprised when their period arrived, like Brooke Shields in *The Blue Lagoon*. She wasn't just sitting on a kitchen chair in her overheated apartment waiting for something to happen. She was out there *living* when her little visitor showed up. Besides, I was freshly Jean Natéd and ready for the world. I ventured down the stairs and out onto the street.

It became clear to me in that first sunlit moment, and remains crystal clear to me now, why (aside from systemic sexism and the attendant glass ceiling) it has taken so long for women to achieve social equality. It is fucking impossible to do anything when you are wearing a maxi pad. *Anything.* It is like trying to hold a wet soda bottle or a flopping adult mackerel between your legs. As you walk, you look like a circus performer executing a highly challenging contortionist's trick. You can think of nothing else, and your facial expression betrays it.

I walked up and down my block a couple of times, taking my new installation out for a spin. The more I walked, the more it migrated, downward then backward, slowly creeping out of the rear of my pants until it looked like I had shoved a roll of toilet paper down my jeans. I surreptitiously reached down to adjust it as I walked, before slamming smack-dab into a million-year-old lady rolling her rickety wire cart to the supermarket. She was annoyed, then disgusted, then confused, then alarmed, as she looked down to see my entire forearm down the front of my pants. And then she ran. As much as a million-year-old lady can, anyway.

I couldn't blame her.

It was hot outside, and the pad was getting damp. I was sweating, maybe from the heat, maybe from anxiety, maybe from the tension of trying to hold this floppy rolled up newspaper at the center of my burgundy corduroys. It had started out annoying and then moved to truly uncomfortable. No wonder the woman in the commercial was splashing herself with Jean Naté like it was made of gold; these pad things held on to every bit of moisture, every drop of sweat—condensed, concentrated, magnified it—and sent it booming back upwards like a cotton-filled version of a smell megaphone. They were uncomfortable, impractical, totally detectable, and much like having a wedgie or something green and cruciferous lodged between your teeth, made you feel unbearably self-conscious. I was beginning to rethink the whole "I can't wait to get my period" thing.

I took the pad for a few more laps before half-skipping, half-limping back to my apartment to fling it, and the entire box, into the trash in a huff. This period stuff was no fun, and what's worse, it had cost me the value of four Salisbury Steak repasts. I could have been sticky with brown gravy listening to Steely Dan on the Ankyo next door, and instead I was lying in a pool of sweat, my face pressed against the cold linoleum, wondering how I was ever going to handle womanhood if I couldn't manage a simple test stroll to the bus stop. Apparently becoming a woman required more than cheap cologne and some bulky sanitary apparati. It seemed easy when you looked at it, but it was clear I was going to need more time to figure this shit out.

After a while, I pulled the box of pads back out of the trash. I then stuffed them one by one inside an empty TV dinner box, and took it out to the garbage can by the curb. My father had enough to worry about without thinking his daughter had gotten her period.

Or worse—that she was walking around for an entire afternoon wearing a sanitary pad in the summer heat for no apparent reason.

A girl that bored should really be in summer camp.

(11)

The Time I *Actually* Got My Period

Well, this just sucked.

(12)

The Time I Snuck Out of My Home in the Night Like a CBS After-School Special

"Better to die ten thousand deaths than wound my honor."—Joseph Addison

"I literally want to die."—Aisha Tyler

The summer before my freshman year in high school, my father and I moved to the Haight-Ashbury neighborhood of San Francisco. You may know this area, because it was made famous by the hippie movement of the 1960s, and was canonized in many of their songs, manifestos, and hysterical scrawlings in poo on the walls of LSD dens.

The Grateful Dead lived there. The Human Be-In happened there. Hippies converged upon it during the infamous 1967 Summer of Love. And now my father and I were living there.

Things were about to get decidedly less interesting.

An atmosphere of daring and creativity still permeated that neighborhood, even decades after that infamous summer. Maybe it was the murals, or the street artists, or the buskers, or the head shops. Or maybe it was the roving gangs of pot-smoking hippies who refused to accept that it was 1984 and time to put on some pants and get a permanent street address. But there was an excitement and a danger to the place, and it soon began to infuse my life in a variety of ways.

Even though we didn't have a lot of money, I had good grades, and I was able to attend a progressive high school that year, one that was full of the children of rich people who felt guilty about being rich and so sent their children to an alternative learning environment where grades and evaluation ran secondary to personal growth and achievement, and where everyone was encouraged to express their ideas freely without fear of judgment or censure. It was also a school where a bunch of dirtbag rich kids drove European convertibles and did unholy amounts of cocaine. I don't think things were going exactly as those parents had planned.

But hey, they were rich, and rich people like to throw money at their problems,[1] then throw money at the problems their money causes, then get their kid a BMW. This is just the way of things.

The other thing rich people like to do is make sure that a couple of poor people get thrown into the mix, so that the rich people can feel better about themselves because their kids get to interact with one or two select, articulate, and very hygienic poor people. Meanwhile, the poor people get to go around all day being hyperaware of how lucky they are to be around all these lovely, special rich people in a school where no one is shooting at each other and you can call the teachers by their first names and there are actual books to read and when kids are mean to you, it's only because you make them feel uncomfortable culturally and not because they're going to stab you in the parking lot later. Boy, are those poor kids lucky!

Hey, wait! I mean me!

The kids at this school were not particularly nicer than other kids I had known. Kids everywhere are pretty mean, regardless whether they are attending school at a run-down urban cesspool or a fancy liberal hugfest. But they were weirder than other kids I had known. And so it

---

1 You may be thinking, "Hey, your dad threw money at the boy problem you had in grade school." Of course, the difference here is scale. He was empowering me to be brave, and also buying me stir-fry. That is way different than giving your kid a European sedan to make up for being emotionally remote.

was here that I met some of my first really interesting, creative friends, and got to be a little more of a creative kid myself.

There were kids at this school who were into Goth, and the Smiths, and Bauhaus, and eyeliner, and for a black kid who had been living in Oakland,[2] this was akin to worshipping the devil. Also, for that self-same black kid, this was an opportunity to throw everyone into a serious tailspin by acting even more off-stereotype than I had previously. I mean, how the hell do you grok a 5'10" black girl dressed like Siouxsie Sioux? You cannot. It cannot be grokked, my friend. It is ungrokkable.

And so it was that among all the condescending rich kids I made a couple of cool, offbeat friends, who were into weird music and liked lying around all day being melancholy and diagramming Talking Heads lyrics. This was also at the time when underground dance clubs were all the rage in San Francisco, and so naturally, being full of youth and our own importance, as well as fully convinced that we were smarter and more interesting than all other teens, we decided to infiltrate.

Despite our being underage, this was not that difficult. Two of my friends and I were scratching six feet, and the third was adorable on the order of a Pikachu. We were in.

Underground clubbing, at least the kind that was going on in San Francisco in the mid-eighties went like this: somehow, someone you kinda knew told someone else you kinda knew that there was going to be a club on Saturday night at a certain address. They knew, and you knew, that the party wasn't *actually* going to be at that address. That was a dummy address. But you would get all dressed up, in your torn tee and your lace gloves and your eyeliner and your ennui, and you would splash on *Poison*, and go with your friends to this spot, whereupon some weird skinny creep wearing super tight jeans with meticulously rolled cuffs would wander out of the shadows and give you another address to go to, where hopefully this fucking thing was actually going down.

---

2 Yes, *that* Oakland. Which is actually not as terrifying as all the rap songs and contorted hand signs would imply.

On occasion this bait-and-switch would occur two, or even three, times, after which you would arrive at the actual club location— usually in an empty airplane hangar or abandoned factory or burned- out school bus in an overgrown lot—sometime after midnight, dance to two or three songs,[3] get perilously thirsty, realize there was nowhere on-site to get a beverage, these things being makeshift, haphazard, and completely illegal, and leave to get giant burritos at two in the morning.

This was how I spent my weekends my freshman year of high school.

This quickly started to get frustrating. We were teenagers, and so had limited resources, limited time, and limited patience. We did not have cars, and so were generally forced to do all this running hither and yon on the bus. The bus! Granted, San Francisco had a kickass public transportation system, and does to this day, but anyone can lose their party shine jumping back on a hot-lit bus for another ride across town when they realize their last transfer is about to expire and they are out of money. We needed a more reliable place to go pretend as if we were older, cooler, and more bored than we really were. We needed a sure thing.

We found it in a club in North Beach called the Palladium. Looking back, I can't believe I ever hung out there, because in retrospect it was a dump, and probably crawling with sexual predators. But these were the eighties, and Dead or Alive's "You Spin Me Right Round (Like a Record)" had just come out, and all I wanted to do was dance. And because I was unnaturally tall, the security guards were kind enough to look the other way whenever we came in. The club was 18 and over, so we couldn't buy alcohol, which was just fine by me, because it was usually all I could do to afford the cover charge and buy a soda to nurse for the evening, despite a recent allowance increase. I slowly ingratiated myself with the staff until the guards would keep an eye on me and the bartenders would refill my drinks for free, and I thought to myself, "Self, this is much better than being parched and dancing on a

---

3 One *always* being "Master and Servant" by Depeche Mode.

burned-out, unstable school bus perched precariously on marshy land at the edge of the Bay. You have it *made*."

I spent a bunch of gleeful and strangely wholesome Fridays and Saturdays at this club, until city crackdowns started to make it harder for them to let in underage kids,[4] so the club started encouraging some of us to come on weekdays, when things were quieter. This worked for me, as my father often worked late, and was occasionally on dates, and I could manage to get out and jump around wildly to Onyx's "Slam" and still make it home before anyone was the wiser.

Of course, my father started to smell a rat. My grades weren't slipping, and I was as well behaved as ever, but he knew something was up. What normal black kid wears an entire armful of *rubber bracelets*? It was unnatural. Like most fathers, he had no idea exactly what was going on with his teenage daughter, but he knew he didn't like it, and he was going to put a stop to it. Immediately.

So he put me on "punishment."

Mind you, my father and I had a very good working arrangement at this point. It was simple, it was transparent, and it was highly functional.

A bit about his parenting approach: my father was a single parent. As single parents and the children of single parents know, that shit is *hard*. Like inexpressibly, soul-crushingly, universe-closing-in-on-you hard. You don't sleep, you don't always eat, you are in constant low-level panic, you bargain, cajole, wheedle, manipulate, anything and everything to keep your child alive, in school, and generally facing forward, without neck tattoos or an addiction to aerosolized glue.

And, for the most part, you do it alone.

This requires some creativity. Some single parents keep their children with them constantly, dragging them to work like bedraggled attachés or tiny bodyguards, leaving them in the corner to brood or nap or make a terrible mess of cracker crumbs and peanut butter on the office leather couch. Others, in desperation, are forced to leave their children to their own devices completely, hoping that they will be

---

4 Booo! Judge all you want, but this was a tragedy.

somewhat self-guiding, and that adulthood will get them before boredom, the lure of the streets, or a freak lightning strike.[5]

My father chose a middle path: neither total freedom nor total encumbrance. This was accomplished through clear-cut boundaries and expectations, enforced by rigorous psychological intimidation, and punctuated by intermediate threats of total loss of freedom and/or threatened (but *never* delivered) violence.

Here was the deal: as long as I did my homework, kept the apartment neat, didn't get in knife fights, smoke PCP, or come home pregnant by a guy named Crank who lived in the science lab of an abandoned high school (or any other guy for that matter), essentially everything else was up for grabs.

But if the man got even a *whiff* of an inkling that I was veering off course, even a smidge, I was immediately slammed back to a sunset curfew and long periods of academic drills, followed by a diet of lukewarm tap water and sawdust.[6] This resulted in some knee-jerk groundings, especially as I got older and tried to game the system a bit more.[7] In retrospect, his disciplinary responses were perfectly reasonable and totally commensurate with my typically reckless behavior. At the time, however, it felt as if my entire world was crashing down around my ears in tiny, crumbling morsels.

At the time of the dance club fiasco, I had been working a good angle for a pretty long run. Good grades, no run-ins with the law, my room was immaculate, and I was generally pleasant to be around.[8] So I felt like I had built up some equity here, and this grounding was completely unfounded, unfair, and without justification. You can't just

---

5 Parenthood is a metaphorical thicket of terror punctuated by small delights and mercies. I fear it unreservedly.

6 Not really. I ate pretty well in high school. But the man could wield a boss threat.

7 Because I was a *teenager*. And that's what teenagers do. Trying to get away with shit is in their nature, along with an innate lack of curiosity, an invincibility complex, and terrible taste in music.

8 As pleasant as any sullen teenager who listens to The Smiths incessantly and cuts her own bangs with kitchen shears can be.

ground someone preemptively because you *think* they might be up to no good![9] It's akin to fascism. Plus it was going to totally ruin my plans to go dancing. So, I thought, I would do what any normal teenager would do when faced with a great injustice: completely blow off my dad's wishes and do exactly what I wanted to do.

What could possibly go wrong?

Fortunately, on this fateful day, my dad was exhausted from working late, and, in my opinion, in a prime mental state to have the wool pulled over his eyes—eyes that, while shut, he claimed, were "not sleeping, just resting." And in my defense, my plan was perfectly conceived and even more perfectly executed. I made dinner. I did my homework. I did the dishes. I made sure the apartment was immaculate. I *dusted*.[10] I then turned out the lights, went into my room, and waited until my dad was asleep.

In the dark of night, night being about 9:30, I made up my bed to look like I was still sleeping in it,[11] tiptoed to my window, eased it open, and climbed through the window and into the freedom of the night, to dance my life away, or at least the portion of my life between then and midnight, when I needed to get home, because I had a major dissection in biology class the next day and really needed to focus.

It is instructive to point out here that this was not an original idea. Teenagers have been trying this parlor trick on their parents for centuries.[12] I was not original. I was not innovative. What made this particular effort so unique (or uniquely stupid), was that my father and I lived in a postage-stamp-sized apartment, one so small that the turning of a book page in my room rattled window frames in the kitchen.[13] The

---

9 Tell that to George W. Bush.

10 This was my fatal mistake. What teenager fucking *dusts*?

11 With a tip of the hat to *The Brady Bunch*.

12 Granted it was probably harder to sneak out of the third floor of a Victorian walk-up and into the London night, but easier to sneak out of a Brazilian hut and into the damp and verdant jungle. Each epoch has its triumphs.

13 This was San Francisco in the 1980s. We were lucky to afford something that wasn't already squatted on by a stony tribe of Burning Man refugees.

idea that I could have snuck out of my apartment was beyond ludi-crous. I couldn't sneak into the bathroom to *pee*.

My father told me later he heard the window the minute it opened, and immediately knew what I was up to. By then I was skipping down the street to meet my friends, confident in my own genius and the obliviousness of my sweet, yet gullible, sleeping paterfamilias.

My father played it cool. He followed behind, slipping in and out of traffic like a two-wheeled wraith, completely undetected by me. He let me get all the way to the club. He let me get inside. He let me dance to exactly seventy percent of "Master and Servant."

And then he dropped the hammer.

When the security guard came to get me from the floor, the look on his face said it all. He did not speak, but the look in his eyes spoke volumes. A very angry, very intimidating black man dressed head to toe in leather and rage was waiting outside to take me away, very likely to a place where I would never be seen again. I had seen my fate in this man's eyes, and my fate was doom. I could do nothing but comply.

When I walked outside, he was at the curb. He just looked at me. No command. No admonishment. Nothing but a silent flick of the head that indicated "put on your helmet. I don't want a motorcycle accident to kill you before I get a chance to."

And that was the last time I ever went dancing at the Palladium.[14]

It was also the last time I ever tried to pull something over on my father. He was too smart, too fast, too good to fool. I was but a young Padawan to his Obi-Wan. I was hopelessly outclassed.

I do think back fondly on how eager, how optimistic I was to think that a strategy for sneaking out of the house that I had only seen work previously on crappy afternoon television would work on my ninja-like father. This was a tough, no-nonsense man reared on the mean streets of Pittsburgh, living through the heart-gripping agony of raising

---

14 My father grounded me, of course. For a year. But after a few weeks of confinement, he realized that if I had to stay in the house, he would have to stay in, too, to keep an eye on me. The grounding ended prematurely, after a stern admonition that if I ever tried anything like that again I would be in *serious* trouble. I was smart enough to take him at his word.

a daughter alone. To think I could pull one over on him was fresh-faced, pure, and totally naïve. I have never been that blindly optimistic since.

I miss that bright-eyed young girl. She had no idea what she was in for.

(13)

The Time I Got Drunk the Night Before Taking the SAT

"Words are like weapons; they wound sometimes."—CHER

"I don't even know if I'm still speaking English right now."—AISHA TYLER

The phrase "youth is wasted on the young" is a complete and total fallacy.

The implication is that when young people are young, they don't know how good they have it; that if they knew then what old people know now, they would spend their time more wisely, live more fully, love more wildly.[1] They would fully experience everything life has to offer before age and infirmity cruelly whisk it all away.

But I would offer that this is exactly what young people do. They take this strong, pristine vessel, with its soft unscarred knees; pink, unmarred liver, unbridled optimism and unmatched recovery time; and they drive that fucking thing into the ground. Young people know

---

1 But seriously, who loves more wildly than teenagers? Every crush is the end of the fucking world. I once spent three months in the same pair of overalls after a breakup with a boy I was particularly into. I do not miss those times. Or those overalls. They were so disgusting at the end they refused to even burn properly.

what to do with a fast car. You drive it. You drive it until you can't drive anymore.

Youth is not wasted on the young. The young are busy wasting youth as hard and fast as they possibly can, so that not one single drop of it is left over for later. They are getting while the getting is freaking good. Guileless and stupid as they are, young people know this whole invincibility thing is utterly temporary, and they are hell-bent on testing it, pulling at it, running it ragged until it breaks, until there is nothing left but retained fluid, osteoarthritis, and a faint ringing in their ears.

Young people get it: youth is transient. Youth is fleeting. Youth will abandon you without warning or remorse. Youth does not love you.

Burn that shit to the ground.

After a dizzying freshman year spent rubbing elbows with the offspring of the rich and ambivalent, I left my private school idyll for the warmer and more terrifying climes of public school. Specifically, my father couldn't afford to send me there anymore, which was good, because I was starting to chafe at my golden restraints anyway. The private school was small and cloistered, and didn't find my consistent tardiness and sarcastic asides in class amusing. I needed a place where I could be myself, among others who were as weird and bewildered and, well, *poor* as I was. And after years of avoiding it, in my public high school I finally found a social home.

High school was when I truly stopped being a loner and made a solid group of friends. Misfits, oddballs, loudmouths, and weirdos, yes, but a group of friends nonetheless, some of whom are still my friends to this day.[2] And now that I finally had a group of friends, I was going to make up for everything I had missed until that point. I was still a nerd, still obsessed with grades and hell-bent for college, but I finally had a social life, and I was highly aware that it might disappear at any moment.

I became obsessed with counting how many times I had spoken on the phone the night before, and for how long, and with whom. Any

---

2 I *really* hope none of them reads this book.

opportunity to go out, to party or interact with others, I took, because up until this point most of my teenage socializing had been between me, a bowl of instant pudding, and a certain private investigator with a rocking mustache, hot pants, and the professional credential of P.I. I don't know that I cared about being cool, but I definitely cared about having friends, and being included, and if there was going to be some fun had somewhere, I was sure as shit not going to miss it.

But oh, for the strength and resilience of my youth! For the ability to stay up all night drinking malt liquor out of a wide-mouthed bottle sheathed in brown paper, in the poorly lit parking lot of a middle school without a care in the world, to eat two-thirds of a monster burrito at two in the morning, sleep for forty minutes, eat the other third, and then go to class and not miss a beat! I am at a point now where if I have a second glass of wine at dinner I wake in the middle of the night hearing voices and wondering if the deep vein thrombosis I acquired over years of cross-continental air travel has finally come home to roost.

My friendships and my true self were often at odds. Even though I had a little circle now, I was still an inveterate nerd, still driven by a desire for excellence and an abject fear of my father's disapproval. I still needed to get good grades and get into a good school. My life was a swirl of keg parties and study groups, beach bonfires and flash cards. I was living two lives, shuttling between identities, juggling lies and falsehoods and façades, and sometimes I didn't even know who I was anymore.

Like Channing Tatum in *Step Up*, I tried desperately to keep my worlds separate.[3] And like Channing Tatum in *21 Jump Street*, I would deny that I cared about school, and make fun of people who *tried*. But I could not keep these worlds separate forever. It was inevitable they would collide, and with disastrous results. I could only hope to emerge from the wreckage relatively unscathed.

Alas, this was not to be.

---

3 How would my cool street friends understand my love of classical dancing? And how would my formally trained ballet dancing partner understand that occasionally a sista just needs to get her crump on?

It all came to a head on the night before I was scheduled to take the SATs for the second time. Everyone who does this, and everyone in the family of someone who does this, knows that you take the SATs twice, because one stomach-churning anxiety-ridden morning full of tears and puke is simply not enough. You do it twice because you are allowed to take the better of the two scores, and sometimes after you have suffered through this four-hour morning of abjection, the agony of it deadens somewhat. You do better the second time around not because you have the answers figured out—you don't. The morning has been a blur and the most you will remember about what you were asked is that some of the answers began with the letter C. And not because you have figured a way to game the system—you haven't. Even the most confident of students stumble away from the test proctor feeling as if they have urinated on themselves during the test. Many of them have.

No, the reason some people do better a second time is that they don't care as much. That is the reason. The first attempt killed something deep inside, and they just don't give a shit anymore.

Or at least, that is what I told myself when I decided, the Friday before I had to take the SATs, to go on a road trip with my friends to Santa Cruz and hang out on the beach all night instead of getting some sleep and focusing on my shaky and increasingly uncertain future. I was excited just to have a group of friends, let alone a group cool enough to come up with an activity as awesome as taking a road trip to the beach at night. Plus, there was a good chance someone might start making out. Whether participating or watching, there was no way I was missing out on that shit.

As for my dad, I had been on my best behavior for a while, so he was off high alert. Furthermore, as he had established with utter clarity, my academic success was my own responsibility. It was his job to feed, house, and clothe me. It was my job to get good grades. He was not going to chase after me about tests, homework, or anything. If I got into a good college, he would pay. If I flunked out, he would silently fling me into the street at eighteen. I knew where I stood.

And where I stood was I wanted to go party with my friends.

It *seemed* like a good idea at the time. I had done pretty well on the test the first time around. I hadn't really done anything in the interim to increase my score, other than tell myself that I had suffered through this god-awful thing once and what was the worst that could happen? I had good grades, great citizenship marks, a position in student government, excellent extracurriculars.[4] And if all that failed, I had a sob story about being the daughter of a single father who was forced to drive me around on motorcycles because he couldn't afford the two extra wheels.[5] Who needed a killer SAT score when I could go drink warm and very inexpensive beer in the backseat of a 1983 puke green Chevy Nova on the beach with a boy I had a crippling crush on?[6]

The math on this was too clear. Too definitive. That test didn't stand a chance.

My friends did nothing to dissuade this cockeyed plan, regaling me with stories about people they knew who had stayed up all night or overslept or not studied or taken the test drunk and gotten a perfect score. They assured me that these were scientifically provable cases, neither conjecture nor anecdote, but *science*. This had really happened to a guy that knew a guy that knew my friend's cousin. And that was proof enough for me.

The whole way down, and the whole way back, I kept telling myself I was doing exactly what I should be doing—not taking the test too seriously. Letting myself relax. Mental excellence required rest and hard work in equal measure. If I didn't know that now, I wouldn't ever really know it, right? Best to take it easy and let the parts of my brain associated with math and reading (and, apparently, intelligent decisions of any kind) lie fallow for a while so they would be rested and ready for the test in the morning.

We had fun. We engaged in hijinks common to the typical Amer-

---

4 I was a whitewater rafting guide for deaf underprivileged teens. Seriously. A black whitewater rafting guide for people who cannot hear but want to experience extreme sports. I was not fucking around on this college application stuff.

5 Massive bullshit.

6 Hold your moralizing horses. There'll be more on high school drinking and poor decision making later. Wait for it.

ican teen with access to a car, a beach, and cheap beer. We yelled the words "road trip" at the top of our lungs as many times as our vocal strength would allow. It was a good night.

Was it worth it? Well.

My friends dropped me off at the test site with ample time to take the test. Somehow, I had remembered to bring my number two pencils, which was impressive, because I was still wearing the same clothes from the day before and smelled suspiciously of Miller High Life and boxed donuts. I walked into that classroom, running my own flimsy internal pep talk about how I was smart and prepared and the answer was almost always "C," and I sat down to ace that test.

When I awoke from my nap four hours later, it struck me that a different strategy might have served me better. It also struck me that wooden high school desks are the single most uncomfortable place to sleep off a hangover.

My SAT score did not go up.

And also, the answer is almost never C.

Thank god for those deaf whitewater rafters.

The Time I Puked All Over the Car of a Boy I Liked in Broad Daylight

"It ain't how hard you hit; it's about how hard you can get hit, and keep moving forward."—ROCKY BALBOA

"I can't breathe. Is this what a ruptured spleen feels like?"—AISHA TYLER

I do not miss any part of being a teenage girl.

Not the confusion, the awkward gait, the emotional instability, the lack of income, the righteous indignation, the fact that my hands and feet were insanely large for my frame, that I had the same haircut as Morris Day of The Time, or that after my mod phase I started dressing like Boys II Men had gotten in a fight with an angry thrift store, all fifties-era letter cardigans and Z-Cavaricci parachute pants.[1]

People romanticize high school. Hollywood likes to portray it as a time when everyone is cute, twirling their ponytails, and meeting up at the Peach Pit for a chocolate malted and a quick handjob from Slater behind the dumpster before glee club practice. This is a pile of utter steaming bullshit, concocted by people who never got a handjob in high school and would like to "re-create" that experience for them-

---

1 Ugh. Just . . . ugh.

selves as adults. This version of high school is a fallacy for all but the very rich, the very slutty, or very rich sluts.

I was not a cute teenager. I was not graceful, bubbly, or precocious. I did not cheerlead, work on the yearbook, organize spirit rallies, or plan dance-offs between opposing gangs of sexy brooding outsiders. I was large, clumsy, constantly lovelorn, snerked when I laughed, and ate yellow mustard on my microwave burritos,[2] which made me smell like a one-woman AV club. I was one slim behavioral quirk away from being Booger Dawson in *Revenge of the Nerds*.

The duck sauce on this tragedy dumpling was that I was a hopeless romantic. This trait did not make me different in any way from every other teenage girl on the planet, or, indeed, in the galaxy. If your enemy formed a massive and invincible force of superhuman teenage girls, all of whom could shoot rays from their eyeballs, fly, lift super heavy shit, and generally kick massive intergalactic ass, you would not need to raise an interstellar navy or arm your arsenal of nuclear weapons. You would just need to organize a small group of cute, brooding, emotionally remote teenage boys, and then send them out into the light of day to lay waste to the oncoming army.

Those boys would kill them all dead and return before lunch, thus proving an axiom, true and immutable, which has held fast since the beginning of time:

Girls are powerless against boys.[3]

I was a living example of this axiom in action.

I didn't crush very often when I was a teenager. There weren't very many guys who were as weird as I was and also not either cripplingly socially inhibited, or gay. Even way back then—far before *Sex and the City*, *Will and Grace*, or that turd *The Object of My Affection*—I knew what a self-brutalizing exercise in futility it was to crush on my hot gay friends. I sensed it would only end with them making out with some boy *way* cuter than me while I ate a gallon

---

2 I still snerk when I laugh. This is neither here nor there.

3 Unless you are a lesbian. And then you are powerless against girls who look and act slightly like boys. Either way, boyishness is girl kryptonite.

of Rocky Road ice cream beside them on the couch and tried not to watch.[4]

And after the crushing defeat of the Great Chinese Food Date Incident way back in grade school, I knew better than to give my heart away recklessly. Sure, I had crushes in the interim, but so many were unrequited that I had pretty much given up on ever liking a person at the same time that they liked me. I figured two people crushing on each other simultaneously was akin to finding a pearl in a live oyster, or winning the Nobel Prize—something that only happened to white people. I had relinquished hope.

So I kept my feelings bottled up, preferring to write bad poetry and eat Häagen Dazs in bed whenever anything resembling a feeling for a boy reared its horned and repulsive head.

Then I fell, and fell hard. And my dignity was never quite the same again.

I developed a crush on a boy my sophomore year so deep-rooted, so epically sweeping, that it lasted almost the rest of my high school career. It was like an emotional tumor, worming its way into every part of my thoughts and affecting all of my behaviors, turning me from a bookish artsy weirdo into a bookish artsy weirdo who stared at points mid-distance for hours and generally acted one thousand times weirder than she ever had prior. This crush was so big and all-consuming that almost immediately, everyone I knew, and shortly after that, everyone in my school,[5] knew about this humiliating and totally debilitating crush. It was tragic on an operatic scale, and there was nothing I could do to stop it. I had taken my elementary school crush, multiplied it by my now much larger bra size, and given it fangs.

When you are a teenager, and you like someone, it takes over everything. It is all you can think about when you wake up, and the last thing you reflect on when you fall asleep. Everything reminds you of them: your schoolbooks. Your favorite television show. Walking. Food. Air. Being.

---

4 To mutilate Tyler Perry, I can eat ice cream all by myself, thank you very much.

5 And shortly after that, I am sure, everyone in the greater Bay Area.

If there was a way to bottle the chemicals produced by a teenager's brain when they have a crush on someone, and we could weaponize it, turn it into some kind of aerosol of want, we could end world war, eliminate poverty, and create a race of super-dedicated athletes focused on world domination. If we could distill and control the unfathomable focus with which teenage girls obsess about the boy they like, turn it into a pill, and give it to everyone, we could solve all of humanity's problems in a matter of days.

Teenagers, however, would never, ever, finish their homework.

I could not think. I could not function. I could not sit still in class or hold a conversation. I could not eat (and, as previously noted, I *love* to eat). I couldn't be a person. I was, for all intents and purposes, very, very sick.[6] And the more I realized that I was embarrassing myself, oddly, the less I cared. That is the thing about humiliation; if you eat enough of it, it starts to taste like normal. Once you have endured the worst embarrassment you can think of, and you have lived, the next sling or arrow is nothing. You have formed a psychic callus over your soul, and now nothing can touch you. The world is your oyster.

Your aloof, humiliating, affection-rejecting oyster.

This boy was not requiting my crush in any way. He did not like me in the way that I liked him. We had mutual friends, and so he was serviceably polite to me, and, at his best moments, tolerated me, which to a teenage girl is tantamount to a marriage proposal,[7] but that was cold and fleeting comfort. Based on a few well-placed and workman-like interactions over time, I was able to fan the flame of this emotional tragedy for a couple of years, as my friends, acquaintances, and the general population of my high school marveled at both my infinite stamina, and my infinite sadness.

I can't say exactly why I was crushing so hard, and honestly, it's irrelevant. It does not matter what was wonderful about the boy. When

---

6 And by "sick," I mean people would look at me and go, "That poor girl. There is something seriously wrong with her," right before they rolled their eyes in disgust and walked away, cackling hysterically.

7 We girls have a way of turning a sidelong and totally casual glance into a romantic gaze loaded with emotional portent. Chicks can parse some shit out.

we are crushing on someone, they are a swirling blur of dimples and crooked smiles, hair flips and skateboard tricks. They make us feel drunk, confused, outside of our bodies. They are a small planet, drawing us in with invisible gravitational force. But when we look back, we can't figure out what specifically made them so alluring. Sometimes we can't even remember why we thought they were awesome in the first place. That's the thing about crushes. They are magic. Terrible, dark, evil magic.

Eventually the crush faded, as it had to. The heart can only take so much rejection, or, in my case, total indifference. Plus I had shit to do. I couldn't just sit around pulling petals out of flowers and making cootie-catchers for the rest of my life. I had to move on. And I did. Slowly, with a lot of effort and focus, the help of my friends, and a few well-placed make-out sessions with other guys. And just when I thought I had gotten my shit together . . . the boy liked me back.

What the fuck!!!

Not okay.

Instantaneously, all the hysteria and internal emotional damage of the previous two years came rushing back, and I was incapacitated again. Like, in seconds. This was not fair. Deep down, I knew I was at the top of a very long, very perilous emotional slide, one made of jagged edges and razor blades and cut lemons and really bad germs that were going to get inside me and render me a weepy, sloppy, oozing mess. I didn't care. It was like I had been standing at the top of a high dive for two years and now I finally had a chance to jump. It didn't matter that when I looked down I saw the pool had been drained and was now full of broken glass and silverfish. I had climbed up here, and I was going to fucking do this thing.

So me and this boy hung out one night, and when it was clear we were going to hook up, it made me crazy nervous, so I drank.[8] I definitely drank too much. At this point, I was just trying not to have a

---

8 I don't care what you saw in movies or on *The Big Bang Theory*. This is *never* a good idea. And also, spare me your moralizing about kids drinking in high school. High school kids drink. It is a bad idea, but it happens. We are not here to judge my sordid past. We are here to dissect, exploit, and mock it. Stay on track.

nervous breakdown. I would have drunk diesel fuel if it had been on hand and someone told me it would take the edge off and make me not feel like a great ugly babbling idiot. And it was a fun night, at least in the beginning, because after a bit, I was more buzzed than nervous, and that was good. And then I was just more drunk than buzzed.

And then I was just fucking *drunk*.

And then we did hook up. And it was awesome, or as awesome as it could be considering I'd been fantasizing about it for half of my high school career,[9] the kind of awesome where you want a burger all day, and then when you eat it, it's good, sure, but it's just a freaking burger, not heavenly ambrosia or Green Lantern's ring. Just a burger.

The next day, however, I remained stoked. Very stoked. Hungover, and sick as blazes, but very, very, very stoked.[10] And it was a Saturday, sunny and perfect, and the boy and I decided to take a drive to the beach, but first we decided to get something to eat. Which I thought was a perfect idea, because I was the kind of hungover that makes people dig out their own eardrums with a broken pencil. So a nice cold soda and a giant hot falafel, full of garlic and tahini and a bunch of other gloppy shit that is hard to pronounce and even harder to keep down when you are hungover, seemed like the perfect idea at the time. In fact, anything the boy said seemed like a perfect idea to me.

I was still very, very lovesick.

We got the food. I ate the falafel. I smiled at the boy. Falafel. Boy. Falafel. Boy. All my dreams were coming true. I turned to look out the open window, thrilled to be with this boy I had been obsessing over since the beginning of time, the cool breeze on my face, blowing my hair back, making me feel happy to be alive, my eyes full of sunshine, my soul full of bubble gum, my heart full of . . .

Puke. My lovesick heart, replete with puke.

Which was now flying out of my mouth at Mach Five like demons

---

9 I honestly can't tell you what it was like. It was a long time ago, and the whole time I was like, "I can't believe we're hooking up!" which I'm sure ruined the vibe a bit. I'm assuming it was pretty boring and punctuated by a lot of high-pitched teenage girl squeals from me and eye rolls of annoyance from him.

10 Teenagers get *stoked*. This is just what they do.

expelling from the pit of my being, propelled outward by the incantations of a wild-eyed priest. And then it was being blown right back into my happy face by that cool breeze, and into my hair, and my face, and my falafel, and the car.

And all over the boy.

And that was the beginning, and the end, of the first great romance of my young life. I had finally found my threshold of humiliation. And the boy had found his threshold of having vomit shot around the interior of his car by a human Gatling gun.

So we had both found our limits. Which was something.

I got over him very, very soon after that. And I learned two things. One, it is a waste of time to love someone who does not love you.

And two, never eat a falafel when you are hungover. Seriously.

Both will end quite badly for you.

(15)

The Hot Wasabi and the Infinite Sadness

"Our vanity is most difficult to wound just when our pride has been wounded."—FRIEDRICH NIETZSCHE

"I can never set foot in this place again."—AISHA TYLER

It may be difficult to imagine, but there was a time in this country, before the Internet, and Gawker, and Pinkberry, and ringtones and Spanx and indeed, civilization, when you could not purchase sushi at every corner store, mini-mall food court, and supermarket in the country.

And stick with me here, as I know this is hard to comprehend: there was a time when Americans, gulp . . . *did not eat sushi at all.*

Years ago, barely anyone even knew what sushi *was.* The word conjured images of slabs of raw, unmasticable flesh, when it conjured any image at all. More often, if you said the word sushi, people would blank out as if they had just remembered they had left their iron on at home. There was no dynamite roll, or firecracker sauce, or crispy rice, and you certainly could not get your crab creamy and spicy. Sushi was exotic, unpronounceable, and very *other.*

And it was raw. Fish. What the fuck is wrong with you?

At the risk of dating myself, this dark age of dining coincided with my junior year in high school. And in keeping with my lifelong philosophy of running headlong and blind into things that I was neither familiar with nor completely understood, I had somehow found a sushi restaurant near my house and set about trying to become an expert in Japanese cuisine. This being San Francisco, we had a higher than normal percentage of Asian restaurants, but the really authentic ones were ensconced deeply in parts of town where most non-Asians did not dare venture out of xenophobia or bewilderment. But there were some Asian restaurants outside San Francisco's Chinatown or Japantown that catered to the uninitiated (read: white people), and it was in one of these that I began my soft initiation into the world of adventurous eating. Which was not very adventurous at all.

The restaurant was called something innocuous and welcoming, like "Sushi Fun Time," or "Rock 'n' Roll Sushi" or "Come On In, White People, Almost Everything is Cooked," and it was perched on Church Street near my favorite bakery, just in case I pussied out at dinner and needed to fill up on more familiar foods afterwards. Nothing got the taste of oddities like eel out of your mouth better than seven or eight carrot cupcakes.

I was determined to master this cuisine, and quickly, because I wanted to impress others with my internationalism and modernity, and because I had seen Molly Ringwald eat sushi in *The Breakfast Club*, and if that waif could do it without gagging, so could I. So I would go, sometimes with friends, sometimes alone, and try everything on the menu, or at least everything that had been cooked first, which, because it was a non-Asian-friendly restaurant, was almost everything. If you wanted shrimp or egg or something called "sea legs," along with copious piles of gut-impacting white rice, this was the place for you. I have no doubt that the sushi chefs there laughed their asses off as they counted their money on the way home each night—they were serving the Japanese equivalent of Spam and eggs.[1]

Eating at this restaurant was part of my larger plan to become more cosmopolitan. And during the execution of this plan, which also in-

---

1 Although the Asians do love their Spam. The Hawaiian ones, anyway. And the Filipinos. You haven't lived until you've had Spam sushi. Well, maybe you have, but it's still delicious.

cluded shopping at consignment shops, smoking unfiltered cigarettes, writing terrible poetry, and eating Wor Won Ton soup—way cooler than regular Won Ton soup, of course, because of the "Wor" part—I met a boy.[2]

This was a boy I liked, one I wanted to impress. So naturally the next step was to take him on a date to the Japanese restaurant and dazzle him with my extensive knowledge of foreign cultures and their cuisines.

So I asked him to come with me to this restaurant. Naturally, because he was a regular old American, and not of Asian descent, he had never heard of sushi, let alone eaten it, so I was already batting a thousand in terms of mysterious woman-of-the-world points. The restaurant was unusual, it felt cool and fancy, they gave you wet towels when you sat down, and it reeked of pickled ginger and danger. I was on fire.

I ordered for the both of us, which felt dazzlingly modern.[3] If I had broken out a cellular phone at the time, I would have taken some kind of world record for forward-leaning behavior. I showed the boy how to mix his soy sauce with his wasabi, and how to scrape the chopsticks against each other to remove any wayward splinters.[4] And when the food came, I explained the strange green substance on the plate as "wah-sah-bee," a "kind of Japanese hot sauce." I knew the boy liked hot sauce, and I wanted the boy to like me, so I wanted to show him that we were alike. That I could take it. That I liked it hot.

With a flourish, I took a nice, generous gob of wasabi on my piece of shrimp sushi, popped it into my mouth, and chewed with a look of sly confidence, mixed with a judicious amount of world-weary boredom—just enough to show him that I was happy to be there with him, but not *too* happy. I mean, I liked him and all, but I did this kind

---

2 Good lord. When would I learn? Nothing good ever comes after the phrase "and then I met a boy."

3 Of course, it was all very pedestrian sushi. Thinking back, I can hear the waitress's eyes rolling in their sockets as she wrote down my California roll order.

4 Both of which are probably about the rudest behavior you can engage in in a sushi restaurant and should have gotten me flung into the street like an unruly hooker.

of shit all the time. Who knows? Maybe after this I would go skydiving. That was the kind of thing sushi eaters just *did*. We defied death, and we ate our sushi *spicy*.

I chewed. I smirked. And then, I exploded.

A masticated combination of shrimp, rice, wasabi, snot, saliva, tears, and shame sprayed across the restaurant like pea soup from a possessed child. There was no table, no corner, no patron untouched by the spray of fluids shot outwards by the combination of truncated sneeze and deep belch of despair that erupted violently from the floor of my being.

And the boy. Dear god in heaven, the boy.

The boy took the full force of the explosion at dead center mass. The boy was at ground zero of the explosive device that was my head. If I had been entertaining any fantasy about making out with this boy, about us ever swapping spit, well, that fantasy had come fully and horribly true. His face was full of it. He had gotten plenty of my spit without any of the sweaty, groping, dry humping fun that usually accompanies it.

As we sat there frozen, me with my hand over my face, trying to hold in the last bits of sushi and my dignity, him trying not to hurl a little bit into his own mouth, the rest of the restaurant poised in that heady electric moment between surprise and gales of shaking, involuntary laughter, I thought to myself, "This is why Americans eat bland food. You can't injure yourself or others with a nice, soft bowl of Spaghetti-Os. A Rice Krispies treat never made anyone explode."

I gathered myself. I took that damp towel (thank god for that damp towel) and handed it sheepishly to the boy with a head tilt that indicated "for your face." There were no words, no need for protestation or explanation. This thing had happened. There was no coming back. My fluids were all over the interior and patrons of a fine dining establishment, and there was nothing to do but hold my head high and plow ahead, sinking the experience deep into my subconscious like a hastily buried corpse.

We finished the dinner with diminished enthusiasm and a marked reduction in eye contact. But despite my humiliation, I didn't die. I made it through the meal, and it was delicious, even if I did eat de-murely and with a bit less gusto after my eruption.

And against all odds, the boy and I did go on another date, and there was nothing for me to do but screw up my bravery again, because I had set the bar for experimentation (and failure) so high that all I could do was keep running at things or admit defeat. And I was far too young and reckless to let a tiny bite of something spicy turn me into a food pussy. So we ate other exciting foods together—Thai and Ethio-pian and palate-searing Hunan—and the boy and I dated for quite a bit of time after that, although we never ate sushi together again.

Since then I've become an even more adventurous eater. I have eaten spicy things and raw things, smelly things and moldy things, animal guts sautéed in butter and set before me with a flourish. Some have been delicious, some confusing, and some have been downright disgusting. But I have never lost my love of culinary adventure, because life is too short to be afraid to bite something on a plate that cannot possibly bite you back.

Well. Not literally, anyway.

(16)

The Time I Was in an A Cappella Group

"A knife-wound heals, but a tongue wound festers."—Turkish proverb

"Could someone lick the salt out of this?"—Aisha Tyler

When I struck out from home, I struck out big.[1]

I had this idea rattling around in my soft and delusional teenage head that I was going to do something great and unconventional in life. The group of colleges I chose to apply to fit my cockeyed grandiose vision. They were all institutions I could barely afford—elite, expensive, culturally and geographically remote—places where I would be financially panicked, academically stressed, and socially isolated. I had realized, after twelve years of teetering on the fringes, excelling academically but struggling socially, until finally finding my home among a group of like-minded weirdos, that I excelled most under adversity; a bit of stress kicked my survival instincts into gear. I had suffered through high school, and academically, at least, things had gone well, so why should college be a breeze? I equated challenge with excellence. And I can see now, looking back, that my unspoken goal was to make my college experience as discomfiting and miserable as possible.

Just to see if I could take it.

---

1 Is this pun intended? I haven't decided yet.

There is a strong possibility I had some kind of undiagnosed psychological problem. That problem may persist to this day.

Based on this self-abusive criterion—essentially "where will I be the most uncomfortable?"—I formulated my college choices. It was a canonical list of oddballs: Bard College, a school as diverse as the front row at an Ani DiFranco concert; Reed College, most famous for its extremely high rate of academic-related suicides; UC Santa Cruz, which eschewed traditional grades in favor of pass/fail grades, accompanied by gold stars and "good job!" hemp cookies; Oberlin College, a school somewhere in fuck-all northeast Ohio, a place I could not have located with Google Maps' assistance, if Google Maps had existed back then; Marlboro College, a Vermont liberal arts school where for all I knew they ate their own composted feces; and Dartmouth College, about which I knew only two things: that it was an Ivy League school, and that they had their own ski mountain, which was highly important to me, as I had recently taken up snowboarding.

None of these schools, with the exception of UC Santa Cruz, was anywhere near my home, and all of them were in remote locations where I would not know anyone, nothing would be familiar, and the weather would be bewilderingly frigid for a good part of the year. Up until this point, I had lived my entire life in California. The warmest coat I owned was a Members Only jacket.[2] I had no idea why I wanted to go somewhere remote and cold. I just knew that every time I told someone I was thinking of going to school in New Hampshire or Ohio they had a million reasons why it was a bad idea. This only made me want it more.

I could say that I was being rebellious, but the fact is that to rebel you need something to rebel *against*. Perhaps I was rebelling against what I *thought others thought* I should do: go to the safe school, the one close to home, where I would feel most comfortable, with a culture most similar to the one I had experienced thus far. Of course, I would miss my parents, the things and places and people I knew. But like my

---

2 You mock, but everyone had one of these. We do not choose the era we are born into. We assimilate or we die.

parents, who moved across the country, far from their families, when they were young and in love, to start a new life, I wasn't afraid of change. I wanted to make a bold gesture, to do something expansive, frightening, life changing. I wanted to go to the metaphorical ends of the earth, to flirt with the unknown.

Or at least get to wear some really cool sweaters.

My years of apple polishing and obsessive-compulsive academic fastidiousness had paid off, along with that summer of guiding the hearing impaired precariously along the razor's edge of near drowning. I got into every college to which I applied. I had a surfeit of options. Of course, the obvious choice was Dartmouth. It was the only Ivy League school in the bunch, it was the farthest away from my home, it was in the mountains of New Hampshire and so guaranteed to rest comfortably in frigid temperatures for a good portion of the year, and it had a reputation for being unapologetically, even threateningly, conservative.[3]

It also had two other very critical things going for it. It was a huge party school, and it had way more guys than girls in attendance.

Copious quantities of beer and dudes? And all I had to deal with was a few supercilious assholes in crested blazers? Sold.

I arrived on campus in the blazing heat of a late New England summer, sporting Birkenstocks (so as to more clearly define myself as *From California,* I thought) and dragging all my shit in a couple of suitcases: one full of clothes, the other full of terror. This place was the opposite of everything I had known previously: East Coast, old, wealthy, full of kids who had come from privilege, few of whom had ever worried about where they would live, or how they would pay the

---

3 There was an incident on campus the year before I attended, where students protesting against apartheid (I mean, who purposely comes down on the wrong side of that issue?) had their makeshift shantytown destroyed by sledgehammer-wielding conservative kids—*while they were still inside.* No one was hurt, but this was mainly luck. The only explanation I can imagine was that everyone was so drunk that the sledgehammer wielders were swinging wide and the kids inside were in that limp physical twilight where blows don't cause damage because the body is so malleable and floppy. This is why it is a good idea to always get very, very drunk on a plane. That way if it crashes, your limp body will be least likely to take damage. I read this on the Internet.

bills. And none of them, I was sure, had ever lived through the horror of watching a chicken peck a litter of baby bunnies to death.

These kids had not experienced adversity. They were loping about in well-worn boat shoes and crisp new L.L. Bean sweaters, laughing about the staff at the country club and their time on the Vineyard, and wondering what kind of cookies their maid would be baking and sending to them in a care package labeled to look as if their alcoholic mother and emotionally remote father "cared" about them. They all spoke the same language, thought the same thoughts, were cut from the same cloth. They were a school of very confident, very well-dressed, yet casually offhanded fish. For the millionth time in my life, I felt completely out of my depth. But this time, I was thousands of miles from home.

This time, I was on my own.

There are two ways to go when you find yourself on the outside looking in. One is to walk firmly in the other direction, embrace your isolation, and celebrate your outsiderhood. I had taken this path my entire life. For the most part, it had worked, if for no other reason than that I didn't have to worry about rejection if I never sought acceptance. Also, over in the corner alone, no one would notice me talking back to the voices in my head.

The other strategy is to walk boldly toward the center of the crowd and embrace what everyone else is doing and, if you're lucky, beat them at their own game. I had been on the outside for most of my life. College was a fresh start. I figured now was the time to see what it was like on the inside.

Not everyone else was on board with this strategy.

One of the things that embodies the Ivy League experience, something that is most archetypically *Ivy*, is the a cappella singing group. This bastard child of the collegiate Glee club and barbershop quartet has been around since the late 1800s, proliferating at a time when the Ivies were the sole domain of men.[4] Every Ivy League college has one (or more) of these precious groups, with such sickeningly confection-

---

4 Who were no doubt profoundly sexually frustrated and so had to pour all that energy into *something*, and that something became standing around twirling their waxed mustaches while singing in mildly effete four-part harmony.

ery names as the Princeton Nassoons, the Brown Jabberwocks, the Yale Whiffenpoofs, and the Dartmouth Aires. They are a blast to see perform, generating a combination of feelings akin to eating chocolate-covered bacon: it tastes strangely delicious, but you can't divine exactly how you feel about it. Is it a brilliant stroke of genius or an abominable chimera that defies the laws of nature?[5] Are you in on some great joke? Are they? Is there a visionary puppet master pulling the strings, or are we all riding in a horseless cart, bobbing our heads blissfully to a marginal arrangement of an even more marginal Boston song?

Not that it mattered. If you wanted to live at the epicenter of Ivy life, to be most quintessentially collegiate, the a cappella group was the way to go. The only way to be more fully Ivy would have been for me to get a trust fund and a coke habit and start sleeping with sorority girls. I figured I couldn't get to the third thing on that list without slogging through the first two, and, as far as I knew, my family wasn't concealing some secret fortune I could use to fuel a drug habit.[6] So, a cappella it was.

The problem is, the established a cappella groups didn't want me. I don't blame them. My voice was okay, but I still hadn't outgrown my gawkiness, and I had stubbornly spent most of my freshman year wearing my Birkenstocks around campus in a hideous act of fashion defiance.[7] Birkenstocks did not go with the overweeningly preppy style of a cappella groups. They were bright-eyed and fresh-faced and sang like angels and knew lots of things about white wine and would all work on Wall Street when they graduated. I was sleep deprived and my hair was a mess and my voice was untrained and I would be lucky to get a job as a receptionist at a medicinal pot dispensary if I kept rocking those ridiculous shoes.

---

5 This is pre-*Glee*, way before teenagers singing pop songs without instruments and dancing around with no sense of irony was even *remotely* cool.

6 As I had been systematically going through my father's pockets since grade school, I had a pretty clear grasp of his net worth.

7 Yes, even in winter. I wore wool socks when it got cold, which had the effect of making me look like a Women's Studies professor, or a vegan bean sprout farmer who lived in a yurt.

I was not a fit.

So I continued with my freshman year as best I could, considering I was trying to navigate an icy campus with an armful of textbooks and unsuitable footwear. I soldiered on. And then halfway through the year, something miraculous happened. All the girls that had been rejected from the other a cappella groups decided to form their own group, and they asked me to audition. This was my shot! I imagined myself vacationing with Muffy on the Cape, sipping minted iced tea, and wondering what the riffraff down at Princeton were up to. I auditioned, I got in, and I was thrilled. My nefarious plans for infiltration were finally coming together.

Unfortunately, this group was brand new, and so had none of the gravitas, elegance, or fashion sense that over a hundred years of elite East Coast Ivy League snobbery had conferred so delicately on the other groups. We were earnest, we loved to sing, we adored ironic arrangements of mid-eighties New Wave songs, but other than that, we were making it up as we went along. And because we were outsiders and had no history to respect or traditions to hew to, we decided to reject the conventions that defined the other groups and go our own way. We would blaze a new creative path.

Honestly, we just had no freaking idea what we were doing.

We struggled. We had a few music majors, but no one who could actually arrange music. We had a few people with rhythm, but no one who had ever conducted a musical group. We had some people who could sing, but no one who knew enough about vocal theory to help develop their voices. Rehearsals were an orgy of confusion, punctuated by brief, satisfying moments of harmony, followed by more delirium, and ending in chicken sandwiches. We knew where we wanted to go, but we had no idea how to get there.

We were all *Idol* contestants, no Randy Jackson.

But we were determined. Motivated. Obstinate even. Willing to feel our way in the dark. To suck terribly in the pursuit of excellence.

And let me tell you, we fucking sucked.

Because we were so rough around the edges, early on we decided we needed a gimmick, a special look. Our singing was still quavering and unsure, so we figured if we had a flashy presentation, people might not notice dropped lyrics and wobbly key migrations. We also figured this would set us apart from everyone else and make us seem more professional.

Sure.

We kicked this around for a while—how to come up with a look that was casual yet polished, accessible yet refined.[8] We struggled with every thematic idea, every visual trick, our brainstorming hampered severely by the fact that we were college kids whose daily uniform involved a college sweatshirt and jeans that smelled of Bic pens and taco salad. We couldn't afford uniforms, eveningwear seemed pretentious, and just showing up in whatever we were wearing that day would make us look like an assemblage of slovenly singing street urchins. We got tired, then bored, then quietly annoyed.

We finally settled on an idea that was simple, affordable, and easy to execute: a set of variations on the mock turtleneck.[9] Why? Because this was the nineties, the United States was completely devoid of any style whatsoever, and the mock turtle was the height of sartorial edge. Functional yet fun. Business at the collarbone, party at the neck. We had settled on the mullet of clothing items.

But how to make this special? Indeed, how *do* you make a group of college women in mock turtlenecks look like anything but a team of foodservice workers or a large modern jazz collective?

The answer was in one of our first songs, a maudlin and forgettable piece by the group Yaz called "Mr. Blue."[10] The name said it all. We would all wear different tops, of different colors, and we could introduce ourselves to the audience according to the color of our shirts. As

---

8 I think we also hoped, much like the people behind artists like Justin Bieber or KISS, that a distinctive look would distract listeners from the fact that we were a bit flimsy in the art department.

9 Much like Steve Jobs, we recognized early on the functionality and versatility of the mock turtle. Unlike Steve Jobs, we got off that shit quickly. However, if I had known that wearing them might have led to founding a multibillion-dollar technology company, I'd still be rocking that shit now.

10 There were other maudlin and forgettable New Wave songs we performed. Norwegian pop supergroup A-ha, anyone?

in—and I am not exaggerating here—"Hi! My name is Aisha, and I'm Mr. Green."

I am Mr. Shattered Pride.

This weirdly non sequitur and socially self-destructive performance bit continued the entire first year of our group's existence, and into the second. We were earnest, we were determined, and we were undeterred. There was a wholesomeness to our ham-fisted approach, a sweetness that balanced out the off-putting peculiarity of it all. We were adorable, the way a yipping puppy is adorable right before it scoots its filthy bottom on your heirloom rug.

But we kept at it. And we practiced, and squawked, and blew on those infernal pitch pipes, and we eventually got better. And then, we actually got good.

The big badge of acceptance at Dartmouth was being invited to "Spring Sing," an a cappella concert that was held—yes, each spring— and involved some rotating segment of all the on-campus groups. Not all of the groups were invited, mind you. This was not a democracy, and every year the group that got to plan the Spring Sing and invite the other groups let us know it.

We'd been around for three years at this point, and had been snubbed by the group that organized the Spring Sing every year. It hurt, because we had actually gotten very popular, selling out shows and even recording an album. We had finally lost those infernal mock turtlenecks. But somehow, not being invited to the Spring Sing reminded us that we were still outsiders. We were the Nickelback of our school, loved by the masses but rejected by the establishment. We acted like we didn't care, but we did. We cared a lot.

Each year, when the Spring Sing lineup was announced, we would be eager and bouncy and puppyishly confident that *this* was going to be the time we got an invitation, then bitterly stung when we realized we weren't on the list. But, like most wounds do, each time we got stung it hurt a little bit less. And eventually, like a wryly funny but socially awkward wallflower in some high school swarming with viciously exclusive cliques, we resigned ourselves to never getting invited to the big dance. And that was okay. We continued singing and performing and writing sketches that made people laugh and making our "art," sometimes good, sometimes bad, but always ours. We got better outfits. We forgot about pleasing others, and started pleasing ourselves.

And then, one day, we finally got invited to Spring Sing.

I am Mr. Shrieking Delight.

I won't lie. This was one of the greatest days of my young life. I had been acting like I didn't care if we ever performed at this thing, but I was freaking thrilled. We were going to sing in front of a theater full of our peers, some of whom I really wanted to lord this over. This was rewarding. This was validating. This was utterly satisfying. It would have been a dream come true, but there was something oddly anticlimactic about it. After all these years of wanting this prize, yearning for it, and crying over it, now that we had it, it felt a bit . . . meh. We had put the Spring Sing dream to bed long ago. If we had never been invited to that concert, it wouldn't have changed how we saw ourselves. We were making the music we wanted to make, and every time we stepped on to a stage[11] in front of an audience, our heads raced and our hearts fluttered. We loved what we did, and after a long slog through insecurity and self-doubt, we finally didn't care what anyone else thought. We knew who we were.

Getting the chance to show our classmates how super hot we already knew we were was just icing.[12]

The show was a triumph. We weren't perfect by any means, but we were enthusiastic, and mostly in tune, and we broke out some sexy new choreography,[13] and we blew those other pinstriped crooners out of the water. And in the name of all that is good and holy, we were not wearing those insufferable fucking turtlenecks. We killed it. We had arrived.

Years later, the group we founded still performs, with a new crop of

---

11 Or a fraternity basement drenched in beer and urine, which was our usual milieu.

12 I am Mr. Smirking Self-Satisfaction.

13 Nothing particularly complex, however, as I am utterly uncoordinated. Add singing to dancing and you've got a quick way for me to poke myself in the eye. Which I have done, unprovoked, on more than one occasion. Ta-dah!

inductees joining with each freshman class. They have recorded multiple albums and given concerts all over the world. If you had told that ragtag group of girls that first freshman year that what we were doing would create a musical legacy that would last more than two decades, we would have laughed until we cried all over our polyblend mock turtlenecks.

We didn't know we were renegades. We weren't trying to be rebels. We just wanted to sing. But you never know what you can create if you put your heart into it unreservedly, and never let anyone else make you feel as if you don't belong. Because a rebel is just a guy who doesn't have the good sense to go the same way the crowd is going, and the composure to act like that was his idea all along.

For the record, I take credit for starting the whole mock turtleneck trend.

You're welcome, Apple.

(17)

The Time I Danced Tragically in Front of My Entire College

"There are some wounds that one can heal only by deepening them and making them worse."—Auguste de Villiers de l'Isle-Adam

"I have no idea what the hell I'm doing. Let's just get out there and see what happens."—Aisha Tyler

Just because I could sing, doesn't mean I could dance.

People often make this unfortunate extrapolation. If you can carry a tune, the assumption is that you are a crunk beat away from getting your Usher on and doing a backflip into the faces of the evil opposing dance team while a crowd full of hard-luck kids with hearts of gold tauntingly intone "ooooooh." I could not manage a backflip with a gravity harness and a team of assistants, but this matters not; it is a skill set people assign to me anyway. The fact that I am black does nothing to help disabuse people of the notion that I can drop it down and back it up.

I cannot drop it down and back it up, unless you are talking about a shitty car with a weak suspension into a parallel parking spot.[1]

---

1 It is definitely *not* getting hot in herre.

In fact, being black has not helped me at all in this regard. I know that is typically our domain, but I spent my childhood making tiny villages out of mud and sticks when I should have been booty popping and krush groove locking. The boogie wonderland passed me by; I missed out on this skill development completely. And much like learning a language, I'm pretty sure the neural pathways that govern dancing form at a very tender age. If you don't start learning early, after a certain age you are reduced to the dancing equivalent of only being able to speak barely functional English. I have mastered a limited number of dances that I interchange with gusto, much like the facial features on a Mr. Potato Head. They are rudimentary and visually lackluster, and they have served me for years.[2] It is far too late for me to change now.

I will never be the lead in *Step Up 17: Old Lady Finally Gets Around to Krumpin'*. I have made my peace with this.

But in college, I had not yet come to terms with my lack of dancing skills or with my utter lack of physical dexterity of any kind. In my head, I was a gazelle, lithe and graceful, gliding across campus like a wayward angel fallen to earth, strewing fragrant blossoms and opals in her path.

In reality, I was a massive, galumphing klutz. Towering, awkward, and completely oblivious to anything happening around me. I was insanely accident-prone. I had the unique ability to find the one sharp item in a room full of down pillows and dandelion fluff, then impale myself on it violently and repeatedly, perhaps nicking a few bystanders in the process. I was the human equivalent of Mechagodzilla, crushing all in my path to dust in an orgy of carnage.

I would often write off my clumsiness to context or exhaustion, or the thoughtless interference of others. But these were feeble and groundless protestations. One night, walking alone mid-winter across the icy campus quad with an armful of books and a large cup of coffee, on my way to a last-minute study session the night before midterms, I

---

2 I can do an excellent Wop, and under pressure I can deliver a serviceable Running Man. Honestly, that's about it. I'm more of an ideas person.

managed the kind of feet-in-the-air, ass-over-teakettle earth-shattering tumble that you might see in vintage animation classics like *Scooby Doo* or *Hong Kong Phooey*. You could literally hear the "whip-eedip-whip-whip-whip-whip-whee!" of my feet slip-sliding on the ice, then soaring far above my head, as books, coffee, my backpack, and possibly a tooth went airborne—then clattered with a thud to the solid, unforgiving ice. As there was no one around for a quarter mile, I could not blame *this* fall on anything but my staggering inability to control the movements of my own body.

My ass throbbed like a bongo drum for three months after that. When it came to pratfalls, I didn't fuck around. Major irreparable personal damage was the name of my game.

So why I ever thought it was a good idea to enter a lip-syncing contest where I would be expected to fake sing, *and* dance, to a popular song, on stage, in front of others, is a mystery. I mean, my fellow students were drunken college kids, sleep deprived and starved for entertainment, but they weren't drooling imbeciles. Someone was sure to notice my total lack of dancing ability and highlight it to others in the kind of "point-and-screech" physical stance used by body snatchers to alert their fellow aliens that someone among them still possesses their human faculties. Even going in, I knew there was no way for this to end but terribly, humiliatingly, and with someone possibly losing an eye or a digit. Or both.

I forged ahead anyway, mostly because my best friend assured me that we would have really cool outfits. Still stinging from the shame of that abominable mock turtleneck, I would have agreed to a public stoning if it meant I could change perceptions about my fashion sense. A public stoning would have been less painful than this performance. At least with a stoning there's no choreography.

Of all the professions people fantasize about, pop star is the only one people assume they could do right away if given the opportunity, without experience, training, divine gift or dumb luck. People may armchair quarterback their favorite football team, but no one thinks that if the coach reached out through the flat screen and tapped them on the shoulder they could suddenly shake the D-line and make a mad scramble for second down. And while we may complain about, crit-icize, or abhor politicians, very few have the stomach to stand bare before the nation while people dig through every filthy detail of their pasts, poring over offhanded comments and questionable investments, parsing letters to ex-girlfriends and drunken photographic tweets. We all talk a good game, but most of us know when we're outclassed.

That is, in every discipline but pop performer. As evidenced by the litany of teary-eyed, bleating tragedies that stream past the camera at the beginning of every season of *American Idol*, every bobblehead with half a vocal cord and a Hot Topic half-shirt thinks they have what it takes to be the next Bruno Mars. Never mind that they've never had a voice lesson or held an instrument in their lives.[3] Everyone thinks that all they need is the right lighting and a copy of Pro Tools to be the second coming of Gaga.

I, apparently, was one of these bobbleheads. And this was my shot to show everyone how selfless I had been to choose academia over my true calling: uplifting lives and devastating hearts while jamming to a funky beat.[4]

My friend and I entered the contest as a duo. Concept was every-thing, and the song would drive the look, so we set about picking an anthem. This being the nineties, we immediately chose Janet Jackson, and us being idiots, we settled almost as rapidly on a song that was completely out of our league. Remember, this was the zenith of MTV, when it was still relevant, impactful, and hit-creating. Oh, and it also actually played music videos rather than just a litany of reality shows featuring drunken train wrecks in desperate need of parental guidance stumbling about like human pinballs in search of a hole. MTV was still Music Television at the time, and the videos that were kicking the most ass were ones where everyone wore leather and looked like background actors in *The Crow*. Janet was awesome then, and we were all part of the "Rhythm Nation."

---

3 Guitar Hero does. Not. Count.

4 Even using the phrase "funky beat" disqualifies me from ever being able to recognize one. I sound like a character from *Yo Gabba Gabba*.

We had this thing locked up.

Except for the fact that neither of us could dance. At college, I had accumulated a group of friends whose favorite pastime was sitting around eating bacon-topped pizza, arguing about the feasibility of large-scale organic farming, and drinking cocktails that had been mixed in an industrial garbage can. None of that involved dancing, choreography, or physical exertion of any kind.[5] The most physical we ever got was getting drunk and running outside in our shirtsleeves to construct a life-threatening ice slide in the frigid wee hours of a January morning.

No matter. Pop stardom was my destiny. Bring it on.

After watching the video for "Rhythm Nation" one thousand times and finding ourselves able to replicate absolutely nothing therein, we decided we needed a ringer, someone who could make us look better and, failing that, dance around wildly to distract everyone. Luckily, the house I lived in had a resident dancer and choreographer who was a fantastic dresser with a scintillating personality and killer stage presence. We threw ourselves on his mercy, much like a frumpy housewife might fling herself at the feet of RuPaul, begging him to make her more feminine. We were failures at dancing, but more than that, we were failures at being sexy girls. We needed serious help. We needed a gay man.[6]

Buoyed by his agreeing to be our resident visionary and *sergent instructeur*, and encouraged by his faith in us,[7] we set about remaking ourselves in Janet's image. Naturally, I thought I should be Janet, being tall and hard to camouflage. My best friend was short, blond, and adorable—not particularly Jackson material.[8] We wrestled with this, and since we valued our friendship more than we cared about what was quickly turning into a massive drag on our free time, we agreed to split responsibilities. Much like Stevie and Paul, we would live side by

---

5 Using a visibly unwashed hand to stir vodka into fruit juice is not exercise.

6 In retrospect, no one could help us. We were a lost cause.

7 He didn't believe in us at all. We offered him tears, then booze, and finally money.

8 Although in Michael's latter days, he resembled her far more than he resembled me.

side on the piano and share the spotlight, offering up a shining example of racial harmony for all to see.

None of this was top of mind, particularly. Most of the time, we were drunk on vodka and grapefruit juice. But it did seem as if, executed properly, we could change the world with this shit. Or at least get laid.

We were renewed, our vigor and commitment made fresh. Unfortunately, the initial enthusiasm sparked by the addition to our two-man band lasted about a day. College students are notoriously lazy, veering madly between floor-sprawled apathy and manic all-night productivity. The diagnosis of bipolar disorder—where a person swings from wild bouts of intensely effective hypermania and elation to long dark periods of depression and inertia—should be voided for college students. Embracing bipolarity is the only way you can actually get through college: weeks of procrastination, defined by days huddled in the dark of your dorm room in unwashed sweatpants, weeping and eating Snickers bars by the fistful, followed by forty-eight hours of mind-boggling effectiveness, during which you clean your entire room, including your roommate's sty of a side,[9] take apart your computer, rearrange its guts to make it n^{17} times faster, put it back together, throw away the leftover parts (which were just decorative anyway), make a seven-layer lasagna using only your hotplate and a bunch of leftover ketchup packets, write three research papers, and finish an entire semester's worth of clinical psychology reading in one night. Rinse, and repeat.

Our first few rehearsals were pretty high-energy and motivated, and then we just fell apart. We were exhausted, and not very good. Also, as college kids, we were prone to easy distraction—the lure of a party, or a half-eaten pizza, or an extra hour of sleep proved irresistible. Instead of actually dancing, we began engaging in mental training—you know, the kind where you think about something a lot without ever actually doing it. I am a professional at this kind of training. I visualize myself winning the Olympic Pentathlon, inventing a phone that can be controlled by brain waves, or doing the laundry. I do not actually *do* these

---

9 Where did this person grow up, a Russian gulag?

things, but I see myself doing them, and that is almost *more* satisfying, because I am also lying down.

By the night of the performance, we were not even close to ready. We did not know the choreography, we had not memorized the lyrics, we could not dance, and I was developing an epic leg cramp. But this thing was happening, so we put on our best approximation of the wardrobe from the "Rhythm Nation" video—black leotards and tights, borrowed leather jackets, and ballet flats—a combination that, I hoped, would magically make me a better dancer. I prayed fervently that beefy white tube socks stuffed into delicate slippers might have some kind of transformative effect. It did not.

Panicked, at the last minute we decided to pull in a fourth, a girl-friend of ours who was bored and avoiding homework, and who knew even less of the choreography than we did, but had a great body and was willing to wear lingerie. We figured if nothing else she could parade around and distract everyone from noticing the cat pile of madness that was our dancing. She was game, and played her role with gusto, striding back and forth for no particular reason, gesticulating wildly, blowing kisses to the audience, and generally shaking her moneymaker.

We, on the other hand, could not have shaken our moneymakers if they had handles on them like giant human maracas. But we did our best to communicate the spirit, if not the actual choreography, lyrics, look or anything else of that music video. We stumbled back and forth across the stage, straining to keep time to the beat, faces masks of concentration, bodies a tangle of arms and legs, flailing and pulsating with utter lack of rhythm. We were an aerobics class in an insane asylum. But we sold it with everything we had, and as the song ended we froze, posed in triumph, arms raised like gymnasts, gasping for air, chests heaving, faces lifted to the sky, feeling like champions. In that one shining moment, we were winners. We were, indeed, a part of the Rhythm Nation.

Also in that moment, we knew, deep down in our hearts . . . that our performance had *sucked*. If there had been a real Rhythm Nation, our passports would have been revoked. We were terrible.

Happily, most of the audience was too drunk to care. There were girls, they were on stage, they were wearing tights, and that was good enough for them. They applauded loudly, and cheered lustily. Whether it was because they loved the performance, or because it was finally mercifully over, didn't matter. We had vamped like crazy in the ultimate vamping contest, and in situations where appearance is everything, it may matter more that you look like you fit the part than that you actually fit it at all.

And I learned that when all else fails, dance your ass off. Preferably in suggestive clothing.

Hey, entire careers have been built on less.

I'm talking to you, Madonna.

(18)

The Time I Created My First Sketch Character

"There's dignity in suffering, nobility in pain, but failure is a salted wound that burns and burns again."—MARGERY ELDREDGE HOWELL

"Boot, then rally."—AISHA TYLER, REPEATING AN OLD DARTMOUTH SAYING, RIGHT BEFORE BOOTING AND RALLYING

Despite the fact that it was an Ivy League school, a bastion of academic excellence, elite accomplishment, intellectual refinement, and *blah blah blah*, the thing that Dartmouth was best at, the area in which it truly excelled, was partying.

Dartmouth was founded in 1789 in the wilderness of New Hampshire to educate the Native Americans of the area. As of 1992, that still hadn't really happened. What *had* happened instead is that a lot of white Anglo-Saxon Protestant dudes went to the woods for four years and drank an inhuman amount of beer. The school is in Hanover, in the wilderness of New England, and from its very beginnings, there has never been much to do up there. The main pastimes of the school in its early years were hiking, clearing woodland brush, building fires, and making underclassmen wear hats with propellers on top. You can imagine a wee dram of alcohol might make the time pass more quickly.

Nowadays, the area around Hanover, New Hampshire, once completely desolate, is only slightly less desolate—a place for which the arrival of a Ben and Jerry's shop is enough to elicit mental breakdowns and uncontrollable tears of joy. This place is in the middle of nowhere. A place full of hormone-filled kids, living on their own for the first time, in the middle of nowhere.

There is bound to be some drinking.[1]

I am not boasting about this. It is just how it is. Young people are stupid. Aggressively stupid. Now put them in a context in which they are essentially unsupervised. And make that place very cold and very far from anything worth doing at all. And now remove girls.

You can see how the social culture at Dartmouth would form almost exclusively around drinking.

Dartmouth College is not special in this regard. All colleges have drunken dummies.[2] And I don't think Dartmouth is even the biggest, or even the tenth biggest, party school in the country. But it is the preppiest. And the one where you are most likely to get terrible frostbite if you pass out in the wrong place.[3] When Dartmouth kids party, they are *serious*. There is a saying at Dartmouth—more like a war cry—that people use when they are partying: "Boot and Rally." This is when you drink so much you have to throw up, then turn right back around and put more booze into the happy void created by all that vomiting. This is not just a slogan, but a rigorous practice and source of pride among students. If you are on the verge of "booting," you may even pull the trigger to get things started, something that might be shameful if you are a thirteen-year-old girl trying to lose weight, but is a puke-green badge of courage if you are a nineteen-year-old premed student with an organic chemistry midterm on Monday morning.

---

1 Yes, it does get out of hand. No one can organize and structure shit, even binge drinking, like the kids of the Ivy League.

2 Our country is lousy with drunken dummies. We have elevated it to an art form. Witness the popularity of *The Hangover*.

3 If cold is a problem for you, I suggest the University of Hawaii. You could pass out on a street corner every night at UH and the worse that would happen is someone would tuck a hibiscus bloom behind your ear while you snoozed.

You are tough. You are motivated. You love fun like it gave you a blow job once. You will not let a little nausea or overindulgence put you on the sidelines. This is your last chance to let loose before you pull a thirty-seven-hour cramming marathon (remember that college bipolar disorder I explained). You. Will. Not. Fold. You boot. You rally.

Blood vessels and brain cells be damned.[4]

Because the school is so isolated, not only has it developed an intensely competitive culture around drinking, but it has also developed an intricate and hoary social structure revolving almost exclusively around fraternities and sororities, or "Greeks."[5] These organizations have had a death grip on the social life of the campus since ale was transported to campus in casks on the backs of pack mules, along with hardtack and smallpox-infested blankets. Members of the Geek culture will tell you they are critical to promoting a sense of brother- and sisterhood, responsibility, civic-mindedness, and philanthropy. Mainly they are just ways for people to feel like they belong, for other people to feel like they don't belong, and for *other* other people (girls, and a few boys) to flirt with guys and gain access to mass quantities of free beer.

I don't know how it works at other schools, but at Dartmouth, all the houses had beer on tap, pretty much all the time. When I arrived, this was akin to entering an academic building and realizing it was made out of marshmallows, with candy cane rails and hot chocolate faucets. Beer. Available any time, from beer taps. Unsupervised beer taps.

Heaven.

I did not behave delicately when I found this out. I have never had an excess of self-restraint, but in this case, I lost it. I was Augustus Gloop at Willy Wonka's place. I had my mouth around those spigots like they were dispensing test answers. As any proud American wan-

---

4 By way of context, the man who wrote *Animal House* attended Dartmouth and was a member of the Alpha Delta fraternity. He based that script on his experiences as an undergraduate. And from what I can tell, he toned them down considerably.

5 No, fraternities and sororities were not invented just to give you someone to hate in movies like *Revenge of the Nerds* and *Van Wilder*.

dering a Costco with a tummy full of "some kind of meatball" will tell you, anything free is absolutely worth having, and worth having twice.

I didn't even really *like* beer that much at the time, but let's be reasonable. Turning down free booze is like turning down free money. It's just not done. Not only should you accept when it is offered, you should do your best to drink more than your fair share, just in case someone finally gets their wits about them and decides to bring a halt to this whole Christmas-morning-all-the-time thing that's been going on.

Now, this beer may have been free to me, but it was not truly free. It came out of the fraternity dues that members paid their respective houses, all of which was put into purchasing alcoholic beverages, and none of which was put into improving their infrastructure or caring for their landscaping or hiring some kind of hazmat team to spray out their biological hazard of a bathroom with toxic chemicals *Silkwood*-style. All of their money went to beer. The floors were sticky, the windows were missing panes, and several brothers were missing teeth due to falling through broken treads on the stairwell. But there was *always* beer.

And because non-house members knew this, we would sneak in at odd hours to slake our thirst, or perhaps try to impress visitors from other campuses with the beer-soaked wonderland that was our beloved alma mater. I distinctly remember doing this with a visiting high school friend. "You can have beer anytime you want! At one-thirty! On a Wednesday! Rich people are awesome!"

The houses got hip to this and started to lock up the taps, but this felt rigid and un-American (and super un-fun), so they started to assign brothers to watch the taps and make sure that the beer was dispensed fairly and properly, which is to say, only to brothers, the friends of brothers, and any girl within a twenty-five-mile radius who looked even remotely thirsty. If you were a female student at Dartmouth with most of your faculties, you could be sure that a plastic cup of lukewarm beer would be sloshed into your hand by an overeager fraternity brother the minute the previous cup even approached empty. *Gee, thanks buddy! Can't wait to choke down another eight ounces of Milwaukee's least finest!*

But it was free. We've established how I feel about free.

The concept of tap duty started to dominate the social conversation sometime around my sophomore year. You'd be talking to a guy, and if he wanted to get out of the conversation, or seem important, or had to pee something fierce, he would say he had "tap duty." This quickly became a target of wide ridicule. "Tap duty" is not a job. Saying you have "tap duty" is akin to saying you have to go home and wash your hair. It's a non-activity. You can *say* it's important, and act like it's important, and even tell yourself it's important, but really, it's total bullshit. You might as well say you have to run home and finish your needlepoint pillow. There are plenty of dudes to run the taps. *Beer* comes out of them. Trust me, there are always volunteers.

This annoying self-importance got to be so pervasive that I would make fun of it constantly. No matter what was happening, tap duty was more important. Adopting a low timbre and douchey facial expression, I would smolder in masculine fashion and wail to my friends about how tap duty was eating my life. In the soul-crushing throes of a breakup with your boyfriend? Can't talk, I have tap duty. Parents getting a divorce? Would love to talk you through it, but people need beer. Berlin Wall coming down? Sure, would love to watch this once-in-a-lifetime coverage, but how will people get lager out of those faucets without my expert supervision? Want to have sex? Man, I do love to bang, but how can I make sweet, sweet love to you when tap duty calls, like a siren in the night? Duty cannot be shirked.

Of course, when one of my friends was on tap duty, I took total advantage of it. I'm no dummy.

After a while, we decided our singing group needed something to separate it further from the other groups, an element that would distinguish us and make us special, or at least more special than our workmanlike abilities and overweening earnestness had done so far. We decided to do some comedy sketches in between songs, as a way to break things up and increase the length of our shows (which to this point had been on the brief side, as we were still building our repertoire). We worked on a bunch of less-than-SNL-worthy ideas, settling finally on a bit built around this douche bag fraternity brother for whom duty always called. And naturally, because I was the largest and most masculine of the bunch, I would play him.

For my very first sketch character, I performed in drag, if drag meant that I put on a baseball cap . . . and then turned it backwards. That was all it took to turn me from delicate, feminine lady to giant, lumbering, grunting dude. Sadly, it was not a big stretch at all.

We debuted the sketch at an outdoor concert on the main green one warm spring afternoon. The sketch was poorly written and even more poorly delivered. I rushed my dialogue. I missed my cues and bobbled my lines. I had poor posture and terrible projection.

I was *awful*.

No matter. The crowd loved it. This was a guy they all knew. Some of them *were* this guy. And at least a third of them (not all female) were sleeping with him. We had hit the sweet spot of campus zeitgeist, and it was a damp and beer-soaked bullseye.

Despite my lackluster performance, I loved it even more than the audience. Getting laughs was the most intoxicating sensation I had ever felt. It completely beat drinking watery beer from a cup that only moments before held cigarette butts or chew juice before being rinsed out by a lazy fraternity brother and reused; plus, no hangover. I was hooked.

"Fratman" was a hit. It would become one of our signature bits, and my own signature character, for the rest of my time at Dartmouth. It was my first foray into sketch comedy, and I was completely in love. I didn't know it at the time, but those early laughs, so delightful and addictive, were like the start of a bacterial infection—the spread of which would come to slowly and inexorably change my life forever.

Even though I wasn't very good, I knew what I wanted. And I knew what I needed to do to get it. Work harder. Train longer. Get funnier. Stop sucking so much.

And that's what I did.

I performed. I studied. I practiced. I watched comedians. I wrote sketches. I performed again. I started learning about comedy and how it works, and for the rest of my time at Dartmouth, I made it an increasingly large part of my life. Even though my early performances weren't much to look at, I loved how they made me *feel*. And I wanted to feel that feeling more.

Because it doesn't matter how badly you suck when you start. It just matters that you *start*. And if you hit a speed bump, you stop, re-orient, and start again. And again, and again, until the speed bumps feel like nothing.

In life, like in sport drinking, you boot, and then you rally.

(19)

The Time I Killed a Hobo

"He jests at scars that never felt a wound."—William Shakespeare

"This is definitely *gonna leave a mark."*—Aisha Tyler

Calm down. I didn't actually kill a hobo. My big pile of middle-class guilt just made me *feel* as if I did.

And as any recovering Catholic or cookie stealing preschooler will tell you, guilt is a dastardly bitch.

When I graduated from college, I returned immediately to the welcoming, familiar bosom of my hometown. San Francisco, besides being perfect in every way, is a city renowned for several things: hilly terrain, a killer food scene, and a kickass rotating army of fierce gay fabulosity.[1] What people may not know about SF (or what we self-obsessed natives call "The City"[2]) is that it is also the number one choice of residence for our nation's unmoored or, as demographists like to call them, the homeless.

Or as I often refer to them, hobos.

Wait for it.

I prefer the term hobo because it sounds jaunty and upbeat. A home-

---

1 Snap.

2 Yes, we call it THE City. Suck on it like a lozenge, New York.

less guy smells like pee and is struggling with mental illness or addiction. A hobo rides the rails and roasts his baked beans and hot dogs on an open flame, harmonica 'tween his lips and a song in his heart. This is, of course, a concept that dismisses entirely the fact that most people on the street *are* struggling with mental illness and *do* need help with addiction. But it helps (me at least), put the hobo-pedestrian relationship back on even footing, and gives the homeless person some transactional parity. Instead of feeling pity or looking down on them as less fortunate, I choose to see them as equals, with hopes and dreams of their own and a colorful, vagabondian history. Plus, hobos get to carry that little stick with the gingham kerchief on the end. See? Jaunty!

I am not making light of homelessness. I grew up with very little, and there was a portion of my time in high school when my father and I lost the lease on our apartment and were without a place to live. Luckily I was able to stay with a friend's family and continue to go to school, study, and live life, for the most part, uninterrupted. I was incredibly fortunate. That said, we had a working-class existence, living paycheck to paycheck; there were moments when my father was in the grocery store with his last twenty-dollar bill, wondering what to do next. So while I would never have claimed to be in legitimate crisis, there were times in my youth when we struggled, and where the line between us and the street seemed razor-thin.

So no, I am not making fun of homeless people or homelessness. It is no fucking joke. The fact is, I grew up around homelessness, and spent a good part of my life seeing, talking, and interacting with homeless people on a daily basis, in a way that emboldens me to speak of them in brazen fashion, but definitely does not make me in any way uniquely qualified to speak about them or on their behalf.

That does not mean I will not do so anyway.

Homeless culture is a part of life in San Francisco, unlike almost any other urban city in the world. There are more homeless people in San Francisco per square mile than any other American city.[3] When

---

3 I have no idea if this is true. It just really seems like it is.

Ronald Reagan signed the Lanterman-Petris-Short Act into law as governor of California in 1967, he dramatically altered the healthcare landscape for those struggling with mental illness in the state. While seen as a great step forward in the movement for patients' rights (the law made it harder to commit and hold someone against their will), the Act had another effect, which was to greatly reduce the facilities and services available to people needing psychological help. For those who aren't criminally insane, but just good old-fashioned batshit crazy, the system was no longer welcoming, and many people struggling with mental illness were catapulted into the street. That single act, and the budget cuts that followed, unleashed a small army of the unmoored that has since grown legion. And because San Francisco is such a bleeding-heart fruitcake lefty hippie bastion of a godforsaken city, full of lovey-dovey huggers and soup kitchen hipsters and people who live on quinoa and fermented flower petals, it is homeless freaking Mecca.

The homeless seem to migrate to San Francisco, drawn by temperate weather and promises of organic milk and fair trade honey in the streets. And they are *everywhere*. In city parks, bus stop benches, subway grates, street meridians, in doorways, down alleyways, obstinately guarding the entrance to your favorite Starbucks like a bobbing, nattering sentinel. They are numerous, they are perceptive, they are driven, and, most of all, they are organized. The homeless are so organized here that San Francisco has a hobo town, an organized tent city with hobo police and a hobo mayor and a tiny hobo coffee stand.

I am only mildly exaggerating.

The homeless people in San Francisco are so focused and effective that several years ago the city drafted a law to tell them where and how they could conduct their panhandling, as they were loitering perilously close to ATM machines and hitting people up as they stumbled away with their pockets full of Jacksons. This may have made the withdrawers uncomfortable, but as a strategy, it was unimpeachable. It's hard to tell a dude sleeping on a piece of cardboard with a broken radio and a hairless cat that you can't spare any money when he just watched you pull a wad of green out of a magic hole in the wall.

So if you live in San Francisco, you quickly come to the realization that interacting with the homeless is a part of your life. This is not necessarily a negative thing. Firstly, it brings you closer to your own humanity and the humanity of others. Living in Los Angeles, as I do now, one can quickly become divorced from the reality of poverty and suffering, especially when one is whipping around town in a Bentley doing blow off the perfect ass of a reality-star-slash-hand-model-slash-yoga-instructor.[4] The homeless are not in evidence here, and even if they were, people in Los Angeles are dead inside and feel nothing unless they are told to by a director, or unless the feeling is surgically inserted into their chest under general anesthesia alongside a couple of plump sacs of saline.

Living in a place where you don't actually see poverty and its effects every single day can have the effect of muting your response to it, and perhaps your compassion as well. It can make you forget all about poverty, skew your sense of need and entitlement, until you think it is perfectly normal to spend $200,000 on a car and $1,700 on a bottle of wine that you saw someone drink in a rap video. People who live a rarified life gradually forget than any other kind of life exists, especially if they never have to confront it at close range.

You can see how the homeless could have a generally positive effect on people's behavior, if engaged properly.

In San Francisco, you see real poverty every day. What's more, you talk to it, engage with it, and occasionally step over a running stream of its urine as you hustle to work each morning. It is a part of life there, like biodiesel and vegan pot cookies. It is just *something that you do*.

And do you must. When I worked there, in my first job out of college, I made very little money. So little, in fact, that when I would get paid every two weeks, most of my money was gone before I even deposited it. Each pay period I would have twenty dollars with which to recreate. That's right. One crisp, disposable twenty, to do with whatever I wished, for the following two weeks. Which, it turns out, wasn't very much.

The twenty was usually rationed out early in the pay period for

---

4 Typical Saturday.

lattés, which at the time were a new and heady import from the mysterious continent of Europe. Managed properly, a single double latté could be made to last a day, and occasionally two. This involved the judicious application of office coffee once the beverage had been drunk down somewhat, followed by office creamer, sugar packets, and periodic strategic microwaving. Thus handled, my morning latté could last all day and be riding home with me on the bus at night, as steaming hot and (somewhat) delicious as the moment it had been delivered some twelve hours afore.

I was very good at being thrifty, at stretching my money, at making every dollar work.

That is, until I came in contact with a homeless person.

There is nothing like another human being lying on the ground in the cold to make me want to turn my pockets inside out like a virgin frat boy at a strip club. I feel crazy. I feel sad inside. I want to take them home with me and feed them Stouffer's Turkey Tetrazzini. This is a compulsive reaction, and it is unavoidable. If I see a homeless person, I *have* to give them money.

You can see how this would be a problem in a city where homeless people litter the street like sleepy dandelions.

After several weeks of navigating the gauntlet that was the two blocks between my subway stop and my office while choking back tears and the occasional murmured "good lord, the humanity," I stopped buying coffee and started packing my pockets with small bills and "spare change." [5] Rather than feeling horrible at the fact that I had food and a guy on the corner seemed to be eating three-day old Spanakopita from the remains of a sock, I coughed up money to whomever asked. This saved me the overwhelming wave of guilt that was sure to ruin my afternoon and weekend, and saved him from having to call me a stingy cunt at the top of his lungs. So it worked out well for both of us.

---

5 Let's just get one thing out of the way right now. There is no such thing as "spare change." Spare change is just small pieces of money that you haven't assembled into bigger pieces of money and spent yet. That being said, if you can spare a quarter, you can probably spare a dollar, so stop being such a selfish prick.

Before you give me a big lecture about how giving a homeless person money on the street doesn't *really* change their situation in life, I would respectfully like to say, shut up. I know that. I know many people on the street have alcohol and drug addictions and will turn right around and use that money to get high. And even if they do use the money to eat, it's not like they can carve the middle out of that scone they bought and live in it, you self-satisfied little prick. I *know* that. That's not the point.[6] The point is to be kind in the moment, to treat another person who is looking you in the eye and asking for a little help with respect, if you can manage it. Plenty of people treat homeless people like they don't exist at all. Just acknowledging them and being kind, just *seeing* them, can be enough to make them feel as if they are not alone.

I believe in being kind in the moment. I can't end homelessness. I get that. But I can give a single person some brief relief from a brutish, unkind, and very chilly existence, if only for a moment.[7] Or, more specifically, relief from a life that is driven completely by concern over when, where, and how to pee, something I can relate to greatly, having attended college.

I quickly acquired a coterie of homeless regulars, including one guy in particular. We'll call him Mitch.

Mitch camped out in front of the coffee shop-slash-bakery across the street from my office building, and from the first moment I saw him, it was abundantly apparent that Mitch was different. Open, engaging, charming, funny even, he had us suit-clad guilt-ridden workaday suckers eating out of the palm of his hand. He was articulate. Self-possessed. He had jokes. His cardboard sign, renewed daily, alternated between some wry, self-aware comment about him needing

---

6 I once had a friend tell me that if I gave a homeless guy money he would just spend it on booze. To which I replied, "If I gave YOU money you would just spend it on booze." He had no retort for that.

7 For the record, I do give to charitable organizations now. But I also still give money to homeless people. It's nice to see what you give end up in the fingers of the person who will actually get to spend it. On booze, or hamburgers, or whatever. His dollar, his choice.

money for a drink and a profound Buddhist quote.[8] He would engage passersby for hours on end, delighting them with his knowledge of current events and his understanding of world affairs. Even when he would sink into a funk (totally understandable, since he was living on the street), he would still find time to give a grateful smile or wave to anyone who would drop money into his cup. He was a model hobo. Absolutely perfect.

Everybody loved him. After bending to give him money, you would stand and smile at the person next to you, who had coincidentally also just given him money (he was that beloved), both of you now feeling that somehow you had made the world just a tiny bit better in that brief, shining moment. The walk to work was made better by passing him on the street, by seeing his smile, and by thinking a) this is truly a great world, where someone in his situation can still be so upbeat, and b) what a great light he is, that he still finds energy to share his joy with others, and c) holy fucking shit, I am late for work. He was wonderful, and it was a pleasure to give up my morning latté so that Mitch could take my money, pool it with a bunch of other people's money, and do whatever it is that homeless people do with their cash at the end of the day.[9]

And then, one day, he was gone.

No explanation. No note. Of course, we all expected the worst, we fatuous yuppie commuters. Where was our hobo? Where was our reason for feeling morally superior? Where was our Mitch?

We never saw him again.

After several months of Mitch's absence, we slowly moved on, in the way that people do. Human beings possess a unique capacity for letting their concern for others fade quickly in favor of other critical worries, such as what kind of sushi would be at the salad bar that

---

8 This is pre-Internet, so this was a real feat.

9 I'm spitballing here—buy a giant bottle of Mad Dog, fourteen Filet-O-Fish sandwiches, and a pack of cigarettes, and bury the rest in a hole of undetermined location to be retrieved by their executors when they die and are discovered to have left thousands of dollars to a neighborhood school or local YMCA.

day for lunch, or when shoulder pads might come back into style. But I couldn't entirely forget him, and I would occasionally ask people around the office if they knew what had happened to him. And one day, finally, someone breathlessly reported that they found out that Mitch had passed away. They weren't sure, but they believed it was substance-related.

It wasn't a surprise, but it was shocking nonetheless. Mitch was our golden boy. Mitch was special. Why I thought he was saving the money he received for an apartment and two weeks at a yoga retreat instead of booze or drugs, I have no idea. This was all part of the illusion, an illusion I had created to assuage my own bullshit guilt. I couldn't get entirely comfortable with the idea that Mitch was truly in crisis, so I made up my own backstory, one that made me feel comfortable with our daily transactions. Mitch was there because he wanted to be. Mitch was a gentleman wanderer. And I was his venture capitalist, a floor-level investor in his quixotic quest.

But that was fantasy. In reality, Mitch was homeless, struggling with addiction, living day to day in a world fraught with danger. A few bucks and a smile didn't change that at all.

I felt immediately that I, with my proffered dollars and friendly asides, had paved the way to Mitch's demise. Somehow I had taken this special man and led him down the primrose path. By gleefully giving him money, instead of ignoring his pleas, or pushing him to get professional help, I felt I'd enabled him—I'd helped put him in the bottle, or the bag, or whatever substance it was that killed him. And I felt guilty, and helpless, and awful, and small, and all the things one feels when one grows up and realizes that the world's problems are sprawling and complex and utterly massive, and can't be solved with spare change or good intentions, and that trying to romanticize the life of a man who has no home is a naïve recipe for tears.

That doesn't mean the world's problems can't be solved, or that we shouldn't try for fear of disappointment or loss. Nothing great was ever done by someone who let a fear of failing stop them. But it's going to take much, much more than a handful of coins and a smug sense of false intimacy with a single homeless man who was clearly extraordinary but suffering nonetheless from the same devastating problems as so many others who struggle to survive on the street.

Later I found out, from another member of Mitch's fan club who had done some investigating, that Mitch was, indeed, a very special homeless person. In his earlier life, he had been a scientist, an Ivy League graduate. This explained his charm and intelligence, his sophistication and manners. He had lived a "normal" life, until mental illness, addiction, and other unknown tragedies drove him into the street.

And so, I suppose, Mitch was just like other homeless people—like all people in general. Flawed, imperfect, in need of our compassion, in need of more help than just financial. And even with exactly the right kind of help, with the right intentions and in the right amounts, Mitch may have still been destined for an unavoidable and tragic end.

While it sometimes felt futile, I didn't stop giving homeless people money. I hope I never will. You don't give up trying to help just because one gesture of kindness doesn't work out the way you had hoped. You keep at it, because kindness is its own reward. It has to be. And inasmuch as your kindness may or may not transform the lives of others, it will transform your own without fail.

Since I was little, I have wanted to save things. I am not likening rescuing a baby bunny rabbit to trying to save a homeless guy. For one thing, you can't keep a homeless guy in a shoebox. But I am saying that it is important to tap into your own compassion, and never let that capacity for kindness die, no matter how many times it breaks your heart.

Or takes your money and spends it on booze. Delicious, delicious booze.

Hey. Spot me a twenty.

(20)

The First Time I Did Standup

"Search not a wound too deep lest thou make a new one."
—Thomas Fuller

"If I think about this fully, I will piss myself in fear."—Aisha Tyler

There's an adage, pretty well known, that warns "If it ain't broke, don't fix it." My mother loves a cute variation on that phrase that admonishes "Fuck with it till it breaks!" She never misses an opportunity to glecfully use that phrase. She is like a sweet, adorable trucker.

That adage has been a governing principle of my adult life. If I find myself feeling comfortable, if things seem to be going *too* well, I immediately feel panic, and am gripped by an overwhelming urge to leap up and go running down the street screaming like a banshee. I like things to be difficult, insurmountably punishing even. And if my life is feeling too easy, it's time to start breaking shit. The charming thing about me is that I never saw a good situation I wasn't willing to completely fuck up.

After college, I was incredibly lucky to get what, by any set of measures, was a perfect first gig: working for an environmental non-profit organization in my beloved hometown of San Francisco. I had wrested my degree from the reluctant jaws of my alma mater—major in political science with a minor in environmental studies—so this was my bullseye: working for an organization that bought up unused urban land and converted it into parks for communities that lacked safe, green places to play. We actually *made* parks for inner-city kids. I mean, could we be any more selfless? I had landed my dream job.

Now, I realize this is not a dream job for anyone who wants to do stuff like make money or get laid or not smell like wheat grass, but, for me, it was awesome. I really did care about the environment, I really did love my hometown, and, even more than that, I really, *really* needed a job.[1] This position hit all three of those criteria, so I was thrilled. This was all I had ever dreamed of. The only thing that would have made it more perfect would have been an unlimited supply of free office chocolate and a desk made of angora sweaters for snuggly lunch-time micro-naps. I showed up for my first grownup job all bright-eyed and bushy-tailed, my tummy full of bubbles made of hope and angel's wings.

My tummy angel bubbles popped pretty fucking quickly.

If you haven't yet noticed, working sucks. Unless you are a racecar driver or an astronaut or Beyoncé, working is completely and utterly devoid of awesome. It is hard, it lasts all day, the lighting is generally fluorescent,[2] and, apparently, drinking at your desk is frowned upon.[3] If you ever needed to ruin someone's fun, I mean really poop a party, just move things to the workplace. Fun terminated.

This particular workplace had a very specific set of elements *not* going for it. First, it was a not-for-profit organization, which I real-ized they took *very* literally after I saw my first paycheck. I made so very little money that I would plan large parts of my workday around opportunities to scavenge for food leftover from office meetings and departure parties. My favorite thing to do was to plan a birthday cel-ebration. It didn't matter if it was actually someone's birthday—if I

---

1 Dartmouth was punishingly expensive—my college loans were like a mortgage—and that was a zillion years ago. Nowadays, you'd have to form your own SuperPAC to raise enough money to send a child there.

2 *So* unflattering. Walking into a corporate office is like stumbling across a team of reani-mated cadavers tapping listlessly at keyboards, trying very hard not to seem dead.

3 Who am I hurting, *really*?

could find a way to wrangle a supermarket sheet cake out of those tight-fisted bastards, I was doing it. A third of a leftover cake was like four meals for me. I was desperate and borderline diabetic, but I did what I had to.

Second, having to go to a place every day where I had to be organized, sit in a cubicle, not use curse words or eat with my fingers, and wear *panty hose* (argh!), seemed like a particularly cruel kind of torture.[4] Just months before I had been floating down the Connecticut River in an inner tube, drinking beer out of an upcycled spaghetti sauce jar, and now I was wearing L'eggs and a polyblend skirt, trying to figure out how to answer a phone that had more buttons than the Starship Enterprise. It was bewildering: I had a dream position, doing something that was important for the world, with like-minded people, in the city that I loved, and yet I was totally miserable. I believed in what I was doing, and I forged some good friendships with my coworkers (some that persist to this day), but otherwise, this whole work thing was sucking major ass.

Also, panty hose make your knees itch.

The problem was, like most people on the planet, I really didn't have an alternative plan. I had been on this path since I was little: work hard, behave yourself, get good grades, follow the rules, give up your dreams of being an astronaut, go to college, get a good job, go to law school, become a lawyer, die a little inside each year, and then eventually actually die. This had been the plan from the beginning, and so far I had executed it perfectly. My parents were *thrilled*—I had hit all their benchmarks: I had an Ivy League degree, I was gainfully employed, I had my own apartment, I wasn't lurking around asking for money or raiding their cabinets for food. They had raised me properly—to work hard, be polite, and stay out of their hair—they'd done their job. Now it was time to do mine.

The only problem was the "die a little inside" part of my plan

---

4 To this day, I do not believe in panty hose. I'm not saying I don't wear them (although I don't; a few visible scars on a lady's shins show she's lived a full life and fears nothing), I'm saying I don't *believe* in them. To me they do not exist, much like Santa, unicorns or black water polo players.

seemed to be kicking in a little early. I felt strange and off-kilter and I had no idea why. I didn't want to do anything. I didn't want to talk to anyone. I would sit alone in my remote corner of the office and stare zombielike at a computer screen while I gnawed droolingly at an everything bagel (which, along with those long-nursed lattés, were one of my only delights at this time). I was completely bewildered.

And then, finally, I figured it out—the long bouts of catatonic silence, the dependence on carbohydrates, the itchy knees—I was depressed.

Even though I was clinically blue, it didn't mean I didn't work hard. I believe very deeply in the concept of industry.[5] I care about what I put into the world, and I believe in doing my best in everything. If my name is on something, it is going to be the best something I can possibly produce. The best macaroni collage, the best book report, the best budget analysis, the best round of kamikaze shots anyone has ever pounded in under a minute. I believe one hundred percent in being the best. It's just hard to be the best at something you find supremely dissatisfying.[6]

I kept at it, though. I like winning more than I like being happy, and I am also a blockheaded and blindly stubborn ramrod of a person, so I threw myself into my work. And that non-profit really was doing good things in the world, which gave me some slim shreds of satisfaction. Trees were protected. Endangered birdies saved. Little kids got green places to play. But as the months wore into a year, I realized I could not go on like this. I needed to make a change. Thankfully, I had very few responsibilities (by design) and even fewer belongings (as I was broke as fuck), so I had absolutely nothing to lose. I had no idea what I wanted to do, but I knew I missed performing. Plus, I was starting

---

5 This philosophy persists to this day. If you aren't going to put everything you have into something, dude, don't bother. You can always kill it at sitting on the couch fucking up some Hot Pockets. For guaranteed success, aim for the middle.

6 This is why they always say: "Find something you love, then find a way to make money at it." That way, the excellence of your own work will be its own reward. Of course, if what you're good at is smoking pot in the morning in front of your Xbox, it's gonna be pretty hard to translate that into gainful employment. Put down the bong. What are you, twelve?

to eyeball sharp objects around the office wistfully. I decided to cast about for some way to get back on a stage of some kind. Any kind. I wasn't picky. I needed to perform.

But I had absolutely no idea how to start.

I started thinking of what *kind* of performer I wanted to be. I could have joined a band, but I couldn't play any instruments. I had three years of violin in grade school but that skill was utterly erased by my general apathy about the violin as an instrument. Plus I doubted any rock bands were looking for a backup string section that only knew the first two movements of Pachelbel's *Canon*. I would have auditioned for a play, if I knew anything about theater or the audition process, or if most regional theater productions didn't test the limits of human patience. Television acting seemed attractive, but of course, I knew as much about that as I did about astrophysics. I actually knew *more* about astrophysics, thanks to my childhood obsession with sci-fi and my current obsession with *The X-Files*.[7] And I was as likely to find a talent agent as I was to find a pot of gold in the side alley next to my apartment building. Getting discovered seemed like something magical that happened only to anorexic twelve-year-old blondes when they went to the mall with their mothers for frozen yogurt.

Unfortunately, I was no longer twelve, I had never been blond, and the only way I would ever become anorexic was if I suddenly lost the ability to chew.

This left standup comedy.

I didn't know much about that either, other than that I had seen some live comedy shows while I was in college, and had found them indescribably delightful.[8] I remember emerging from one such show, after laughing so hard that my stomach muscles ached (at an act that I would undoubtedly find insanely hacky now—something about Tyrannosaurus Rex trying to play the flute—wait, actually it's still

---

7 They talked about science on that show, right?

8 Comedy, even comedy done poorly, is like candy. Even butterscotch has a bland yet sticky appeal. If you laugh just once during a show, even if it is *at* the comedian rather than *with* them, you have laughed. That is all that matters.

pretty funny), and feeling as delirious and amazed as if I had discovered fire. That was when I fell in love with comedy. But several years later, I was still only a secret, slightly lurky admirer. I had no idea how standup comedy worked, how you made funny come out of your face, where you went to do it, or anything of any value whatsoever that would help me become a standup comedian.

Serendipitously, comedy was in its boom time in the nineties. You could find it everywhere: late-night talk shows, syndicated standup series, coffeehouses, strip mall comedy clubs, and a brand-new cable network called "Ha," which was the single worst name for a cable network before "Starz." "Ha" played standup twenty-four hours a day, and because this was still relatively early in the advent of television comedy, they played a lot of the same execrable crap over and over again. Dude in a blazer in front of a brick wall. Dude in a blazer in front of a velvet curtain. Chick dressed like a dude in a blazer in front of a piano in front of a brick wall. All of it tepidly amusing, none of it very good.

Being an arrogant little snot with a freshly minted Ivy degree and no money to go out and do stuff like normal people, I sat on my dumpster-rescued futon and watched a lot of comedy on this channel while eating Smartfood by the fistful. And inevitably, after each set, I thought arrogantly and snottily, "Man, that sucked. I could *totally* do better than that guy."

It was this kind of unfounded and breathtaking hubris that made me quirkily adorable, and also highly likely to lose a limb or get stabbed by an itinerant tattoo artist someday.

Buoyed by my enthusiasm and total lack of experience, I immediately set about writing down my joke ideas in a little spiral notebook. Anything that struck me as funny, I would jot in my book for later consideration. I threw myself into this task with relentless focus. I would scribble all day long in tiny wavering script, the ink-riddled pages of my notebook starting to resemble an unhinged rant penned by Kevin Spacey's serial murderer in *Seven*. My coworkers thought I had some kind of late-surfacing OCD that caused me to write things down compulsively. They started avoiding eye contact. They started calling me Rain Man. They started reporting me to Human Resources. No matter. I was undeterred.

Mind you, I was not writing down good jokes or even jokes at all, really. I was writing down *ideas* for jokes. Comedians call them *premises*. These are not anything you can actually say in front of people. They are unformed, ill-conceived, malnourished *concepts*, and no matter how much potential they have, or how well-intentioned you are when you deliver them, they will not get laughs.

I did not know this at the time.

Seven months after I started scribbling things down in that notebook like the foreword to a hermit's manifesto, I screwed up enough courage to actually perform. My obsessive-compulsion in full bloom, I had done extensive and meticulous research on where and how to do a first comedy set. I may have hated my job, but I sure did love the organizational skills and access to clerical resources that came along with it. I had addresses, show times, and phone numbers all charted and cross-referenced—every opportunity for soaring comedic triumph or agonizing creative demise arranged meticulously in an easy-to-read grid. I had discovered after several phone calls that the best open mike for beginners (well, the *only* open mike for beginners) was at a club in the Sunset district called the Holy City Zoo. They had a show on Sunday nights, and the fee for performing was two dollars for a hefty three minutes, which to me seemed inordinately fair and a bargain besides. I didn't know much, but I did know you couldn't pay two dollars to get on stage anywhere else, except for maybe the world's saddest strip club.[9]

So I settled on a scant list of wobbly "jokes," and rode the bus to the club on a Sunday night with my boyfriend in tow, both for moral support, and so he could carry me home should I happen to bomb and try to drink myself to death after the show in despair. I felt optimistic, breathless even, over what was about to happen as we disembarked from the bus in the evening fog. And as we arrived at this adorable

---

9 Man, if you have to *pay* to let other people see you naked, you need to reexamine your entire life approach and make some serious changes. Having to make it rain on yourself is a Moebius Strip of sadness.

little shack of a club in the middle of a block of used bookstores, thrift shops, dive bars, and walk-up dim sum counters, I was struck by one very apparent truth.

I was *super* fucking late.

I hadn't realized that a part of the transaction for getting stage time at this place was that not only did you have to pay for your stage time (utterly disproving any misconceptions about meritocratic ideals ruling the entertainment biz), but it was also first-come, first-served. Now, people have called me many things, but one thing they have never called me is first-come. I am nice, reliable, trustworthy, charming, supportive, and I make a mean Manhattan. But I am never, ever first-come. The earliest I have ever been is second-come, and that was remarkable enough for me to take a few snapshots and tweet about it, which also tells you how recently in my life this moment occurred. "Be on time" is a recurring New Year's resolution for me, getting replay on my list more times than Taylor Swift at a bat mitzvah. The only thing I have resolved more often is to get more sleep.[10] You can also see how those two goals might be at odds with each other. I have definitely succeeded in getting more sleep, but it has directly and severely undermined my efforts to be on time. One cannot have it all.

So I get to this club, and I'm terrified, and I'm confused, and I'm anxious, and I'm late. What's worse, the seductive aroma of *char siu bao* is wafting over me like college sex, and I can't decide whether I want to do standup or eat a fuckload of dumplings and pass out in a puddle of pork. But my boyfriend encourages me; we've come this far, and on the bus no less, and what do you have to lose except for your sense of self-worth and respect? He has a point, and when he promises me as many steamed buns as I can eat afterwards, I reluctantly agree to move forward.

I get in line. I am dead last.

This means, I discover when I finally get to the front of the line and plunk down my two scrills, that I will also go dead last on the lineup for the night. Again, I know very little about comedy, but I'm

---

10 Late *and* lazy. I'm a keeper.

crystal clear this is a bad thing. The only time going last on a lineup of performers is good is when you are Jay-Z and you are headlining Coachella. And even then, half of the audience is drunk or on Ecstasy and the other half made a break for their cars right after deadmau5 so they could get out before traffic turns the parking lot into an actual parking lot, and they are forced to sleep off a tummy full of pot brownies in the backseat of their Priuses. Still, I have come all this way, I have been bribed with dumplings, and when there are dumplings involved, I deliver.

That night was *long*. My set was right before closing, at 1:52 a.m., which allowed three minutes for me to perform, and a couple of minutes for the show host to say good night and sweep out any remaining customers or sleeping itinerants before they shut the doors. The show started at nine, and after the host did ten minutes, each comedian got three to perform, which meant there were approximately *one million comedians* before me.

I know this may shock you, but not all of them were good.

Some were. There was some real talent in there, some inspired ideas and well-crafted jokes, and even a few true geniuses in the bunch. But mostly it hurt. Hurt to watch, hurt to listen, hurt to laugh, hurt to think that would be me in just over three short hours. It was terrifying, and it went on forever. I almost fled several times, but I did not want to lose my two dollars. That was like ten percent of my $20 recreational budget. There was no going back.

When I finally went up on stage, I felt brave. I had seen almost every possible iteration of a comedy set performed onstage: some killed, some bombed, separated by every possible configuration and result between. I knew I wouldn't destroy, but at the least I might do better than the guy who ate powdered donuts while reading aloud from *The Tao of Pooh*. As I climbed up there, I said to myself, "Be brave. No matter what happens tonight, you won't die." And that, at least, was true. I did not die.

Not *literally*, anyway.

The silence of a darkened nightclub at 1:52 in the morning after three-plus hours of comedy can be so oppressive as to feel like a weight.

Like a giant has climbed upon your shoulders and taken a seat for a few hours to think. It can squash you, push the air out of your lungs, turn everything dark. I can't tell you what jokes I did that night, because honestly, they weren't jokes. I can't tell you what unformed premises I presented, because I blacked out soon after ascending the stage, the rest of those three minutes unfolding like an out of body experience of which I have no memory, just the faint sensory recall of sweat pooling in the hollows of my collarbone, the deafening bass drum of my racing heartbeat, and the crisp, dry taste of pennies in my mouth. All I know is that I was not funny, and I was not getting laughs.[11]

Except for one.

Just one.

I got one laugh, around eighty percent of the way through my act. I don't know what got it, and I was never able to reproduce that exact laugh ever again. The next twenty, or fifty, sets I did were exercises in how long someone could stand before a group of utterly silent people.

The rest of my set was workmanlike, shot through with terror, and preeminently forgettable. I shambled offstage to a smattering of applause, and by smattering, I mean the bartender, who wanted to go home, and my boyfriend, who wanted to go home. I was exhausted, confused, and like a soldier with PTSD, I just wanted to forget. I might have hated my job, but at least the entire office didn't get together to critique my work while I stood at the blinding center of an overhead klieg. Spending the rest of my life in a nice quiet cubicle with my instant noodles and my broken hopes and dreams suddenly seemed like a perfectly fine way to die.

But that one laugh, like a single transcendent experience on a highly potent drug, was enough to change my brain chemistry forever. Afterwards, my boyfriend and I went and ate our weight in dumplings.[12] And after that, he got laid.[13]

The next day, when people at work asked me how my big debut had

---

11 My boyfriend laughed but that didn't count because he was trying to get laid.

12 Sweet, sweet *char siu*, how did people ever live without you?

13 He laughed at my jokes, *and* he bought me dumplings? Come on. Double score.

gone, I told them the truth: it was terrible. And somehow, I couldn't wait to do it again.

I had decided to try something terrifying, I had tried it, and it had been, indeed, terrifying. But I had done it. And that was my first step out of being mired in a frustrating and unsatisfying dream job, and into being mired in an even more frustrating but supremely rewarding dream career. And while that night was traumatic and on the whole pretty scarring, it did drive home another old piece of pabulum: you've got to venture if you want to gain. And if you actually get off your ass and try to follow your dreams—make yourself a little uncomfortable in pursuit of what you want—holy shit, you might just achieve them.

Or at the very least, get to destroy a plate of *char siu bao*, ride home on the bus, and have hot dumpling sex. Which is the best kind, because you get to use up all the leftover duck sauce.

(21)

The Tenth Time I Did Standup

"Truth alone wounds."—Napoleon Bonaparte

"Truthfully, I suck."—Aisha Tyler

This was as awful as the first time, only without the dumpling reward at the end. So, actually, this was *way* worse than the first time. Suck minus dumplings equals super suck.

If I could go back in time and tell myself not to do this set, I would.

No, wait. I wouldn't, because bombing so hard you get a bruise on your ass is the only way you get any funnier. We learn from our mistakes.

And if the bigger the mistake, the more we learn, well then this elevated me into genius territory.

So, yeah. This time *really* sucked.

(22)

The Hundredth Time I Did Standup

"Great is the power of habit. It teaches us to bear fatigue and to despise wounds and pain."—Marcus Tullius Cicero

"I can't feel my face."—Aisha Tyler

Comedians have a name for newcomers who have only been doing standup for a few years. We call them babies.

Baby comics, specifically.

We don't call them baby comics because they are infants. Sometimes they *are* literally young—high school students, or worse, precocious middle-schoolers full of moxie and innuendo whose parents have to drive them to the club and wince delicately through five minutes of wobbly material on jump rope and homework. But just as often, they are a middle-aged cubicle jockey who decided to recklessly chuck it all—job, relationship, kids, self-respect—to become a comedian.[1] These people are called baby comics because they have absolutely no idea what they are doing, stumble about aimlessly, are prone to outbursts and tantrums, stare at you uncomprehendingly when you

---

1 Good luck with that, buddy. You're a braver man than me. And much more willing to be utterly and completely alone.

offer help, and occasionally shit their pants.[2] Regardless of their age, baby comics are immature, undisciplined, hysterical, emotional, self-centered, and totally without humility.

It is hard to believe I was *ever* one of those.

Baby comedians are all the same, and they are very easy to spot if you know what to look for.[3] No matter their age or provenance, they all have the same complaint: nobody *gets* them.

It is an almost universal refrain: every comedian who has been doing comedy for three years or less will tell you that they are brilliant, before their time, the next coming of Richard Pryor, and others just don't recognize their genius. People are trying to stand in their way, keep them down, cockblock their stardom. Every baby comedian is confident they've got what it takes, that stardom is just a shortcut away, and if people would just give them the respect and adulation their startling brilliance deserves, they would have their own sitcom by Christmas.

And every comedian who has been doing comedy for ten years or longer looks back at their three-year-old comedian self and thinks, "Geez. What an intolerable douche."

When I was a baby comic, I kept looking for the *secret*. The hidden key, the magic trick that would help me bypass all the waiting and sucking up and bombing and suffering and zip straight to comedic stardom. I was convinced it existed, and that older comedians I admired, who told me that the only "secret" was hard work multiplied by time, just didn't want to share what they knew. Like some MLB home run phenom or blood-doping cyclist, they all kept claiming their success came from focus, discipline, and drive, when I knew it really came from a shot of something clear, potent, illegal, and undetectable. All I needed was a phone number or shady address. I needed the BALCO of comedy. I was positive it existed; people just weren't coming clean.

---

2 Metaphorically most of the time, but yes, occasionally, literally.

3 You might think you'd be looking for someone who keeps bombing over and over again, but it's not as easy as you think. Some baby comedians *are* preternaturally talented, and are hilarious right from the get-go. Of course, we'll never tell *them* that, but it does happen.

What is most charming about youth, both literal and comedic—enthusiasm, optimism, bright-eyed hubris—is also what sucks most about it. Young people are swaddled in delusion. You think you are more awesome than you are, the world more interested in you than it is, your countenance more dazzling, your ideas more captivating, and that LeBron James was just a natural talent recruited from a neighborhood pickup game. You don't want to practice, you don't see the value in sacrifice, and you are convinced there is some vast comedy conspiracy to keep you from buying your first Bentley and dating a model by the time you are twenty-five.

Wow. You *are* a douche.[4]

Unfortunately, much like the actual process of growing up, there is no shortcut out of metaphorical comedy childhood either. Every baby comic is looking for an easy way out, a secret door or magic bullet, a red pill that will make everything go away—make the shitty open mikes and stone-faced comedy bookers and sleazy club owners evaporate, leaving in their place a late night spot on *Conan* and a week of sold-out shows at Madison Square Garden. These babies are convinced that anyone with a moderate amount of comedy success has figured out this chute-and-latter secret, and if they can just prize it from their elders, they'll be well on their way to hosting the Emmy Awards.

Sadly, like friendly aliens or gay Latino Republicans, this shortcut to fame just does not exist.

Sure, there are people who have shot to infamy quickly and without serious effort. I am thinking, of course, of the ilk that populate such heady dramatic fare as *Jersey Shore*, *Pregnant and Sixteen*, and any of a variety of surgically augmented and mentally demented *Real Housewives*.[5] They have, indeed, lucked out. Their main talents seem to be their proclivity for psychotic outbursts, the ability to funnel their husbands' money into fresh sets of breasts, a love of getting drunk on

---

4 I am speaking, of course, of the royal you. And by royal you, I mean royal *me*.

5 Also: *I Don't Use Birth Control and so Deserve My Own Show*, *I Am Using My Child to Fulfill My Failed Dreams of Being a Beauty Queen*, *I Am a Self-Involved Asshole Using Television to Find Myself a Date with a Similarly Self-Involved Asshole*, and *The Apprentice*.

boxed wine in the middle of the day, and a deft proficiency at snatching the weave off a bitch.

But that is not fame, and it is not earned through any real talent, or by putting anything meaningful, helpful, or good into the world. It is *infamy*, not fame. Ignominy, notoriety, celebrity—they are poor substitutes for actual ability. Infamy is not real. It does not last.[6]

Real success and accomplishment, at whatever it is you are passionate about, requires real work. Real sacrifice. Real disappointment. Real failure. And it requires the ability to scrape your sorry ass up off the floor, stumble to your feet, wipe the rivulets of watery drool from your face, and do it again, like an obstinate toddler running against the wall with his head in a bucket.

This is the thing that baby comics do not understand. It is the thing that I did not understand, until I had done my hundredth set. It was not a memorable set, or even a particularly good one. I don't remember the jokes, or the crowd, or the club, the town, what night of the week it was, or how much I got paid. What I do remember is how I *felt*. Because somewhere around set one hundred, I realized something that had evaded me up until that point: it was going to take hundreds more sets, just like that one, to get where I wanted to go, and in all probability I would never actually get all the way there. I was in this thing for the long haul, and that haul was going to be much longer than I had hoped. But that night, I realized for the first time that I loved what I did, that the comedy itself, the elation of creating art, expressing ideas, making other people laugh, was its own reward, and that passion for my work was more important than fame or the false adulation of a bunch of people I didn't know or care that much about anyway.

That, I realized, *was* the secret. And that night was the moment I finally saw it clearly. The work is the reward.

That's what I tell baby comics now. Don't do this because you want

---

6 Just ask the lady with the eight kids. Or that other guy who contributed the sperm. I forgot their names.

to be famous, or rich, or get laid.[7] Sure, everybody's gotta make a living. But don't get into comedy because you imagine yourself riding in a Bentley with a bevy of porn starlets and a shitload of gummy bears. Do this because you love it, because it imbues your life with meaning, because you have something you want to say—no, *need* to say—and you cannot live without saying it. Because in all likelihood you won't become famous, or you will run out of stamina way before you run out of road, or the rejection and thanklessness of the business will grind you to a bloody smear on the pavement, and if you don't have your passion to drive you forward, nothing will. It's great you're talented. It's fantastic that you're unique and there's never been anyone in the history of comedy quite as amazing as you. But that guy over there—who is half as talented as you—gets up twice as early and works twice as hard. *And* he can snatch a mean weave. You've got work to do.

Here's the thing: you may truly be talented. You may be a creative genius or a mad scientist or the next Larry Page, running around with the next decade's life-changing technology scribbled on a cocktail napkin. You may be the third coming of Richard Pryor,[8] funnier than Eddie Murphy trying to get into the hot tub when the water's too hot. You may, indeed, be fucking *awesome*.

No one gives a shit.

No matter how incredible you are, how naturally talented and touched by greatness, you still have to do the work. Chris Rock still goes to dive bars and open mikes and struggles through thirty minutes of wobbly new material to get three great new minutes. Michael Jordan, cut from his high school team, practiced for hours and days and weeks and months to become the player he was, and then after that, he practiced some more. At his height, Tiger Woods was on the

---

7 Although it will get you laid. Being funny is like people catnip, which is why troll-like comedians who would never get play otherwise are always draped in giddy waitresses and swirling clouds of smug.

8 The second coming has already been claimed by like seven hundred people, so it's pretty much locked up.

range drilling for hours every single day.[9] Talent is not enough. It's not even close. Hard work is far more valuable than talent. The world is littered with brilliant, talented, lazy nobodies. Almost the entire workforce of Starbucks is populated by a bunch of geniuses that "nobody gets, man." If you have talent and you don't have the stones to get up every day and perfect that talent, accept criticism, look at yourself honestly, suck on the hard lozenge of failure, and try to constantly and consistently improve, well then, you don't have shit.

Baby comedians are generally wallowing in talent. Dripping with it. An army of undiscovered superstars sleeping in their cars and living on chicken wings, expecting that any minute a dude in a suit is going to knock on the glass and ask them to roll it down so he can whisper through the opening, "I've been looking for you everywhere. Follow me! I'm going to make you a star." [10]

Grownups, comedians or not, realize that excellence requires not just early, but constant, unrelenting work and sacrifice, and that reaching a peak does not mean you will stay there. There will always be someone more talented than you, younger than you, hungrier than you, better looking. This is an immutable truth that comes with living on a planet where people are humping like rabbits and making more people as fast as they can, hoping the next one down the chute is going to be Miss Toddler and Tiara 2027. Do you think that girl who's been greasing her teeth with Vaseline and holding a microphone since she was three years old, who remembers what it was like to sleep in the back of her parents' pickup truck and live all day off the free breakfast buffet at the Holiday Inn,[11] is going to feel even a morsel of remorse when she passes you up like a rocket and knocks your star out of the

---

9 I will refrain from making a bunch of jokes about Tiger drilling women here, because I am mature and disciplined. He did drill a lot of women, though. Sorry. I couldn't resist. I am not mature at all.

10 As previously established, this will only happen to you if you are drunk, from New Jersey, impossibly tan, possibly on steroids, and in the middle of a broken-bottle bar fight. Something to aspire to.

11 I have done this more times than I care to remember. Until you have constructed a breakfast sandwich out of Pop-Tarts, hard-boiled eggs, and margarine, you have not lived.

firmament with a satisfying *pop*? No. That creepily precocious little girl is not just headed your way. She is *gunning* for you.

So what are you going to do about it? Whining about how you are brilliant and no one is giving you a chance ain't gonna do shit. You better get to fucking work.

And yes, you may work your ass off, all blood and sweat and tears and sacrifice and long nights and burned weekends and failed relationships and a transmission falling out of your shitpile of a car, and you still may not get to where you wanted to go. That is a reality of life. Shit happens, people are mean, puppies die, and things don't always go your way.

But even if you never quite accomplish your dreams, if you try your hardest, you'll never look back and think, "If only I had gotten up off my ass and given it my best." You'll look back and think, "Man, I put my heart into that. It sucks that I didn't make it, but at least I know I really gave it my all. And it also really fucking sucks that puppies die."

Life is short, and no one gives a shit about your problems. Get up, get out there, and as the kids say, get to grinding. Do that hundredth set, and then do the hundred-and-first. And then do one hundred more. You're just getting started.

Talent is what you're born with. Success is what you do with it.

I'm gonna use mine to save puppies.

(23)

The Time My Worst Standup Nightmare Came True

"Fools, through false shame, conceal their open wounds."—HORACE

"I would feel embarrassed, if I was capable of feeling anything at all."—AISHA TYLER

Everyone has a nightmare scenario about what they do for a living, a recurring bad dream they have had about something going terribly wrong in their workplace.

For most, it is suddenly waking up at work naked, or oversleeping on the morning of the biggest meeting of their careers, or being completely unprepared for a major presentation, or having the boss walk in while you are banging his/her wife/husband/cousin/daughter/housekeeper/other hot relative over their desk in mid-stroke.[1] Everyone's got a subliminal hell scenario—elaborate, humiliating, disturbing or just plain terrifying—that crops up every once in a while in your subconscious to scare the shit out of you. This is one of the realities of being human. We are afraid of a *lot* of stuff.

For me, after the naked-in-class nightmare and the one where I can fly and it's awesome and then suddenly I can't fly but am already in

---

1 Don't lie. You've had this fear/fantasy. Stop being coy.

mid-flight and tumble end over end screeching wildly down to earth, at first very disappointed, then after that very dead, the main irrational fear I have is performing with my fly down. I don't know why I am so afraid of this happening. It's not such a big deal. Unless you are rocking it commando, most women with their fly down don't risk exposure of any great magnitude. Maybe people see your underwear, but I am so OCD (and was so drilled by my mom on that whole hysterical "wear good underwear in case of a car accident" scenario) that mine are always at least minimally presentable. And indeed, the times that my fly has been down and I've noticed, it has usually only involved a bit of minor placket exposure. Nothing to freak out about.

So why is this such a bugaboo?

I could throw out a bunch of theories around the "laughing at me versus laughing with me" concept, and I suppose that might be part of it—the idea that you get up on stage and you're destroying, everyone laughing in merry and unbroken lengths, and then halfway through your set you realize that the audience isn't laughing at any of the right parts of your act, or any of the right times. Instead, they are just tittering away through the entire show, regardless of pause, pretense, or punchline, and you realize with horror that none of the laughs you got count, because they weren't earned by your brilliant material, but because you look like an Abercrombie & Fitch ad gone awry, your pants gaping like a just-caught marlin on a schooner deck.[2]

But I can't be sure that is all of it. I think this fly-down fear is irrational, like a fear of clowns or ducks, or a love of lite country music. You can't explain why you feel this way, you just do.

For years, this was my number one fear when it came to performing, and I would check my fly obsessively and repeatedly to make sure it didn't happen. If I ever develop an Asperger's-like behavioral pattern, this would be it. I would check my fly repeatedly in the bathroom. I would check my fly repeatedly in the back of the club. I would tell

---

2 The vision of a marlin gaping for air on a slick schooner deck is a prime trigger of night hysteria. I have heard.

myself it was zipped, then look down to make sure as I made my way to the stage. And occasionally, I would surreptitiously try to check it while I was actually performing, either by trying to look down without looking as if I was trying to look down, which was insanely hard to do and made me look like I was trying to avoid the gaze of the audience in a fit of snobbery, or as if I was in the throes of a grand mal seizure. I would occasionally supplement this behavior by trying to work the fingers of my left hand stealthily toward my fly to check that it was firmly secure without anyone seeing, which is impossible to do discreetly when you are standing on a stage illuminated by spotlights and keenly observed by hundreds of people. I'm sure it made me look as if I had some kind of itching condition of the crotch, or was trying to masturbate in public.

None of this was any good of any kind. Period.[3]

This fear grew, slowly becoming more and more debilitating. If we lay this scenario against the Hitchcock Axiom of Suspense—which holds that what is feared and anticipated but unseen is most terrifying—then me striding on stage with my fly splayed open to the world was slowly becoming more frightening than the shark in *Jaws*.[4] I could not stop thinking about it, and, much like the shark in *Jaws*, it made me never want to get in the water again. Only the water was comedy, and I was a comedian. I was gonna need a bigger boat.

Things came to a head (ahem) one night when I was having a particularly thrilling bout of OCD that peaked with me being afraid I would have to pee on stage (a lesser paranoia, but just as fun-making). Any comic will tell you that they never have to pee right before they go on stage, and then the minute they step up there and remove the microphone from the stand, the Falls of Niagara begin raging behind the flimsy muscular dam that is the gateway to their bladder, and all they

---

3 I guess people might have also assumed I was on my period and was adjusting my undercarriage. This, I don't have to point out, would not have been good either.

4 And much like that shark, once seen in all its mechanical glory, would be both terrifying and deeply disappointing.

can think of is running faucets and Malaysian monsoons and the slow tinkle of pelvic release.[5] I had been going to the bathroom right before my set for weeks at this point, trying to avoid the lower-quadrant discomfort that came with having to pee and realizing you still had to stand before a room full of people for twenty more minutes without crossing your legs like a whizzy third grader. I would work to time this perfectly so that when I emerged from the bathroom, freshly evacuated, the show host would just be in the midst of thanking the previous performer, right before terribly and inexplicably mangling the shit out of my name.

This had been working beautifully, because peeing right before I went on stage meant a) I didn't physically have to pee when I went up there and b) I *knew* I didn't have to pee, because I had just peed.[6] So when I would feel the urge to pee, I could say to myself, "Self, you *just* peed. Shut the hell up and get through this bit about how you love meatballs." This strategy had been foolproof, which was saying a lot in my case.

So on this particular night, I had worked my way to the bathroom with what I believed to be plenty of time to pee, stare furtively one last time at my palm-sweaty piece of notepaper with my list of jokes, and ascend the stage. Only, for some reason, on this day, the pee gods conspired against me, and my complex plan came to naught. The guy on stage before me cut his set short for some reason (I like to think he had been paid to, or had some unspoken vendetta against me; I can't be entirely sure), and as I sat down on my carefully constructed little pillow of toilet paper assembled atop the toilet seat[7] in this marginally sanitary club bathroom, I could hear my name being called—faintly yes, but distinctly and unmistakably—from the stage.

---

5 This also happens to professional athletes, schoolteachers, and rock stars. Although in rock stars' cases, they just go pee right there on stage. Rock and roll, baby. Rock and roll.

6 Sometimes the brain needs reassurance.

7 OCD. I can't help it. Besides, who sits bareback on a public toilet seat? Half the time I have to resist the urge to get out a lighter and a can of hairspray and firebomb the entire joint. How Britney Spears could walk into a gas station bathroom barefoot I have no idea. I can barely enter fully clothed and holding my breath like a champion free diver.

And not in that "this is the first time I've said it" way, but in that "Bueller, Bueller, I've been saying this shit for what feels like hours and I'm about to give up and launch into one of my classic old people driving bits" way. If I didn't get up there, and pronto, I would lose my stage time, which is akin to allowing someone to take your lunch at school when you know you won't have access to food again until seven p.m. at least, or nine p.m. if your dad worked late. I freaked.

I rinsed my hands cursorily (they definitely were not clean), sprinted to the stage, and launched into my set, so breathless I didn't even bother to correct the host's pronunciation of my name.[8] And miraculously, despite my harried start, things were going well.

Until, like Trinity in *The Matrix*, everything the Oracle told me started to come true. People were laughing more than they had before, and longer, and in all the wrong spots. They weren't making eye contact. They were whispering to each other.

There was surreptitious pointing, and the startling tang of a mocking undercurrent. I could *feel* it. I knew it well. Thinly veiled mock. It was like an old friend come home to roost. It was third grade all over again.

I *knew*. I knew right away. As my hand worked its way toward my zipper in classic creepy guy on a park bench fashion, I already knew it. My fly was down.

I touched it, I panicked, and I froze.

What do you do, when your wildest dream, or in my case, worst nightmare, comes true?[9] You adapt, or you die.

Okay, fine. You don't die. You zip up your zipper. You tell the crowd you can't believe they didn't tell you your fly was down—how could they let you hang like that, you thought they were your friends—and you *keep going*. And that was what I did. I kept going. I was embarrassed, I was flustered, I was completely thrown, but I kept going.

---

8 For the last time, it's TY-ler. Like Steven, or Perry, or one *zillion* suburban white kids. How can so many people get my mystifying first name right, and then call me Aisha TAY-lor? It severely boggles.

9 Yes, I admit that my worst nightmare really isn't that bad. Parsing minutiae is what gives me joy.

My set was fine. My pants were fine. I was fine. My underwear, as perfectly immaculate as ever (god forbid that car accident), were fine (and entirely covering the precious cargo within). And as I wrapped up my set and stepped off stage, I realized something: the thing I had dreaded most had happened to me, and I had survived it. I felt a peculiar strength in that. Nothing could shake me now. I was unflappable.

There were still plenty of things to fear irrationally. War, locusts, a zombie apocalypse, or a Palin presidency might still give me a rattle. But being humiliated in front of a room full of people no longer held the same power over me it once had. I had been embarrassed, I had joked about it, and I had moved on.

Once you looked it in the face, that stupid mechanical shark wasn't so scary after all.

Although I still won't get into a pool at night.

The Time I Wore That Awful
See-Through Dress

"The optimist already sees the scar over the wound; the pessimist still sees the wound underneath the scar."—ERNST SCHRODER

"Everyone can see what I've got going underneath this dress."—AISHA TYLER

I blame Jennifer Lopez.

I blame her for so many things—extreme hair extensions, tiny Fiat cars, my deep feelings of inadequacy about the size of my ass—but mostly I blame her for this.

See, there was a time in our nation, not so long ago, when all you could see, all you could think about, all you knew, unless you were living in some kind of government-funded biodome deep inside the Earth's crust, was J. Lo.

She was in every video, every movie, on every red carpet, the cover of both *Vanity Fair* and *People en Español* (so greedy!). She was Jenny from the block, dating first a black luminary (P. Diddy) and then a Caucasian one (B. Diddy) and generally making people from every ethnic group wild with jealousy. She was killing it for a long run there, and whether you were a fan of her music or not, you couldn't help but root for her when she used what she learned in her Tae-Bo classes to beat the shit out of her abusive ex-husband in functional yet flattering stretch pants and that ridiculous short wig in the Oscar-worthy film *Enough*.

J. Lo was on fire.

And the moment that started it all, in the opinion of almost anyone who knows (or at least anyone who agrees with me), was *that dress*.

That unholy Versace dress she wore to the Grammys on P. Diddy's arm, the one that was cut down to *here* and up to *there* and was one thread away from revealing the color, size, and temperature of her fallopian tubes. That dress was crazy and beautiful and confusing and a little dangerous and a whole lot slutty and it was all anyone could talk or think about for months after she wore it.

Including me.

Well, actually, not including me. Including my stylist at the time. She was obsessed. See, a big part of the whole "wear some shit on the red carpet and get your picture taken" thing is that you want to make news. Looking nice and conventional and clean and pretty is boring. Nice doesn't get headlines, especially if you are the host of a cult television show on a to-remain-nameless network that gets only marginal numbers despite broad name recognition of the program. You are a minor star in a minor constellation in a long-forgotten quadrant of the night sky. You want to be noticed, lady, you gotta get out there and *make* them notice you.

Unfortunately, I was married and so could not make news by dating a rapper or dating an actor or dating a rapping actor; I was not a drunk or a drug addict and so could not make news by going into rehab; and I was not an idiot so I could not make news by falling out of an Italian roadster wearing a miniskirt with no underwear and a perfectly groomed undercarriage. Alas, I was just a regular old comedian with a decent gig who worked hard, and what the hell would that ever get me? I needed to make a splash.

My stylist suggested this could be done on the red carpet. I would wear something eye-catching and risqué, something that would be sure to get people's attention and a few inches in the fashion rags, or at the

Ugh. Why am I smiling?

least, on this newfangled thing called the Internet. All I needed was a total lack of shame, a temporary lapse of fashion reason, and a very nice pair of underwear.

I don't know why I let her talk me into this. It was a bad idea, poorly conceived and even more poorly executed. If I had seen another person in this dress, I would have sprinted for a pen and paper with which to write a litany of jokes about how bad they looked. I looked sad, and naked, and confused, and as if I had forgotten part of my outfit at home.

This was not J. Lo material. This was J. NO material. I looked like a drag hooker from Queens.

Somehow, I actually agreed voluntarily to wear this dress. I think at the time I was just excited that I was in decent shape and that nothing was jutting out awkwardly and I had no visible homunculi. In the house of delusion that was my mind, that made me just one step away from Elle "The Body" Macpherson.[1] I agreed, of my own volition, not only to put on this dress, but wear it out. In public. And then stand in front of photographers so they could take pictures of me wearing it. Using flash photography. Pictures that, like the Internet, will never die. Even if in a million years the entire planet folds in on itself like an ouroboros and slowly collapses into dust, the Internet will still persist, and on it will be dozens of photos of me in this awful dress.

I hate this dress. I hate the pictures of me wearing this dress. I hate that these pictures continue to resurface more than a decade after they were taken. I hate to think that people might think this is how I like to dress, or how I ever liked to dress. I hate to think that people are basing any opinion or understanding of who I am as a person on the fact that I wore this dress.

But the fact is, I wore it. And I have no one to blame but myself.

Think about that the next time you dress to go out of the house and decide to wear black socks with sandals, or a top that leaves your threadbare seven-year-old bra-straps visible to the world. The days of

---

1 This is the explanation for why all women wear outfits that look absolutely terrible on them. We all think we're Naomi Campbell. Except for Naomi Campbell, who knows no one else is Naomi Campbell, and will hit you in the head with a phone to prove it.

looking like anonymous shit are over. You may not be a globe-trotting Latina pop star with a multimillion-dollar fortune and two adorable twins, but . . .

Actually, that's it. You're *not* a globe-trotting Latina pop star. Put on a decent shirt. Change your socks. Take off that mesh half-shirt. It's not 1983. Pull those sweatpants down to an area of your abdomen that doesn't make it look like you are smuggling a package of veal chops in your pants.

Pull your shit together. People are looking at you. People are always looking.

And the Internet, unfortunately, is forever.

(25)

And Had That Awful Two-Toned Hair

See chapter 24. What is going on with my hair? Did I not have a mirror?

Again, I have no one to blame but myself. And perhaps a brief bout of colorblindness.

Can you get that from drinking bourbon?

All the Times I Did Those Terrible Corporate Standup Gigs

"Satire should, like a polished razor keen, wound with a touch that's scarcely felt or seen."—Lady Mary Wortley Montagu

"These people must be dead inside."—Aisha Tyler

There are a few rules when it comes to performing comedy.

No matter how much you wish that things were different—that satyrs were real or that your teenagers loved chores and vegetables, and hated drinking keg beer in a strip mall parking lot—these rules are what they are. They have been in existence since time immemorial, and they hold, eternal and fast. The sky is up. The ground is down. Water is wet. Drunk people heckle. This is just the way it is.

I do not make the rules. I just report them.

If you want to succeed—if you want people to laugh—these rules cannot be broken or ignored. They are absolute and immutable, and any success outside their parameter is an abomination, an anomaly, an irreproducible aberrance.

1. Comedy must be performed at night.
2. People must be drunk or on their way toward being drunk.

3. People must be indoors.
4. People must be facing forward, toward the stage. Not at each other, where they will inevitably be distracted by whatever their drunk-ass tablemates are doing during the show.
5. It *must* be nighttime. I cannot emphasize this enough.
6. Under no circumstances can the show be organized, paid for or attended by employees of a corporation.

No matter how many times people try to skirt these rules, no matter how many times some corporate booker insists that *this* show will be different—our crowds are great, they can't wait to see you, they are your biggest fans, insert bullshit sycophantry here—the rules must be obeyed. Comedy must be performed in a nightclub, where people are drunk enough to laugh like hyenas at nearly everything that comes out of your mouth, but not so drunk that minimally complex ideas or adorably clever metaphors confound them. It must be a close space where laughs will become contagion as people flash the whites of their teeth at each other like monkeys and elbow their neighbors wildly in the ribs, and where the noises of mirth will bounce off the walls and compound into a sound wave of irrepressible joy. There must be just the right amount of food served to keep people from getting drunk too quickly and turning into an angry drunken mob, but not so much that gnawing a mountain of chicken wings distracts them from the show, or so little that their gnawing hunger turns them into an angry *hungry* mob. And while it is okay for people to come to a show with people they know from work, they can never, *ever*, come with their bosses, in front of whom they have never acted like a person or given a hint of being even remotely human, and so are highly unlikely to start now.

Here's the thing. Comedy, good comedy at least, is irreverent, and bawdy, and dirty, and outsized, and if done properly, will shock or offend a handful of people in the audience at the very least. If you plan it right, you will never offend more than a handful of people at any one time, and never the same handful of people over again, thus sending that little fist of anger moving around the audience throughout the show, so that at least ninety-five percent of the audience is laughing while that knot of prudishness purses their lips, looks around at all the happy people, feels suddenly uptight and out of touch for not laughing, and lets all that rage slip quietly into another part of the audience, allowing a different group of people to temporarily get their panties twisted into a hot and sweaty bunch. This rule of roving rage allows that there will always be a minimal number of people with a wad of underwear crammed between their posterior cheeks at any one time, but never enough to truly derail a show.

This is the essence of how comedy works. It is inherently prickly, shocking, difficult, and incendiary. Underneath personal style, affect of delivery, physical comportment, subject matter, even whether you decide to curse or not, there is one essential truth: if you haven't offended *somebody*, you probably didn't say anything very interesting.

This is why people must be in a place where they feel free to laugh at things that under other circumstances might be seen as highly inappropriate. A comedy club gives them that permission. Things are racy and broadstroke, and everyone is a little tipsy, with a tummy full of ranch dressing, chicken limbs, and rum. It's okay. You smell like buffalo sauce. You can laugh. No one will judge.

And this is why corporate gigs never, ever work. Never.

NEVER!

I don't know why I keep forgetting this. Every time I do a corporate show, and it goes painfully, soul-scarringly wrong, I say to myself: *self, never again.*[1] I will never again do comedy at nine in the morning for a bunch of convention-goers, many of whom drank too much last night, several of whom are severely hungover, some of whom slept with someone they shouldn't have and are now undergoing an active existential crisis over bad hotel coffee and cheese Danishes, all of whom are sitting next to or within earshot of their boss, their boss' boss, the CFO of the company, and/or pernicious roving moles from Human Resources. These people will *never* laugh. They are physically incapable of mirth. I might as well perform in a bathroom stall to a toilet paper

---

1 I love to talk to myself. I am a scintillating conversationalist, and, sometimes, I am the only person that will put up with my bullshit.

dispenser; at least when I'm done I can stick my hands in that awesome Airblade dryer thing, and I won't have to pee anymore. At a corporate gig, I spend twenty minutes staring down the gaping maw of disdain that is the sales force of a midsized big box store conglomerate, praying I'll have a severe histamine reaction to hotel pastry and pass out so I won't have to finish my show.

And then I blink, and they are still there, staring up at me with their bloodshot eyes and their mouths full of transfats and their brains full of fabricated stories to explain to their spouses why they didn't answer the phone at three a.m. last night—how they lost their wallets, their cell phones, and the phone in their hotel room was broken, and *that's* why they didn't call—and I look at the clock. I am two minutes into a forty-minute set.

And I want to die.

And I finish the set like a soliloquy, not an actual comedy set, more like a long-form poem with no breaks or moments of silence so that it will never be apparent I was trying to elicit laughs, so that when the laughs do not come no one will feel weird, at least no more weird than people already feel at having to suffer through what seems like a tonally inappropriate and very long motivational speech from a giant black girl. One who seems to be doing everything she can not to say fuck but really seems to want to say fuck and is spewing sexual innuendo and doesn't seem to realize that this is a work function and so by its nature joyless and devoid of any potential for fun.

Then I sprint for the door, fast as I can, and I thank the person who has been assigned to be my contact or chaperon or monitor or jailer, and gratefully demur when they offer me coffee for the road, and make no eye contact with anyone, and rush back to my hotel room, to drown my sorrows in twenty ounces of coffee and four Starbucks muffins, because it *isn't even ten in the morning yet and I have already bombed.*[2]

Why do I keep taking these gigs when I know for a fact—I don't

---

2 My only solace is that I can watch *Law and Order* (because some iteration of *Law and Order* is always on) and eat muffins off my chest while lying in bed in a hotel robe. All of these things are very soothing on their own; combine them into one grand action and you can recover from almost anything.

suspect, I *know*—that they will be the worst forty minutes of my life since the last horrible forty minutes I spent trying to entertain people in suits holding corporate training materials and wishing they were somewhere else?

Because of the money.

I am admitting a bit of crass truth here. Corporate gigs always pay much better than club gigs. Corporations have money to spend, mostly because that is what they are in business for—because guys who don't have boners really, really want boners, and they are going to spend money to get those boners, the devil and the details and the price tag be damned. And thanks to those bonerless guys, the corporation's got a wad to drop on their annual training conference or brainstorming retreat or employee recognition dinner, and they are going to spend it on something fun just to make sure that their employees don't think they are dead inside or plotting to slowly grind their workforce into emotional dust, and so they can point to the annual company event and go, "See? Wasn't that *fun?*" [3]

So they hire a comedian, because hiring John Legend or the Black Eyed Peas or Gwyneth Paltrow would blow their entertainment budget for the entire year, and because hiring a magician or a hypnotist is just ridiculous. A comedian is affordable, and a good time, and if you ask nicely and give the comedian a list of names, maybe they'll make gentle, ribald fun of Bob in accounting and the head of Legal Affairs. "Hey, go for it! Jim's super laid back. He *loves* jokes. He won't mind at all." [4]

And the poor comedian, suckered in by the prospect of making this month's rent and more in one night, says yes every time. After all, we are comedians because we love to make people laugh. But we also do it to make a living. If we wanted to make people laugh and not make any money we'd draw political cartoons. And, unfortunately, you do make great money doing corporate gigs. Also, unfortunately, you will not make anyone laugh.

---

3 Beeteedubs, it wasn't.

4 Beeteedubs, he did.

Well, except for one or two young, interesting (and probably gay, and so used to being on the edge) employees who just got to the company and so don't yet know that laughing is absolutely not allowed under any circumstances, and especially not at some comedian's risqué material about how she thinks there should be marriage equality because that way she could hire a husband-husband hair and makeup team.

For the record, I have done many, many corporate gigs. I have always been gracious, and professional, and prompt and focused, and made jokes about Jim from Legal Affairs and how green the new sales force is, and yelled out a rallying cry about how everyone is going to break sales records this year, and so go *out there and get 'em*! And I have thanked the people who come up kindly afterwards and tell me how funny they thought I was, even though they didn't actually laugh out loud, because their boss was at their table, and they didn't want him to think they actually feel anything or have ideas or likes or dislikes or hopes or dreams or anything. And I walk out of the room with my money and my head held high.

And then I go back to my hotel room, eat a bouquet of muffins off my chest, watch five episodes of *Law and Order* in a row, and pass out in a dreamscape of crumbs. And in the morning, I vow that I will never, ever, ever take a corporate gig ever again, as long as I live. Until the next one.

Quality muffins ain't cheap.

(27)

The Day the Comedy Died

*"The deepest wounds aren't the ones we get from other people . . .
they are the wounds we give ourselves."*—Isobelle Carmody

"Those stains will never come out. Just burn it."—Aisha Tyler

Of all the skills and personality traits that my father passed on to me, the one I am most proud of, and the one I utilize most often, is "acting as if." As in, "act as if you belong."

This is not the same as pretending you are someone you are not, or mimicking the behavior of others in an attempt to blend in. This is a bigger, more ambitious, and much more radically personal approach— acting as if you belong wherever it is you are, and behaving as if you are completely comfortable there, regardless of whether on the inside you are completely mystified by what is happening, and do not understand the language people are speaking, comprehend the signage on the walls, or recognize the food that has been set before you on your plate.

My father has always been a guy who has been comfortable no matter where he goes: construction site, French restaurant, board meeting, slaughterhouse floor, underground fight club, afternoon tea klatch. My father can slide seamlessly into any context and immediately not just make people feel as if he belongs there, but that the entire thing may have been his idea, he is on the board of directors or perhaps an anonymous and powerful donor, and they are his esteemed guests. He is the kind of guy who looks you in the eye and claps you on the arm and laughs just loud enough to make you feel included but not self-conscious, and in minutes you have a lemonade in your hand, have invited him to dinner in your home, and agreed to meet him for an evening of vigorous salsa dancing sometime in the very near future. Later that evening, people will wonder who the incredibly funny and charming black man was and where he came from; they will compare stories and slowly realize that he was like a ghost—appearing magically from the mists, delighting and confounding all he encountered, and vanishing just as inexplicably into the night. He is like a full-grown, hilarious, very handsome, potty-mouthed elf.

He is both truly wonderful and utterly nefarious.[1]

This quality, the "acting as if," is a talent both genetic and cultivated. Part of it is just the way he was born. My father is an insanely likeable guy, the kind of person who could sweep all the dishes and food from the table mid-dinner party—just as people were lifting the first bite of something delectable to their mouths—leap to his feet atop the vintage furniture, tell a story comprised of both shocking subject and salacious language, and leave at the end of the night with everyone sighing about how wonderful he is and how this was the best dinner party they had ever been to, even as their stomachs are growling from hunger because he punted their duck breast into the fireplace during an especially explosive punchline. The man is that good.

The phrase "I just *love* your father" is one I have heard uttered so many times as to be able to smell it coming and mouth right along, keeping my irritated eye rolls to a barely detectable minimum. From the time I was very young, people have always thought he was delightful, drifted toward him, fallen into his gravitational pull, even as I was dying of embarrassment on the other side of the room.[2] One of my

---

1 Most people are not cut out for salsa dancing. This is just a truth. You think you are, but you aren't. Leave it to South American lotharios and international spies.

2 Literally on my back, gasping for air, choking on the green bile of my own mortification. Literally.

most vivid memories is of my father swinging my very tiny and argu-
ably brittle grandmother-in-law around the dance floor by her armpits
(she weighed like sixty pounds) to some interpretive jazz song at my
wedding, before gleefully dropping the f-bomb multiple times, then
striding outside to illegally halt traffic in front of the reception hall
with a pile of hazard cones he had obtained from only god knows
where.

Everybody at my wedding just loved him. This is the effect he has
on people.

I'm pretty sure I did not acquire this skill. Sure, I am loud and rude
and love to curse, but the bulletproof likeability thing I'm not quite
sure I received. I talk too much and too fast, am perilously clumsy,
anxious, obsessive-compulsive, and quite possibly the most neurotic
black woman on the planet. These factors seem to counterweight my
more fun characteristics. However, the one thing I did get from my
father, partially from genetics but mostly from ongoing and relentless
drilling from him, is the ability to charge into a situation and "act as
if" I know what I am doing when I have no freaking idea what is going
on, why we are all here, or even what day it is. The "act as if" philosophy has a slutty and unscrupulous bedmate—the "fake it 'till you
make it" axiom, or "keep going through the motions as you learn what
the hell you are doing those motions for and gradually develop the
skills and knowledge required to really and truly belong." In plainer
language, I often have no fucking idea what I am doing.

That has never, ever stopped me.

I believe fully that if you want to do something, you just go do it.
You can sit around, thinking about it, waiting until things are perfect, wringing your hands, dithering and hesitating and slowly twisting
your panties into a perfect little fisherman's knot. Or you can get up
off your lazy fucking ass and *do something*. What's the worst that can
happen?[3]

As I'm sure you've gleaned from these pages, this philosophy has

---

3 Lots. Lots of terrible things can happen. There is a bottomless cornucopia of bad occurrences waiting for you at the other end of this hypothetical. Nonetheless, *excelsior*.

not always served me well. I can attribute several broken bones, a dumpster full of ruined meals, a wrecked racecar, some second-degree burns, and a scrapped short film to this charge-ahead philosophy. However, I have just as often thrown myself into something, studied, watched others, cribbed a bit from the Internet, and come out just fine. And sometimes, much more than fine.

There is something truly invigorating, and also terrifying, about deciding to do something, and then just doing it. Much like ripping off a bandage or touching your tongue to the tip of a battery,[4] the dread of anticipation is usually much scarier than the actual event.[5] But we have all had the experience of wanting to do something, and then dithering and planning and waiting and watching and revisiting and revamping our plan until the opportunity has passed and that unbelievably hot guy or girl has left the bar, never to return. And then we kick ourselves angrily, because we didn't screw up our courage to just do some shit that probably wouldn't have been that hard in the first place. So you get shot down. It's not like you haven't been shot down before. Seriously.

So we wait, and we hesitate, and all the awesome shit we wanted to do—start a rock band, learn Mandarin, take up painting, become master of the Cat's Cradle—have completely passed us by, and we can't play an instrument, barely speak English, resent art, and fear lengths of string.

Don't be someone who is afraid of string. Just pick up the fucking string.

When I decided to become a comedian, I just decided to do it. I didn't take any classes, I didn't read any books, I didn't ask anyone their opinion or get anyone's permission. I just did it. And as acknowledged previously, for a long, long while I wasn't very good at it. But that didn't keep me from approaching it like I had been doing it forever, like it was my lifelong passion and all I had ever been cut out for

---

4 I am not advocating this.

5 I actually cannot speak to what it is like to touch your tongue to the tip of a battery. I have never done this, because I am not a four-year-old boy.

in this world. I didn't worry about rules, or conventions, or how things were done. I just figured that shit out as I went along. Of course, I had doubts, and questions, and more than a few panic attacks, but once I decided to be a comedian, I was a comedian. I wasn't *trying* to be a comedian. I didn't *hope* to be a comedian. I *was* one.

This bold unbridled approach led, in turn, to a pretty intense crisis of faith about six years into my career. I had moved to Los Angeles, because I was sick of the breathable air and delightfully potable water of the San Francisco Bay Area.[6] By this time, I had gotten relatively funny and pretty accustomed to doing well on stage. Don't get me wrong; I was no comedic genius. My act was formalized, stilted, and more than a little gimmicky. But I had honed it into a pretty tight set, with a hook that people could relate to, and my punchlines were reliably effective. Plus, what I lacked in substance, I more than made up for in style, gesticulating wildly and mugging as if my facial contortions might earn me extra points in a clownery competition. My act was adequate and serviceable, and had been working for years, and I was feeling pretty damn confident about it.

And then, suddenly, I wasn't.

I don't know how this happened, and at the time, I had no idea why, either. It was abrupt and cataclysmic: all of a sudden, the same jokes that had killed the week before just stopped killing. No explanation. Nothing I could point to. I just started to suck.

I tried *everything*. Moving my jokes around. Talking louder. Talking more quietly. Making more eye contact. Being more drunk.[7] Nothing was working. I was bombing repeatedly and consistently, and it was quickly eroding my now brittle self-confidence.

I started to freak the fuck out.

The stress of bombing, coupled with the lack of comprehension of why I was bombing or how to fix things, started to manifest physically: anxiety, lack of sleep, dry skin, hiccups. The most dramatic of these symptoms? I started to develop flop sweats. Up until this point,

---

6 I like a little challenge in my life-sustaining elements.

7 This has often been my solution in times of crisis. It has only not worked like half the time.

I had no idea what a "flop sweat" was, but let me tell you, when you experience one, that shit becomes immediately clear. Being "sweaty" is not a flop sweat. Leaving the gym drenched in perspiration is not a flop sweat. A flop sweat is when you go from delicate daffodil to dock worker in 3.5 seconds flat, with no warning and no explanation; when you can leave the house showered and fragrant with a triple application of antiperspirant, and arrive at the club twelve minutes later looking as if you just went three rounds in the octagon with Ronda Rousey. When the most strenuous thing you did in between was *drive your car*.

This is what I was experiencing. My body was in a constant state of fight or flight, but it had no idea who I was fighting or what I was fleeing. It got to be so that I would wear two or three tee shirts to the club at night, assembling them into a kind of bulked-up MacGyvered torso diaper, then bring a change of clothes along so I could whip off my soaked garments right before I went on stage, assemble a new chest diaper, and promptly Whitney Houston the shit out of the second set of tees during my set. I was an unholy mess.

I realized I would have to do something before I slowly dissolved into a puddle of sweat like the Wicked Witch of the West. I wasn't about to abandon standup, but standup seemed to be pretty set on abandoning me. I would have to make some kind of fundamental change or watch everything I loved go flying out the window, or into the hamper, so to speak.

Finally, after one particularly punishing night of sweating it out on stage, both physically and psychologically, rivulets of liquid slithering uncomfortably down the sides of my rib cage and into the sodden waistband of my jeans, taking all hope with them, I realized this shit wasn't working, and it wasn't likely to magically start working again any time in the near future. I needed to do something massive. Something radical.

I had to destroy everything.[8]

I would have to throw out my whole set—every joke I had ever

---

8 Which was even more painful as I didn't have much material to begin with. It wasn't a bonfire of the vanities; it was a tiny campfire of the sadnesses.

written, honed, and performed for the past six years, essentially my entire career—and start from scratch.

This initiated an entirely new and wholly more startling series of flop sweats that graduated from merely tragic to grandly operatic in nature. I was *terrified*.

In almost every job, you build on past successes. You learn, you grow, you fail and succeed, and you take what you have learned and apply it to your work going forward. But in comedy, you are only as good as your last set, and if your material isn't working anymore, you are right back at square one. You can't polish off the old turds and give them new coats of gold. You've got to come up with a whole pile of brand-new turds. It's the only way.

I set about building an entirely new set. For a while I tried to have someone else do some writing for me, because I was so confused and unsure of myself that I figured having someone else write jokes for me couldn't hurt me any more than I was already hurting myself. But what I quickly realized was that delivering someone else's jokes and pretending they were my own felt like just that: pretending. I already felt unsure on stage and trying to find myself within someone else's words felt foreign and odd. Plus, I wasn't any funnier with someone else's jokes than I had been with my own. If I was going to suck, I might as well suck on my own terms.

I threw that set out and started again.

This was painful. I cannot overstate how painful this was. It wasn't like I had lived through a natural disaster or lost a loved one, but it really sucked. The thing I loved, that I had been good at, all of a sudden I wasn't good at anymore. I felt like Michael Jordan during his MLB days—everything I had known or believed about myself was suddenly gone and I had to start over with the fundamentals, something I had never bothered to learn in the first place, because I had just started doing standup half-cocked, chock-full of enthusiasm but short on technique.

So I started over from scratch. I wrote, and wrote, and wrote some more, performed what I had written, threw most of it out, and started again. And again. I did beginner's nights and open mikes, late-night lineups and coffeehouse shows on Sunday afternoons where people were too hungover or full of gas-inducing soy milk to laugh, late night bar shows when people were too busy drowning in lite beer and crushing despair to laugh. I trained like Rocky for a prizefight, minus the raw eggs and slightly pervy sweatsuit. And I tried, as best I could, to be optimistic and open-minded, to trust my instincts, listen to my heart, and relearn what I thought I already knew.

It didn't go well at the beginning. I was paralyzed by fear and insecurity, not a healthy mental state to be in while yelling at a bunch of drunken bikers in a dive bar about interracial marriage and how Abercrombie and Fitch stores smell like sex with a college freshman. When things worked, I was relieved, but I didn't always know *why* they worked. And when things went poorly, it reinforced every negative suspicion I ever had about the world and myself, which was that I should have been a lawyer like my parents wanted, that there was no such thing as Santa Claus, and that a cute golden retriever would just as soon shit on you as lick your face. My very faith was tested.

But I was determined to do the thing I loved, no matter how much, at that particular moment, I hated doing it.

And then, slowly, things started to get better. I started to have good sets again, and then awesome ones, and finally, I started to kill. Even the loud obnoxious open mikes in the back of karaoke pool halls started to go well. Even better, I stopped dreading getting onstage, and started to feel eager to do it again. Excited about a new concept, or a new bit, new punchlines, new ways of saying something I felt confident would turn a joke from just okay to good, or from good to great. And with all of this returned my confidence. I again embraced the idea that I might not be the best comedian in the world, but I was damn good at this, and, even more importantly, it was something I enjoyed, and so if nothing else I would get up there and grin my ass off, be happy when people laughed, and when they didn't laugh, write them off as a bunch of dim-witted idiots with poor taste.

That was almost a decade ago. Since then I have done a lot of comedy performances, in clubs, and concert halls, and late-night shows, and cable programs. I have written two books, and a bunch of articles—

some good, some just okay. I have produced a comedy special, which quite a few people claim to like, and some others think isn't funny at all. And I have reached a place where I love what I do, and I put my heart into it, and I am pretty confident that I do it well, and that no one else does it quite like me.

It took twenty long years and a lot of blood, sweat, and tears to get here,[9] but I can finally say that I don't just act as if I am a comedian. I am one.

Along the way I realized that to be really good at something, to truly excel, you have to love it even when it doesn't love you. You have to be prepared to suck at it, and get good, and then suck again, and that may go on for a very long time, until you want to punch the thing you love in the face and get a job at Home Depot.

But if you really want something, you don't punch it in the face. You stick with it until you stop wanting to hit it and start wanting to hug it, and then kiss it, and finally make sweet, sweet love to it that will leave you both in a shivering puddle of tears.[10]

Until then, it's absolutely fine to fake it 'till you make it. Jump in with both feet. "Act as if." Just remember you've got to actually put in the hours, and do the real, hard work of "*becoming* as if."

Because eventually you will have to put your money, or your jokes, where your mouth is.

---

9 Mostly sweat though. A lot of sweat. Ick.

10 Okay. That got a little weird.

(28)

The Times I Spit on Someone from the Stage While Doing Standup

---

"Forgetting about our mistakes and our wounds isn't enough to make them disappear."—Aɪ Yᴀᴢᴀᴡᴀ

"Let's both pretend this never happened."—Aɪsʜᴀ Tʏʟᴇʀ

I have done this so many times it does not even warrant counting; literally more times than there are stars in the infinite galactic heavens. I have done this Sagans of times.

I have shared DNA with so many drunken strangers that if the government wanted to spread some kind of engineered virus aimed at thinning the world's population so that they would be easier to subdue and control, I would be a perfect candidate for patient zero. I run around onstage like a rabid ferret, gesticulate as if I am trying to catch candy as it cascades from an imaginary piñata, and talk faster than a third grader off their Adderall. I could, without trying, without even looking in your direction, spit directly into your mouth as you are laughing at a joke.[1] This is not a skill I am proud of. But it is a skill, nonetheless.

---

1 I realize that none of this is an advertisement for coming to one of my live shows (which are hilarious, in my very humble opinion). But I am dedicated to telling the truth, no matter how painful. Or no matter how likely it is that the truth could give you a cold.

People do one of two things when they are talking and realize they have spit on another person midsentence. They ignore it completely, even though they know they spit and the other person knows they spit and they know the other person knows they spit; or, they make a grand gesture of saying, "Oh my god! I spit on you! I am disgusting! I am also perfectly healthy and impeccably meticulous, so you cannot be catching anything at all from me but my delicate fastidiousness and dedication to personal hygiene!" This, of course, convinces no one, but at least the spitter is off the hook and hasn't completely ignored an occurrence that both parties are totally aware just happened, and are a little grossed out by.

When you are on stage, you are in a position of power. You are above everyone, illuminated by spotlight, wielding your microphone like a broadsword and striding the stage like Eddard Stark about to take a man's head for fleeing the Wall. Showing weakness is the furthest thing from your mind, and in truth, would be a fatal mistake. You cannot show weakness, and you cannot bring the show to a halt so that you can apologize to a guy in the front row for hitting him in the face with bodily fluids. This would be exposing a chink in your armor that anyone, be they affectionate heckler or drunken asshole, could fully and fatally exploit. We cannot have that. People paid money to see you. The show must go on. There are many, many dick jokes left to tell.

When you play the game of microphones, you win or you die.

So you must always go for option number one, which is that not only will I *not* acknowledge that I spit on you, but I will act so oblivious to the possibility that I might have spit on you as to convince you, through my bright and smiling certitude, that it never actually happened. You will immediately cast about for the source of this new-landed moisture, checking first your table mates, then the ceiling sprinklers and your beer glass, and finally your own mouth, with a variety of Zapruder-like theories of how you might have been caught in the face with a droplet of watery substance. And then you will refocus on the show, and why you came, which is to laugh, and you will move on.

In comedy, as in life, fun must be had, my friend. Don't let a little spit derail you.

(29)

The Time I Broke My Arm at Sundance, and the Ensuing Meltdown

"[N]obody likes having salt rubbed into their wounds, even if it is the salt of the earth."—Rebecca West

"If I can't have fun, damn it, no one can!"—Aisha Tyler

I will not do what you tell me to.

In fact, if you tell me not to do something, I will do exactly what you tell me not to do, even though I may have agreed, audibly and in your presence, not to do it.

For example, you may tell me not to eat the birthday cake. When it is gone, I will tell you I did not eat it. Technically, that would be true. Instead, I will have nibbled at it delicately and for an extended period, until it was no more.

You may tell me, after oral surgery, not to eat any solid food for twenty-four hours. I will then immediately order a double cheeseburger with bacon and spend the next four days scrubbing blood out of my pillowcases after chewing up the inside of my mouth.[1]

You may warn me not to put my finger into that highly charged

---

1 But bacon? Seriously. So good. Worth the injury.

light socket. Of course, that is exactly where you will find me, minutes later, right before I pass out and require resuscitation.

Sometimes I do not even do this consciously. I may not even *want* to do the thing you told me not to do. I may actually want to follow your heartfelt and well-intentioned instructions. I may just not be able to. I am powerfully and inexorably—often subconsciously—drawn to do the thing that I should absolutely avoid. I have always been this way.

It is a disease. Seriously. It is some kind of sickness.

It's not that I'm not a team player, or can't follow instructions, or that I don't want things to go smoothly, or safely, or stay out of the hospital. It's just that somehow, whatever I am supposed to stay away from, my brain will keep drawing me toward, again and again, like a mental event horizon, the pull of which I cannot escape. I do not do these things by choice. They just happen. I swear.

I am loyal. I am kind. I want nothing but the best for you and your family. But please do not leave a donut in front of me and say you'll be right back. That donut and me will be long gone. While I am highly trustworthy, I am not a freaking statue.

When I was a kid, this manifested itself in many ways. If you told me I wasn't athletic, I was on three teams by the next afternoon.[2] If you told me I wasn't good at science, I would have signed up for physics classes at the local college by Friday, even though I was only halfway through sophomore algebra in high school. And if you told me I didn't know Kung Fu, I would have spent the weekend trying to break a board with my hand, and showed up at school on Monday with a very, very bruised hand and a very splintery, but unbroken, piece of wood.

The most dramatic occurrence of my young life came when I got into Dartmouth and decided to attend, and my high school counselor told me not to go there because it was too far from home and too different from what I knew, and that I would be martyring my college career.

I sent in my intent to enroll form that same day.

---

2 Man, did cross-country suck. Do you know they run like a zillion miles? Blech.

I really don't like being told what to do. And even less being told
what I am *able* to do.

The most dramatic occurrence of this in my *young* adult life (as I
am refusing to fully enter adulthood, mainly because being a grownup
sucks) was the year my first book, *Swerve*, came out. It was also the
year I had a film in the Sundance Film Festival,[3] which is a big deal,
because I am rarely in a movie, let alone one that gets into Sundance,
which is such an honor and a validation of your work and everything,
and also they have lots of parties and you can drink for free and
stuff. So, of course, I was very excited that my film was going to be
screening there, and I planned a big trip to Utah to party and rage and
snowboard and drink and walk around Park City. Oh, and support
my film. Yeah. That too.

It was a very exciting time, because right afterwards I was scheduled to go on a tour to support my first book, and I was going to get
to ride on a bunch of planes, and take pictures, and meet celebrities,
and do karaoke, and sign copies of my book, and I felt very super extra
fancy.

I invited my oldest friend to Utah to snowboard with me and get
hooked up with all the free stuff I was sure to get there, as I had heard
Sundance is all about free shit. We flew in to Park City on the same
day. On the way in from the airport, I called my husband, who wished
me luck and harmlessly spoke four portentous words: "Don't break
your arm."

I laughed. Of course I wouldn't break my arm! Why would I do
that? Who likes breaking their arm? I was going to rip up the snow and
destroy the mountain and generally have a killer day. I was not going
to break my arm. I hated breaking limbs.

Of course, now it was in my head, so cue the Plaster of Paris.

I didn't *set out* to break anything. I was in a great mood, the sun
was out, and the house I was staying in with friends was huge and

---

3 *Never Die Alone*, alongside the lovely David Arquette and the great actor, rapper, and
police impersonator Ja Rule.

luxurious and had a hot tub and a toaster oven.[4] My friend met me at the lodge, there was lots of snow on the mountain, and life was good. I rented a snowboard short enough to make up for the fact that I hadn't ridden in a zillion years, but long enough not to make me look like a pussy. It was going to be a perfect day.

As it was, I landed at eleven, was snowboarding by noon, and at four in the afternoon my arm was broken. Very badly.

See what telling me not to do something does? Aargh!

It is worth mentioning here that my oldest friend is a guy. A guy I love dearly, but a guy nonetheless. And as such, he is someone I feel competitive with and must beat at everything. Not because I need to teach him a lesson or get payback for some earlier perceived slight, but because he is a boy and I am a girl and I cannot let him be better than me at anything other than having a deep voice and peeing standing up.[5] I love him, and he is better than me at lots of things: computers, knowing things about sports, memorizing old-school hip-hop lyrics, making the shape of a vagina with his thumbs and forefingers, and being dourly sarcastic. He is definitely a way better snowboarder than I am. But I will never, *ever* tell him that.

Ever.

On this day, I had not ridden in a very long time, and it was very important to me to be as good as the last time we rode together, and maybe better, because I was older, and people are supposed to improve at stuff as they get older, right? But my friend rode faster than me from the very beginning, because he *had* gotten better as he had gotten older, while I had gotten soft and puddinglike, which made me mad, so I sped up to keep pace. The faster I rode, the more afraid I was that I might fall and mess up my face,[6] which made me even angrier at myself for being so girly, which made me ride even faster. Soon I was riding a bit out of control, which scared me, but also made me happy,

---

4 I was all about toast at the time.

5 Even there I might be able to give him a bit of a run for his money.

6 It *is* my moneymaker, after all.

because I like feeling a little scared, and also because it made me look like a badass, and freaked out all the rich white people who were already a bit confused at seeing a giant black girl go screaming by on a snowboard.

I was rocking people's world—or so I thought, as I went whizzing down the mountain about to pee myself in terror. I was ripping it up.

At the bottom of a particularly long and harrowing run, we came to a stop at a line for another lift that would take us to another part of the mountain. My friend had stopped before me, because he was always getting to the bottom before me, because he was faster than me and wanted to rub my nose in it like a naughty dog.[7] And I came to a screeching halt right next to him, to show him I meant business and that the only reason I was riding more slowly was because my board was a rental so I couldn't really turn on the afterburners. As I did, I realized that my braking abilities had decayed significantly in the more than four years since I had ridden last, and I wasn't going to stop fast enough, and I was going to crash into him.

But crash hardcore. Because I'm fucking hardcore.

I actually didn't crash into him. I stopped like two inches in front of him, and then I crashed *across* him. I fell over his board, and I realized if I put my hands down to break my fall, they would hit the metallic blade-like edges of his snowboard, and I would sever all my fingers at the palm, and make a really big bloody mess for the mountain patrol to clean up, and ruin my mittens.

So instead, I put my hands out, on the other side of his board, so that I would not cut off my fingers, and so that I could fall in the most painful and awkward way possible, which is what I did.

I felt fine when I stood up, after I swallowed a big bolus of embarrassment about falling in the lift line, and then swallowed a big rash of shit from him about falling at all. But my arm felt funny. Crunchy. Clacky. Maraca-like. I complained. He told me to stop being such a pussy, and I told him to go fuck himself, because this is how we talk to

---

7 I will get him.

each other.[8] And I got back on the lift and rode back up to the top and took another four screeching runs down the mountain.

During which I fell on the same arm three more times.

Because when I fuck something up, I fuck it up but good. I fucking *mean* it.

At this point, my arm was starting to act funny, like pointing in the wrong direction funny, and going all numb and wonky and feeling like the arm of a dead person. This is when I called it. Yes, it took me until my arm felt cadaverous to decide it was time to stop snowboarding. I am bullheaded and obstinate, but I am also willful and slow to admit defeat. So I have all that going for me.

When I went to the mountain doctor, he told me what I had suspected after the second fall: I had broken my arm spectacularly. Lots of little pieces were rolling around in there, alongside a few bigger chunks—the x-ray of my elbow looked like a bag of calciferous marbles. I was pissed, a bit at my friend for making me so competitive, and a bit at my husband for telling me not to do what he knew I would be powerless not to do once I heard it. And, of course, I was mad at myself, for being such a blazing idiot.

But only a little, because of course this was all other people's fault.

I spent the rest of Sundance that year with my arm in a sling. They couldn't cast my arm, because if you cast an elbow, apparently it fuses in place and never bends again, and you're forced to lean casually against walls and bars everywhere so that your bent arm looks like a jaunty pose and not the terrible result of your reckless life choices. I refused drugs because I hate drugs and also because drugs make you say stupid things and I need absolutely no help doing that, thank you very much. And while my plan was to control my pain via alcoholic beverages, this was the most poorly conceived strategy ever, because I could never drink fast enough to get ahead of the pain, and so was both boozy *and* pissy the entire trip, partly because I was drunk, partly because my arm killed, and mostly because I had broken my right elbow and so couldn't zip up my pants and was always holding in all the pee I

---

8 This is us at our most affectionate.

had made trying to drink the pain in my elbow away. And I was a huge party pooper for all my friends who just wanted to drink all night and sploosh around in the hot tub and eat toasted bread in the morning slathered in butter, while all I wanted to do was moan gutturally while wandering around the house like a phantom, muttering about snow-boarding and brittle bones and being hardcore.

I was a fistful of hot, wet, ouchy mess.

After Sundance, I had to spend two weeks on a book tour, during which I had to sign books with my left hand because I had broken my writing hand. Hundreds of people have the signature of one "Asa Tyr" in their books, as that was the best I could manage. Occasionally people just got a giant "A," or an X, or a few well-placed salty tears after they grabbed my broken arm without knowing it was broken (it not having a cast 'cause of the fusing and all) and squeezed it like I owed them money.

Was my life ruined? Not even close. I still snowboard, and I still love my friend, and my elbow healed like new,[9] and life went on. It was only hugely inconvenient that I did the exact thing I was told not to do, and thank god it was only my elbow.

But it did teach me that I needed to find a way not to be so defiant of others, or of safety, or the universe in general, and that maybe it was time to slow down a bit, and not try to prove how badass I was to absolutely everyone all the time.

Of course, I only learned that for a little while. I went right back to the old Aisha as soon as my elbow healed. Because apparently, I will not do even what I tell *myself* to do.

I never listen.

---

9 Although my elbow *can* tell you if a storm front is coming in, and not just my elbow, but also my butt bone, which I broke snowboarding in college. I am like a walking Doppler 5000. Yes, upon reflection, maybe I should stop snowboarding.

(30)

The Time I Broke My Foot, Alone, in a Hotel Room

"You can't patch a wounded soul with a Band-Aid."—Michael Connelly

"You can't fix a broken toe with Scotch tape."—Aisha Tyler

Just to prove that I do not need others, or a high-speed athletic activity, or obstacles, or any reason at all to self-injure, I offer this anecdote.

I was in Miami for a photo shoot,[1] one for which I was very anxious, because it was going to be me and a bunch of models, and they would all be models, and of course, I would be *me*. The thing most people do not realize about models is that when they are all together, they look normal. Thin, yes, but not as abnormally thin as they *actually* are, because contextually they are thrown next to other crazy-thin people and other things that resemble them, like light posts, palm tree trunks, and drinking straws. So compared to those things, they just

---

1 Because this is one of only three reasons one goes to Miami: for a photo or music video shoot, to attend a party thrown by Kanye West, or to find a hot gay Latino man to have sex with. Oh, and to eat fried plantains. So, four.

look slender and fit, like they decided to hit the treadmill or cut out gluten or something.

But! Put them next to someone who is of a normal weight, and eats dairy, and loves gluten like she birthed it from her womb, and something very different happens. The models all look thin, and the normal-sized person looks as if she has some kind of glandular illness that has made her puff up like a manatee. I'm not saying this is what I was worried about in regards to this particular shoot, I'm just saying this is what was shaking me awake in a cold sweat every night for weeks on end in the months leading up to the photo shoot. Those fucking models and their fucking oppressive skinniness.

Don't get me wrong. I love my body. I have a very generous sense of self-worth, and I believe in being healthy. I like to promote responsible and realistic standards of beauty, not terrible and totally unattainable standards that most people cannot meet, male or female, even if they never ingested solid food again, and had their bottom two ribs removed by a wild-eyed surgeon wielding a bone saw and a tapeworm. These model people are *tiny*. They could be used as an example of developing-world malnourishment, if people in the developing world could afford to live on yogurt, cocaine, and organic fair-trade pesticide-free roll-your-own cigarettes.

You might think I'm being catty, but I am talking about the dudes. I actually had one of the guys on this shoot—who had slender little legs and a waist so small that two pairs of his pants could have been sewn together to make a single pair of very depressing chinos for me—tell me my build was "athletic." Which I took as a very nice, very modern way of saying, "Wow, you disgust me." I suppose I should have appreciated the effort.

I had tried to diet in the most responsible way in the weeks between when I was asked to participate in this shoot and when it happened. I did not starve myself. I made sure my meals were balanced. I worked out, but not to the point of self-destruction. I was reasonable.

And I was fucking *starving*. I don't know how people diet. As it is, all I think about is food, all the time—when I am working, when I am driving, when I am on the toilet.[2] And when I am trying to diet, my food obsessing goes from a low background hum to a deafening foreground rumble. I watch the Food Network while I am on the treadmill. I look at pictures of layer cakes made out of meatloaf on the Internet in bed before falling asleep. I make a comprehensive and thorough mental accounting of every single time I have eaten ice cream, and try my hardest not to touch myself. When I am dieting, I am completely unhinged.

So I struggled through this period of dietary restriction and borderline madness because these photos would be committed to the annals of history forever, and I did not want to be the homely bystander who had wandered accidentally into a faerie wonderland of beautiful sylphs, then plopped to her haunches to watch the goings-on, wobbly jowls agape. I wanted to at least kind of look like I belonged. And I was miserable. I hated everyone and everything.

But when I finally made it to the shoot, I felt marginally confident. The photographer was brilliant, the shoot concept was great, and the model I spent most of my time with was sweet and smart and didn't make me feel galumphy or plump at all. It was a great day.

And when I got back to my hotel room I felt an incredible sense of relief, and accomplishment,[3] and I congratulated myself on all my hard work and discipline, and on how focused I had been on my goals. And then I ordered a giant cheeseburger, fries, three chocolate chip cookies, and a bottle of red wine, and ate it all like the world was coming to an end and the eye of the apocalypse was Miami Beach.[4]

I pushed things into my mouth with index fingers, and wolfed

---

2 I have *Lucky Peach* and *Saveur* and *Cook's Illustrated* sitting in my bathroom just waiting for me to get a good hour alone to sit there and let dirty, dirty, gravy-laden thoughts run through my mind uninterrupted. This may be sick. I do not care. I am thinking about food in the bathroom. I don't need *you* to tell me it's problematic.

3 Or as much "accomplishment" as you can feel after having had your picture taken. It's not like I ended world hunger or anything. What a self-important asshole I am.

4 Which it may very well be, should it ever come to that. You can't have that many people sporting man-thongs and not expect some kind of cosmic payback.

things down without chewing, stopping only every few minutes or so to gasp for some much needed but entirely uninteresting air. I finished it. All of it. And then I wandered around the room barefoot, rubbing my shiny, grease-slicked tummy with a sticky hand, and drinking the rest of the red wine straight from the bottle.

There is something about the relief of a stressful experience being over, about the release of anxiety from the body, that is at once highly energizing and entirely discombobulating. The endorphins released when your brain finally realizes "holy mother of Mabel, thank god *that* shit is done" act as both relaxant and accelerant. Suddenly the world opens up to you. All things are possible. You are light as a feather and sharp as glass. You see all. You know all. You can do all . . .

Except navigate a simple hotel room without walking your big drunk ass at stride velocity into the corner of the king-sized platform bed. Which is what I did, bottle of wine in one hand, third choco-late chip cookie in the other, phone pressed between ear and shoulder, as I attempted to pack. Even then, with both hands full, a mouthful of cheap Garnacha, and my shoulder contorted into a phone cradle, I should have known better. I can barely avoid injury when all my limbs are unfettered and I am stone-cold sober. Why I thought I could manage a hotel room in my state of decreased capacity I will never know. Hope springs eternal from the bottom of a cheap wine bottle.

I knew right away that I hadn't just stubbed a pinky toe. I had really broken my shit. My index and bird toe[5] had gone from vertical to an unseemly and alarming l-shape, accompanied by a spreading bruise and a metallic smell that I later realized was the scent my body makes when I have just experienced "what the shit." My toes *killed*. They were tiny, but they were also really fucking broken and radiating pain that made me forget my own name.

I was alone, and injured, and pretty drunk, and I had to leave for the airport in twenty minutes.

A trip to the emergency room was out of the question. I wanted to go home, and what's more, I had to go home, because the magazine

---

5 Are those not the technical terms?

had paid for the hotel room and the flight and I was pretty sure that, much like the boys I dated in college, now that they'd gotten what they wanted from me they would not be interested in laying out any additional money. I had to rally. I wiped away the tears and cookie crumbs and called the front desk. I asked for ice, ibuprofen, and medical tape. The front desk brought me ice, ibuprofen, and wondered if Scotch tape would do. I let them know that this would not do at all, in any way. They scrounged around and found medical tape, that I am sure one of those skinny models with the perfectly unbroken toes had used to tape their mouths shut to prevent themselves from eating food or feeling feelings.

And then I, biting down on a washcloth, pulled my toes into a shape more or less resembling their former selves, and, remembering from my Internet wanderings that you cannot put casts on toes,[6] taped the offending digits to their neighbors, pounded the last of that wine, put on some flip-flops, and left for the airport.

My foot felt terrible the entire way back. On the rattling ride through the airport on a rickety airline wheelchair;[7] on the altitudinous cross-country flight, my throbbing foot jutting into the aisle, where it was tripped over repeatedly by flight attendants, passengers who had to pee, and one really annoying little kid; and all the way home from the airport in the car, which was really the most comfortable part of the trip but by that time I was just *pissed*, as I had fully sobered up and even had a twee hangover. But I bit down and sucked it up, because as usual I had no one to blame but my big dumb self.

When I got home, the podiatrist actually remarked on what a good job I had done immobilizing my toes, and that he couldn't have done any better. Cold fucking comfort, Dr. Bones.

And I learned that dieting is evil, and it is better to live a life of moderation, where you have a little something delicious every day,

---

6 Thanks WebMD! Also, why is it that I seem to break only uncastable bones? What's next, my cochlear bone?

7 Not as fun as it looks. I feel terrible for old people. How they don't pee a little bit while being pushed around the airport in those bumpy jalopies I have no idea. I did.

rather than saving up for weeks on end for one explosive food orgy where you might make yourself sick, undo all the hard work you have accomplished, and in all probability break a digit. Or two.

I will say that while I won't win any awards for being lithe, graceful or having functional motor skills, if the world ever comes to an end, I would be a killer triage medic. With tape, ice, Neosporin, and a cookie, I can fix almost anything.

Bring on the zombie apocalypse.

The Time I Fell Asleep on the Patio Furniture at a Birthday Party

"Wounds are an essential part of life, and until you are wounded in some way, you cannot become a man."—Paul Auster

"I'm really not interested in being a man."—Aisha Tyler

The person who passes out at a party is a very specific creature. They are someone for whom time and space have slowed, and the rules of comportment in a group setting no longer apply. They have set aside all pride or dignity in favor of something much more pressing: the sweet, sweet oblivion of sleep.

I used to make fun of this person. Point, mock, place their hand in a bowl of warm water, cover them in shaving cream, and perch a teacup poodle wearing a sweater vest precariously upon their chest, before taking one million cell phone pictures. They had brought this embarrassment upon themselves, and there was naught to do but teach them a lesson. I was crass and merciless.

Until it happened to me.

You may remember the term "walk of shame" from your time in college, or your twenties, or last week. But you have not experienced a true walk of shame until you have fallen asleep mid-party and awoken at sunrise, birds singing as if it is the dawn of creation itself, and someone has tucked a knit blanket around your knees and put on soothing house music, which made you dream you were at a rave dancing with a very hot guy with very scratchy legs all night long. And you are not in college, young lady. You are a grownup with a mortgage and a job and mutual funds and a car note, and you have absolutely no excuse.

To pass out and wake up alone in the dark is one thing. The damage may not be that bad. Maybe people cleared out without noticing you on the couch. Maybe you were just part of the scenery, one more jacket in a pile of discarded coats. Maybe you were resting your eyes before leaping up spryly for another round of Jell-O shots. Maybe you were meditating.

But if someone has tucked you in, you are completely fucked.

How I *let* this happen, I have no idea. As an adult, I have become supremely disciplined in social situations. This circumspection is not innate, but rather the aftermath of a lifetime of egregious drinking errors. Having made the terrible mistake of being the MVP of a party[1] several times in my twenties, and having experienced the relentless mockery that follows, I know better than to give others even a sliver of an opening. And much like the hazed freshman who becomes a fearsome Pledgemaster her sophomore year, I am a kind but relentless teaser of others when they themselves falter. It is not that I am mean. It is just that passing out is such a party foul, such a calamity of one's own doing, such a perfectly self-inflicted wound (and one I have experienced multiple times) that it demands notice. No one made you drink that much. No one made you do shots on an empty stomach. No one made you curl up in the corner of the futon like a milk-filled

---

1 If you do not know what "MVP of the party" means, just search the next soiree you attend for the person who is *really* giving it their all—drinking, eating, talking, but most of all drinking—with gusto. They care not for the morning, the feelings of others, or their own self-respect. They are there to *win that party*. That is the evening's MVP. They will accept their trophy lying down on the lawn, or perhaps wrapped somberly around a toilet or a jumbo bottle of ibuprofen the next day. And strangely, in the morning, it will not feel at all like winning.

kitten. You have chosen this set of actions for yourself. And you have no one to blame but this self-same selfy self. I know this from painful experience.

So for me to have done this was such a shock, such a foundation-rocking misstep, that for a good couple of minutes I wondered if I was hallucinating. Certainly I, a grown woman, her humiliating college years far behind her, someone who owned a car and the license to drive it, could read, write, and eat with a fork, could not have possibly made the series of specific and terrible mistakes required to result in waking up, cement-faced and groggy, on the porch of a rented house in Palm Springs. This was some other giant black woman, and I wanted my life back.

The worse part of this was how happy I was right before I fell asleep. There is nothing worse than having lots of fun one moment, and then, in what feels like the blink of an eye, sucking on the penny-tang of humiliation the next. It is like you got to the bottom of your ice cream sundae and found a mouse turd. You were so happy one bite ago, and now you wonder how you can ever go on living. And the ice cream is gone, the Jimmies and nuts too, and there is nothing to do but continue, yet all the color has drained out of the world, and it is a dark and joyless place.

I know how it happened. Of course I do. I hit the bullseye on all the clichés. Didn't get enough sleep the night before. Didn't eat enough at dinner. Tried too hard to demonstrate my knowledge of French wine by drinking a lot of it with my pinky held aloft. Entertained every challenge to do shots. Thought I was tougher than a twenty-year-old scotch. Thought I was tougher than a fifth of Maker's Mark. Believed I was strong enough to rest, for just a moment, on a highly plush piece of outdoor furniture. Nothing but arrogance at every turn.

These moves were a series of critical errors, strung together into a terrible necklace of self-destruction.

The worst part about this whole debacle was that the party was a sleepover party, and I had to see all of these people for another twenty-four hours. Sleepover parties are a double-edged sword. Because you don't have to drive anywhere afterward, you feel safe enough to cut loose. Usually the group is a group of friends, and small enough to feel welcoming, so you feel even more comfortable about really letting your hair down. And because you know you can just stumble off to your room or bunk bed or beanbag chair at the end of the night, there is really no reason at all to behave yourself. But because you feel so comfortable, so free to get your rage on, you are more likely to do something you will really regret, and you don't have the crowds of a nightclub or street mob to fade into after you have embarrassed yourself. If you fall through a plate glass coffee table at a vacation rental in front of ten people, it's pretty much guaranteed all ten people saw it. And will remember it. Forever.[2]

And then, of course, there's the next morning, when everyone is bleary-eyed and stumbly and groping for coffee, and they all congregate in the kitchen to drink juice and compare notes, and then you come in. And everyone remembers whatever ridiculous thing you did last night, and while it seemed hilarious at three in the morning in a haze of bourbon, now it just seems sad and a bit tragic. And you wish you were home in your own kitchen, where you'd have no one to answer to but yourself, but you are here, and people are avoiding your gaze, and you still have another twenty-four hours to spend with these people, and you want to die.

When you are trapped at a remote location on a Saturday morning after a Friday night of self-immolation, surrounded by everyone who had warmed themselves at your blazing pyre the night before, there is only one thing to be done: apologize as best you can, hold your head high, and act as if curling up with your head on a hose caddy is something you do all the time at home; that you are eccentric and prefer sleeping outside because you are rugged.[3] These are lies you tell yourself, and others, to cover up for the fact that you passed out, that

---

2 Maybe one guy was in the bathroom, but he still heard it.

3 No mention of the fact that you suck your thumb or were curled around a dog-eared teddy bear that you found somewhere in the house. The neighbors' house.

everyone knows you passed out, and that you are grateful no one wrote the word "jackass" backwards on your forehead with a Sharpie.

This approach is universal, and helpful any time you ever blow it in a major way—workplace faux pas, ethnically insensitive joke, slamming into your boss's car in the parking lot, accidentally touching your mother-in-law's breast at Thanksgiving. You can slink away, tail between your legs like a dog who just urinated on the baby's bassinet, and die alone in a corner, or you can straighten up, look them dead in the face, and say, "I did this. I'm not proud of it, but I'm owning it, and I am going to look directly into your eyes and apologize, while holding your gaze so long and with such defiant pride that you will start to wonder if perhaps it is *you* who has offended *me* in some way. And then I will leave here and humiliate myself terribly in front of others, because that is just what I do."

I did apologize to each and every attendee of that party. Individually, and with great remorse, because I am polite, and also because I needed to find out if I had flashed my boobs at anyone the night before. Thankfully, at least half of them were as drunk as I was, and remembered nothing, and the other half were too kind, or too embarrassed for me, to hold it over my head, dismissing my contrition with a "don't mention it" and sending me on my way, and I was grateful, relieved, and very, very hungover. And the party continued through the weekend and my trespasses were forgotten, because the very next night someone got even drunker than I was and actually *did* flash their boobs at everyone, and I sighed a sigh of sweet relief that I hadn't gone that far.

At least, as far as I could remember.

But I acknowledged my mistake. I moved past it, I made direct if truncated eye contact with everyone there, and I pushed through the pain. And that is all that can be asked after one has humiliated oneself in an enclosed space with a group of near strangers.

The person who passes out at a party is a living emblem of poor life choices. The person who passes out at a party is tragedy personified, and to be avoided lest one becomes like them. The person who passes out at a party is the most unfortunate person in the world,[4] and their impulse is to slink into the shadows, never to be heard from again.

But the person who boots, passes, owns it, apologizes profusely, and then rallies is a phoenix risen from the ashes to rage again. That person is a champion. And also delightfully polite.

Maturity. Now *that* feels like winning.

---

4 I am exaggerating wildly, of course. I can think of a million other people more unfortunate. But none more likely to have their faces written on in permanent marker.

(32)

The Time I Vowed to Stop Drunk Tweeting

"A wound will perhaps become tolerable with length of time; but wounds which are raw shudder at the touch."—Ovid[1]

"People are never, ever going to forget this. Crap."—Aisha Tyler

The night we killed Osama bin Laden, I tweeted some pretty irresponsible stuff.

I admit we were all caught up in the excitement of it all, the heady "look what we done" drama of the night, and we had killed this terrible mass murderer who was responsible for the loss of so many lives, after looking for so long, and after all those whiffed chances and missed opportunities we got the monster. By we, I mean the president, his close advisers, and some very brave and badass highly trained operatives doing dangerous shit very far away from home. Much in the way that "we" have won the Superbowl when the 'Niners were in the midst of their dynasty, "we" killed Osama bin Laden.

Yes. By "we," I definitely do *not* mean me.

But I was excited. That guy sucked. And it was late and I had some wine, and I did some really ill-advised online jubilating that in the

---

1 Yes, goddammit. *Ovid.*

light of day, which was like a few hours after I did it, I really wished I hadn't.

I mean, he was a bad guy. He had signed his own death warrant a thousand times over. But do you really want your definitive statement about the killing of another person to be the tweet

> ### Aisha Tyler
> @aishatyler
>
> ## "America! Fuck Yeah!" [2]

Good lord. Have some composure, lady.

When I woke up the next day, I was filled with regret. I should have shown more restraint. I wished I had thought about the tweet before I tweeted it. Stepped back. Realized a whole lot of people would see this thing, and I might want to consider how I would feel if my grandchildren read it, and how I would explain it to them if they did.[3] And I realized I wouldn't be able to. It was improper. It was undignified. And it was way too late to take back now.

Luckily, the Internet is full of stupid, like to the gills, so it's not like in the grand scheme of things I was going to stand out. The Internet is where stupid goes to find stupider so it doesn't have to feel so stupid. My tweet would pale in comparison to the idiots who think the Apollo mission was staged on a Hollywood movie set or that aliens embed secret messages in cell phone waves or President Obama was born in Kenya and is part of a terrorist sleeper cell bent on overthrowing the American government and establishing Sharia law. Me and my momentary lapse of judgment pale next to the guy with the potted meat and the tinfoil hat.

But here is the thing about Twitter. Like its home, the Internet, Twitter is forever. You can never, ever, ever take it back. You can delete a tweet from your stream, strike it from your memory, end your Twit-

---

2 It's a great song. There is no disputing that.

3 I don't have grandchildren. At this rate, I never will. I spend too much time on Twitter to raise babies.

ter account, and never visit the Internet again, and years from now, decades, centuries even, when whatever life-form is still alive and sentient on this earth strikes up their computing device, your infernal and incendiary tweet will be waiting for them in some forgotten, dusty corner of the interwebs, proclaiming for all the world that you are still, and have always been, a complete idiot.

It does not matter that it is easy to tweet, or convenient, fast, or even brief. Brevity is the soul of wit only if you have wit to begin with. Anything that seems ribald and cutting at four in the morning when you have been nursing a bottle of Bailey's Irish Cream will, by the light of day seem a) sexist, b) racist, c) stupid, or d) all of the above. You cannot beat Twitter. Its sole purpose is to capture the things you have said and amplify them across the Internet in a terrible game of Telephone. Only when your tweet comes back to you, it isn't a distortion of what you said, but *exactly* what you said, and just as terrible as everyone thought, and there is a picture of your penis attached along with a very poor joke about cats and fire hoses, only both are metaphors, and you didn't use the words "cat" or "fire hose."

You didn't mean it. You shouldn't have written it. You regretted it the moment you clicked that little blue button. None of this matters to the Internet. The Internet feels no sympathy. This thing you have said is out in the world, and what's worse, it is being passed around actively by dozens, even hundreds of people, who do not know you and do not care to know you, and so cannot apply any kind of "I know him and he's really a nice guy" temperance to their interpretation of what you said, instead flying to the exact opposite "Oh my god, this person is pure evil and must eat kittens for breakfast and should be bound and thrown into a river" kind of place, from which there is no return.

Here's the truth. As helpful as it may be, and as important as it may seem, the Internet hates you, the people that live inside the Internet hate you, the troll that lives under the bridge hates you, and they are all just waiting, just *dying* for you to make a mistake.

So what should you do? You know the answer to this. It is simple, pure, and utterly impossible.

Don't tweet.

I realize this is completely unrealistic. How can you *not* tweet? How else will people know what you ate for breakfast or what you are listening to on Spotify or what your gamerscore is? Ridiculous. Not tweeting is not an option. I am a dolt for even suggesting it.

So the second option is to never, ever tweet when you are drunk. Not even a little intoxicated. Not even after you have used alcohol-based mouthwash.

I have written tweets I thought were lazy, not funny, boring, dry. I have tweeted silly things, maudlin things, and things that upon retrospect were pretty self-involved.[4] I have tweeted stuff I thought should have been reworded or retracted. But it is only when I am drunk that I tweet stuff that I know will be a source of deep and abiding regret when I am old and my brain is hooked up directly to the Internet via nanochips and a web of fine copper wires. It is then that I will be haunted, day and night, with the images of my vintage tweets, floating back at me like traffic signs on a lonely highway, reminding me just how easy it was in the olden days to write something in 140 characters that you would never say in real life, and then set the hellhound of your own destruction loose upon the world.

Nothing particularly terrible resulted from this regrettable run of tweets. I was not reprimanded huffily by a follower, received no calls from my family or emails from colleagues. Instead, I was just struck by my own regret, and the sense of agony I would feel if what I had said had ended up in print, or was analyzed elsewhere on the Web. These weren't meant to be official statements or repeatable quotes; they were the midnight ravings of a lunatic. But no matter, because we as a nation now take every tweet, every offhanded Facebook comment, or shotgun aside as the gospel truth of a person's sense of the world, when in reality most are typed late at night when people are intoxicated or sleep-deprived or just got in a terrible fight with their spouse. *Most* of what is posted online, especially on Twitter, which by its very nature is brief, temporal, ephemeral—is disposable. But nowadays, when something posted at

---

4 No one cares THAT much about what is #np'ing today, lady.

noon in Buffalo can be duplicated a thousand times across websites by one p.m., nothing is disposable. Like that awful see-through dress that refuses to die, nothing will ever disappear into the ether again.

So let us all say it now, together once more, so that it sinks into your head and sears itself brand-like into mine: the Internet is forever. Forever like sequoias, like fossils, like mountains, like Old Tjikko,[5] like atoms, like interstellar dust, like the ever-expanding universe.[6] You can delete it, you can disavow it, you can strike it from the record, you can beg, borrow, plead, and disable your account, but that tweet is out there, shot through the Internet like a virus, and you can never, ever, take it back.

We are so cavalier nowadays with what we say, tossing out off-handed jokes and saucy commentary via smartphone, typing madly with the thumb of one hand while drinking vitamin-enhanced water with the other. We do not even take the time to type the thing that will be our undoing with both hands anymore, which is probably why we are so quick and so very eager to hit the "post" or "tweet" or, more accurately, "detonate" button, because how can something that was so easy to type, so facile to concept and execute, be a danger to anyone, including ourselves? Easy things are soft, they are gentle, and they present no danger.

At least that's what you tell yourself as you take a cell phone picture of your naked torso in the mirror of your filthy, laundry-strewn bathroom, and then upload it to Facebook accompanied by a tinkling cloud of LOLs.[7] Whom could it possibly hurt?

You, and only you, and you repeatedly, and you will have none to blame but your wayward, thoughtless, and downright reckless right thumb.

---

5 A 9,550-year-old Norway Spruce. That tree is *old*.

6 Okay, maybe not as forever as the universe. But you get my point.

7 Or pictures of you doing shots off a stripper's torso, or of you dancing on the back of a fire truck in your bra, or you with your arm around a woman who is not your wife, or your half-mast erection pressing against your robin's egg-blue boxers, or . . . well, you get my drift.

So think before you tweet (or post, or text, or email, or upload video, or anything that gives others any information of any kind about you or your life), and end up tortured in a hell entirely of your own making, at once delightful and ghoulish, spending eternity drowning, much like Homer Simpson under an avalanche of donuts in his personalized Hades, under a torrential and endless deluge of your own 140-character idiocy.

Man, I should tweet something about that.

The Apologia; or, Shut Up Aisha—a Far From Comprehensive List of My Verbal Gaffes

"All the hours wound you, the last one kills."—LATIN PROVERB

"I'm screwed now, may as well keep going."—AISHA TYLER

I always say the wrong thing. Luckily, I have made a career of it, or I would have no friends at all.

It actually comes in quite handy for a comedian. A big part of our mental energy is spent breaking down the brain-mouth barrier, the mechanism in normal people that keeps you from blurting out the first thing that comes to mind, the on-off switch that says to normal people, "Hey there, why don't you examine this statement before you just fling it out into the world like a word grenade?" Most people have this mechanism in their head, and it keeps them from putting their foot directly into their mouths most of the time, unless they have been drinking or are overly emotional or a character in a meet-cute rom-com blockbuster.

Comedians do not have this mechanism, and those that do spend a lot of time trying to override it. The only way to be spontaneously funny, to be verbally sharp, to be quick on the draw, is to *never* think about what one is about to say, to not ever hesitate, but say that thing, as loudly and theatrically as possible, and *pray*. You open your mouth, turn on the faucet, protect your eyes, and stand back. Most of the time this works, and you are quick, irreverent, off-the-cuff, and hilarious. Occasionally, it backfires terribly and you say something you really wish you could take back, or worse, something that others are going to force you to take back through angry correspondence and the Internet version of a pitchfork mob. You hope for the little mistakes—ones remedied by a simple apology, rather than something you have to call a press conference for, issue multiple statements, and then donate money to an anti-defamation league or animal welfare charity. You pray for the tiny trespasses. After a while, they are your only friend.

I am constantly apologizing for stuff I have said. At this point I automatically default to apology mode, mostly as a prophylactic strategy. It's possible I may have said something that offended you, or that I will say something that offends you, or imply it, or think it, or make you think it, and so let's just get the apology out of the way now, before you have time to get really worked up and send me an angry letter or post something crazy on my Facebook page or try to punch me at a cocktail party. Let's nip all that pent-up aggression in the bud, shall we? It's highly unhealthy.

I'm sorry.

Because I am in a constant state of sorry, I started a segment on my podcast called "The Apologia," the entire purpose of which is to head any offended sensibilities or righteous indignation off at the pass and save people the busy work of dashing off an angry missive and sending it to me in a purple huff.

The thing is, people offend so easily nowadays that letters of outrage almost don't mean anything anymore. Everyone is always mad all the time. Either you were too cavalier about that subject or too precious. You supported your favorite sports team and now children who love opposing sports teams have been psychologically scarred. You gave too much money to shoeless orphans, when you could have spent that money on something that would grow the economy, or you didn't give enough, and you are a heartless bastard who hates orphans.

Everything makes everyone furious all the freaking time, and there is always someone out there deserving of your righteous indignation. That doesn't mean your particular hurt feelings aren't warranted, or even legitimate. It's just that people have made a cottage industry of outrage, an art form of being deeply cut by the words of others. Most of the time this isn't real; this person doesn't actually feel offended, doesn't really feel *anything* at all, just the swelling feeling of power that comes with forcing someone else to backtrack and backpedal and walk back and take back and back up and just plain apologize.

So, again, I'm sorry.

And so you won't skitter to your computer and whip off some kind of hysterical and sobbing demand for restitution after reading this book, I thought I'd just get it all out of the way right now.

I apologize. To you, and to:

white people
black people
skinny people
fat people
rich people
poor people
the homeless
drinkers
teetotalers
straight-edgers
crackheads
theater people
people who hate musical theater
meat eaters
vegetarians
vegetarians who secretly eat meat
people in Texas (this is redundant with meat eaters)
Asians
nail salon owners
Asian nail salon owners
other ethnicities who feel left out

soul food restaurateurs
Whitney Houston fans
hookers
johns
models
Native Americans
Gary Coleman
little kids who are offended by sex jokes
people offended by sex jokes at the expense of little kids
religious people
atheists
babies
kittens
people who hate UFC
infant bunnies
comedians
string figure experts
people who take pictures of themselves in their bathroom mirrors
    with their cell phones
people who love Twitter
people who hate Twitter
people who don't understand Twitter
hipsters
vegans
hipster vegans with inexcusable mustaches
old trees
ballet dancers
people who like unscripted television
people who like scripted television
people who like *American Idol*
people who have terrible taste in television shows
people with goiters
people who fear goiters
people with urophobia (fear of urine)
pitchfork mob enthusiasts

the Kardashians
whoever designed that awful see-through dress
my parents
my husband
my in-laws
my coworkers
people who can read
people who read this book
people who received this book as a gift
people I spit on accidentally at my comedy shows
Kanye West
people who love pigs
people who hate bacon
pigs who have been turned into delicious bacon
and that plump little redneck kid who drinks a lot of
    Mountain Dew

Now, don't you feel better?

The Coda: Stop Doing It to Yourself

"The lessons of life amount not to wisdom, but to scar tissue and callus."—WALLACE STEGNER

"I know there's a lesson here. I just don't know what it is."
—AISHA TYLER

What was the point of all this self-flagellation, other than to use words like self-flagellation in a sentence?[1]

Well, I hope this book can be a cautionary tale—no, 32 tiny cautionary tales—about what can happen when you live your live recklessly and without any caution whatsoever. I have made a lot of mistakes. I mean *a lot*. Way more than I could ever fit into this book, or would care to. I mean, I wanted to write a funny book, not embark on Alcoholics Anonymous's Step 4.

But I have also pursued my dreams, without reservation, and really without much thought as to whether or not they would ever come true. I honestly never worried about that. I just *believed* they would, and then set about making them come true. And if they didn't (and many of them didn't—oh dear lord, so very many), I revised my game plan and went right on running at it using a different play formation. If at first you don't succeed, sack the fucking quarterback. Make that guy *feel* it.[2]

---

1 And how many times do you get to do *that* in a lifetime?

2 Why did I use a sports analogy here? Because I *can*.

My relentlessness paid off. Not so much in "success," or "money," or "meeting Ryan Gosling," although all these things have happened, but more in the fact that I never look back and wish I had gone after something that I didn't. Because I *have* gone for everything I've wanted. Like a crazy person. Like a juggernaut.

Like a motherfucking banshee.

And I am happy, because every day I get to do stuff I love, and feel passionate about, and pour my heart into, because it is what I was put on this planet to do, and so regardless of remuneration, the work is its own reward. Does that sound cliché? Suck it. I don't care.

I also hope this book will encourage you to be even more reckless, more wild, to make bigger, crazier, more frightening choices than I have, to chase your dreams with wild-eyed abandon, to run headlong into the most terrifying situations, to speak freely, to act freely, to do every single thing you have ever dreamed of doing up until this point but didn't do because you were scared that things might go wrong.

Because the truth is, they *will* go wrong. Terribly, mind-blowingly wrong.

But what's the worst that can happen? Maybe you'll be embarrassed. Maybe you will fail. Maybe things will go exactly the opposite of how you planned. Maybe you'll break a limb. But one thing is for sure: if you do nothing, you'll have done exactly that. *Nothing.*

So go out and make a bunch of mistakes. Hold your breath, close your eyes, and jump without looking. Wreck the joint. Break some shit. At the end of it all, at the very least, you'll have a bunch of really awesome stories.

You only live once. You can make it six weeks in a full body cast.

Now get out there and kick some ass.

Acknowledgments

This is my second book. Holy shit.

I really never thought I'd be here, so there's something to be said for blind optimism coupled with dogged relentlessness and an alarming lack of pragmatism. I could not have felt brave enough to make the mistakes I have made, nor recovered from them as readily, without the love and support of an incredibly resilient group of family, friends, and beleaguered colleagues. When you are as recklessly headstrong as I am, the people in your life must endure a lot of blowback and collateral damage. So I better thank these people before I get into real trouble.

I have to thank my husband first, because I am not an idiot, and also because he is the most incredible person ever birthed on planet Earth. He has made every day of my life since I met him infinitely better. He is the man at the starting line firing the starter's pistol, silently mouthing "go" as I leap to my triumph or my doom, and he has been waiting with bandages and ointment for the inevitable aftermath every time. He has always encouraged me to go for what I want, holding my hand every precarious step of the way. He is the blazing sun at the center of my solar system. He totally rules my world.

Don't tell him that, though. I need him to take out the trash.

And my parents, to whom I dedicated this book, and who truly made me, first literally, and then figuratively, into the person that I am. I have been Googling like crazy, but I cannot come up with the words to express how grateful I am for everything they have done for me. And to me. They are artists, and pragmatists, and dreamers, and thoughtful, and supportive, and crazy, and hilarious, and I would not be here without them. I could not have conjured up a better pair of people from whose loins to spring. I hit the jackpot.

I want to thank my sister, who is my spirit animal, and way cooler, funnier, smarter, braver, and more badass than me. And she has more tattoos. Seriously. Why is she so awesome? There are not enough hours in the day for us to talk on the phone. Thank god for texting.

Thanks to Zenobia, who has a mind more complex and delightful than an Escher painting and is one of the smartest, most creative, and most brilliantly beautiful people I know. And Sam, whose passion for art, music, film, history, cultural legacy, and especially my mother, continually inspire me.

My manager, Will Ward, who always tells the truth, even when it hurts, has rescued me from myself more than once (including that trainwreck of a night in Aspen), and has always encouraged my wild-eyed dreaming. He has been there from the beginning, and for a million beginnings that have come since. He is my Jerry Maguire.

My book agent, Dan Strone, who has been smart, elegant, thoughtful, and restrained—everything I am not—and also wildly enthusiastic and supportive, which is the quickest way to my heart.

My editor, Carrie Thornton, who has the patience of a saint. She fought for me, fought with me, and fought through many iterations of this unwieldy woodshop project to get us here, but she never flagged. Because of her, when you pull the trunk, my ceramic elephant lights up beautifully. And thanks to Cal Morgan, Kevin Callahan, Michael Barrs, Joseph Papa, Brittany Hamblin, and everyone at It Books, whose enthusiasm and passion have propelled me forward on a wave of awesome.

My team at ROAR: Jordan, Bernie, Greg, and Jay; and at UTA: Chris, Brett, and Max. You are my khalasar.

I have a bunch of long-suffering friends who have given opinions when requested, endured late-night emails and last-minute queries, come to my standup shows, listened to all of my podcasts, and generally helped me do everything I have ever done. Also, I have exploited the details of their lives on occasion in print, so I suppose I should thank them. Todd, Kimberly, Molly, Ben, Serene, and Michele, thank you so much for bearing up under the punishing weight of my friendship. You deserve a medal. I hope cocktails will do.

I want to thank South Korea for the profusion of awesomely bewildering and wonderful K-Pop bands, to which I listened almost exclusively while writing, and whose totally incomprehensible and yet dazzlingly killer music videos provided fantastic study break material.

And I want to thank my fans, without whom I would have nothing, including the ability to make fun of myself constantly, without relent or remorse. Thanks for laughing. At me or with me, I don't really care. You guys are awesome.

Finally, thanks to the Girl on Guy Army. We made this together.

You are my army, and you are legion.

Late.